JOSIE TOWNSEND

Can't See Around Corners

Third edition

Advisor: Craig Downs

This book was professionally typeset on Reedsy.
Find out more at reedsy.com

Contents

1	Chapter 1	1
2	Chapter 2	20
3	Chapter 3	38
4	Chapter 4	55
5	Chapter 5	72
6	Chapter 6	92
7	Chapter 7	107
8	Chapter 8	123
9	Chapter 9	143
10	Chapter 10	162
11	Chapter 11	181
12	Chapter 12	200
13	Chapter 13	219
14	Chapter 14	239
15	Chapter 15	261

One

Chapter 1

T he two young women eagerly examined their wardrobes and cautiously packed their suitcases. It seemed as though they'd been visualizing this overseas trip in their minds for an eternity, but now, the monumental time had finally arrived. Absent were the grinding days studying for their degrees at Stanhope University; now, they were relishing in the heightened anticipation of exploring the big wide world.

'I can't believe this is actually happening', Annie confessed with a modest shrill in her voice. 'Well, it is, my precious sister, but essentially, we have to face our grueling farewell and graduation party that Mum and Dad are forcing upon us tomorrow night, then we'll be flying off into the blue yonder', Sharon endorsed as she imitated an elevating plane with her right hand.

'Now don't be like that, Shaz. Mum and Dad are proud of us, and it would be an honor for them to share their happiness with family and friends', Annie justified.

'Yeah, I know, but we've spent the last three years studying our butts off and saving up for this trip, and I'm keen to get it underway that's all', Sharon huffed as she examined another blouse that she'd brought into Annie's room from her closet.

'Well, only two more days and our journey won't be just a dream anymore, it will be a reality', Annie encouraged

'Maybe Mum and Dad will be happy to finally see the back of us', she continued, giving Sharon a quick glance.

The girls were the privileged twin daughters of Edna and Warren Karce, who were well-respected and prominent figures within the socialite cluster of Richmond Province. Warren Karce was a resolute and portly fellow with an olive complexion, dark curly hair, and a thick, streaky grey beard. He had made his substantial wealth as an architect and now held an executive position within the largest building company in the region. Edna was the opposite of her husband. She was of slight stature, with porcelain skin and long red hair, which she usually tied up into a majestic bun at the nape of her neck. She had never worked and was the lone daughter of the former Governor Emsley, so she was typically accustomed to the class of nobility and the like. They had both fantasized about raising a large family, but Edna's hardships came in the form of unexpected miscarriages, and she was only able to carry the twin girls to almost full-term due to the fact that she was bedridden and nursed throughout the entire pregnancy.

'Any endeavor to have more children would be foolhardy' Edna's residing doctor warned. So ultimately, she and her husband were handed the sentence of a full hysterectomy.

Chapter 1

It devastated both of them. Without a doubt, Sharon and Annie, their only children, were their pride and joy. The sisters were fraternal twins, so even though they conveyed a striking resemblance to each other, with their father's raven hair and their mother's creamy skin and pale blue eyes, they were not entirely identical. Sharon was the eldest of the two and had arrived into the world two hours before Annie, so she was inherently dominant and took responsibility for her baby sister, chaperoning her wherever they went, which on occasion, exasperated Annie's honest shyness; but regrettably this amplified protection from Sharon had refined Annie into an impulsive, gullible young lady. As young girls growing up, Sharon always had to be the center of attention and pouted when friends and family members showed their warmth and affection towards her delicate sister

'Everyone loves you', Sharon would utter with a harsh tone in her voice.

'Why do you have to be so charming all of the time?' she added.

'I'm not deliberately trying to take any attention away from you, Sharon. I'm just being myself. Maybe if you weren't so difficult, people might want to spend more time with you', Annie would justify.

Annie's childhood memories with Sharon weren't always pleasant. She was willing to forget about the beloved pet budgerigars Sharon had let out of their cage, one at a time. She was always looking beyond her sister's angry outbursts and was even able, she thought, to forgive her sister for turning their adult years into a resolute struggle between them.

As small twin girls, their mother, Edna, would sometimes dress them in similar outfits, and Sharon would make a beeline straight to her wardrobe and change her clothes. Over the developing years, they had locked themselves into an old pattern of emotional tactics where Annie was constantly appeasing her sister and Sharon trying to diminish their relationship by emphasizing the importance of her special friends. Annie had learned to adapt, to get along with her sister, whose goals and interests were visibly different from her own and this made the distinction between them, having a cooperative or a rivalrous relationship. Comparisons from outsiders were inevitable.

Some would make comments like 'Which one of you pretty little girls is the "bad" twin?'

On the other hand, their mother didn't help the situation as she'd frequently used unfavorable comparisons out of frustration in wanting to goad Sharon into behaving better. Years ago, Annie had made a promise to herself that even though Sharon could be a demanding bitch, she was always going to keep the communication between them pleasant and uncluttered, as to avoid creating any obstacles. It would've been less agonizing for Annie if she had made the opposite pledge as she had learned to keep her feelings to herself and hide her true spirit. As the girls grew, their sisterhood matured, and a fierce loyalty developed. They began to support each other throughout the highs and lows of life, looking out for one another when things got tough

Mutual friends they socialized with were a densely woven group and had a powerful impact on the girls' social consequences. They were mainly from advantaged backgrounds who experienced greater ease mingling on their university campus and flourished with less support from the unknowns. Annie felt more supported socially by her privileged hometown friends, but one rookie colleague in her sorority also provided her with some emotional support regarding her academics and, at times, listened closely about her secret anguish with Sharon. This unlikely pair would meet up in the library, share notes, and quiz each other before exams; and to the intrusive outsider, they appeared culturally mismatched.

His name was Liam Cartwright.

'Why is Annie hanging around with that trailer trash boy, Shaz? I saw them in the library yesterday, sitting really close to each other and giggling', one of their elite friends asked.

'Not sure, Deb, maybe she feels sorry for him or something. You know Annie, she's always had a soft heart for orphaned things', Sharon miffed with distaste.

'He looks really scruffy, he reminds me of a hipster with those out-of-date raggedy clothes and long hair. He obviously comes from a deprived family, or worse, from an institution. As you said, Shaz, Annie has a soft heart for strays.'

'Oh, stop it, Deb', Sharon whispered as she lightly slapped Debbie's arm, and the two girls erupted with laughter.

Unlike Sharon and Annie, Liam didn't grow up privileged in the Province of Richmond. He had moved there eighteen months earlier from Southport, an insignificant fishing and surfing village on the coast of the bordering northern rivers territory.

Annie had once asked him, 'I hope you don't mind ... but do you come from a poor family, Liam?'

His reply was simple but profound.

'To me, poverty is an empty heart, my family mightn't have the assets in terms of being financially rich, but we are abundant with love, harmony, and laughter ... that's our wealth, Annie. I was able to score a scholarship to attend university and study the things that interest me, not elevate me to a higher status of wealth. Always remember, Annie, work for your dreams and not for others. How you spend your money or treasures is far more important than how much you earn.'

She gazed at him long and hard, studying his attractive face, his long brown wavy hair undulating down one side of his face, fragments of it catching in his spindly goatee as he tilted his head slightly, looking back at her. She'd never met anyone with the insight into contentment as he'd just described; and as she looked into his big brown eyes, she wondered why he had befriended her and wished that Sharon had been there to hear his wise foresight.

'You're a sweetheart.' She smiled and gave him a kiss on the cheek.

On one particular Tuesday, Liam spotted Annie in the library alone, prudently studying a book. He carefully approached her.

'Hi, Annie', he said, hovering behind her left shoulder.

She quickly turned around towards the raspy voice.

'Oh hi, Liam', she said. 'You scared me', she continued.

'What are you studying?'

'I'm just looking at some of the countries Sharon and I are going to visit during our overseas trip.'

'Yeah? That sounds interesting. Do you mind if I sit with you for a while? You can show me some of the highlights of your expedition, that's if it's okay', he queried.

'Sure, I'd love to, but you might find it a tad boring.'

'No, no, I'm curious about the places that intrigue you, Annie.'

'Cool, well, grab a chair, and I'll take you on a book tour.

I've done some research on the Internet, but I find the older books detail more of the stories that really interest me.'

'Really? And what might that be?' Liam pulled a chair closer and sat down beside Annie as she simultaneously moved the book towards him so as they could both examine it.

'I'm so taken with the mythologies surrounding Scandinavia and the North Germanic people. The Norse paganism stretched from Norway, Sweden, Finland, Russia, Latvia, Estonia, and Transylvania, just to mention a few', she declared, proud that she finally got the chance to share her knowledge on the quirky subject.

dinner room.

'Ooooh, how lovely', Mrs. Hargraves serenaded, pixie-clapping her hands like a ruined child. The group situated themselves around the extended dining table, pausing at their chairs until 'In the world of Norse mythology, you'll find gods and goddesses, giants, strange and powerful creatures, elves, dwarves, and land spirits. It's difficult for people of our era to conceive the viewpoint of the Vikings, which is brimming with such a variety of spiritual beings. There's not a lot of evidence in regards to those ages, except the limited number of tools, some jewelry and ornaments, and stone burial cairns.' Annie continued to enlighten Liam.

'Tales of death and destruction seemed to follow certain famous jewels. There are many stories of ancient warlords fighting bloody battles and kings and queens suffering agonizing ends. Like princesses leaping off buildings, fortunes ruined, careers dashed, and companies bankrupt, all because of sparkling stones. Would you believe me if I told you that blood-red gemstones with sticky spots in them are indicative of a curse?

'Really? Wow, you seem to know so much about these creepy legends.' Liam leaned in closer, wide-eyed at her stories.

'Yes, and there's something else that's very interesting. It's believed that some have even gone insane after complaining of visions of demons due to these ancient pieces of jewelry.' She turned to look at Liam with a proud smile on her face.

'Annie, you're such a cultured lady. What inspired you to take on this enthralling pastime?' 'Oh, my history degree brought it to my attention. In our second semester, we investigated some of these primeval cultures, and it grabbed me like an iron fist. Plus, my life can be so boring sometimes, with Sharon safeguarding everything I do.'

'Yeah, that would be a pain with big sis checking on you all the time. She's very protective, eh?'

'I know. It was alright when I was little but now I'm a grown woman, it's stifling. We get along, but I feel like she is suffocating me most of the time.' Annie closed the book and stood up. 'Well, my free period is nearly over, Liam, so I better meet up with Sharon at the car. Thanks for showing an interest in my "eerie preoccupation"', she mused and placed her hand warmly on his shoulder.

'That's okay, Annie. I like hanging out with you. You're a charming lady.' Remaining seated in his chair, he regarded her, smiled, and offered a cheeky wink.

When school had finished for the day, the girls assembled themselves into their white BMW convertible and turned on the car stereo. Liam watched them from the obscure library window as they cruised out of the car park, and with the music booming, they headed towards home.

He just stood there, long after they had disappeared around the street corner, and reran Annie's kiss on his cheek a couple of days ago and her irrational folklore infatuation over and over again in his head. He thought how adverse she was from the other girls in the group, especially with her twin sister. He'd seen Sharon a few times before in some of the communal lectures they had attended for chemistry and biology. She always sat in the middle row of seats, twirling the ends of her long dark hair, nibbling on the end of her pencil, glancing down periodically at what he presumed was her mobile phone, as every so often he would see her smiling and fidget with something below the desktop. His discernment of her was that of a woman who had immense confidence, had a high opinion of herself, and was very insistent.

One particular day, while attending a lecture, he scrutinized her for so long that she must have felt his eyes upon her, and she turned abruptly towards him, catching his glare.

He instantly dropped his head, facing the desk as she sat there still glaring at him; and when he thought she had stopped, he slowly lifted his head, only to detect her seriously mouthing the words in his direction, 'What are you looking at, River Boy?'

When the lecture had finished, Sharon collected her books and walked towards the exit door. Liam sat there observing her every move and thought to himself, as she disappeared,

'I bet everyone who crosses her path ends up a fucking casualty.'

Liam's upbringing was difficult. He was the middle child of five siblings and was expected to work with his father, mending nets, for their prawn trawler after school and on the weekends. He'd sit there on the dock hour after hour, his skin bronzed, tortured by the sun due to monotonous exposure. His eyes were firm. These were eyes of experience. He had seen a lot, and not all of it pleasant; his hardened look and sometimes stone-cold glaze were a clue to their witness. His suffering relationship with his father was tiresome. All he ever wanted was for someone to really care about him, and he made every effort to encourage himself to strive for his own destiny. He feared for his future and felt powerless with his existing situation, and each day, he'd vigilantly promise to succeed physically, socially, economically, and spiritually. He was searching for a larger meaning to life, and without his promise, he would just feel grey. So consequently, Liam would spend every other waking hour studying in his bedroom, above the kitchen of his family home, all the while visualizing the scholarship to university as his eventual prize.

Annie had been cramming for her bachelor's degree in History, but her core passion was Nordic mythology, while Liam was studying and obtained his bachelor's degree in Environmental Science as his vision was to work as a pharmacist someday. The subjects that Liam and Annie had in common were the Principles of Economics and Introduction to Criminology. They both outclassed the other students at these two components, putting their heads together and helping each other with some of the more problematic tasks involved. It was a harmonious arrangement for both of them.

As the sisters drove into the long circular driveway of their home and pulled up at the front door, Sharon, still seated behind the steering wheel, shifted her body towards Annie.

'What do you see in that unkept Liam fellow?' she probed.

Annie sat there silently for a minute, making a mental list of everything that was 'right' about him

'I know you don't approve of my friendship with Liam, but he has a lot of potential, and he just needs time to travel his own path, to make his mark in this world. He's working extra hard on achieving his goals. He embraces his challenges and has kept a promise to himself to never stop dreaming big. Is that such a bad thing, Sharon?' Annie replied, justifying Liam's impoverished background as she recognized this was the main reason Sharon loathed him so much.

'Yeah well, just be careful, Annie, he might see you as an easy meal ticket is all I'm saying.' Sharon huffed as she opened the car door, stepped out, and grabbed her bags from the open back seat.

'Stop it, he's not like that, we're just study buddies.' Annie replied defensively. 'Anyway, we've nearly got our degrees and university will soon be over, so I won't be seeing him anymore after that,' she continued trying to pacify her sister.

Those few remaining months flew by, and the last day of college came sooner than expected, and the idea of waiting for their voyage to happen made everything more exciting.

Mingling around from one bedroom to the next, the girls continued to examine each other's choice of attire for their overseas trip. As Sharon walked out of Annie's room, she saw the household maid, Tilly, climbing the curved staircase to the landing.

'Yes, Tilly, what is it?' Sharon asked.

'Your mother has asked if you girls would start getting ready for dinner. She's requested that you wear something lovely as there's company joining you tonight. They'll be arriving in an hour'. Annie popped her head around the corner of her bedroom door.

'Shaz, did Tilly just say that we're having visitors tonight?'

'Yep, and mum has asked if we could wear something nice,' she replied.

'I wonder who it is.' Annie queried.

'Don't know, we'll just have to wait and see. But you know Mum, she always loves throwing dinner parties. Hurry up and get dressed, Annie, they'll be here shortly.' Sharon commanded

As the girls entered the informal parlor room, the invited guests were already circulating around with Warren and Edna; filled champagne glasses in hand, they gossiped and chuckled.

'Oh, here they are, my two beautiful girls,' Edna announced, holding out her hand towards them. Annie and Sharon walked up to their mother and gave her a ritualistic peck on the cheek as they simultaneously clasped Edna's hand.

'Hello, Mama, Papa,' they said, greeting their parents.

'You know Mr. and Mrs. Hargraves and Mr. and Mrs. Simmons?' Edna signposted, knowing full well that Annie and Sharon had met them on a number of occasions before.

'Hello, sir and madam.' The girls welcomed their parents' confidential friends.

A waiter moved towards the girls and, attentively balancing a silver tray with one hand, offered the girls a drink.

'So?' Mrs. Hargraves conveyed directly to the girls. 'I hear you're both heading overseas on a holiday soon.'

'Yes, ma'am, we are. University has finished, and before we begin our careers, we're taking a little break', Sharon initiated with a firm tone in her voice.

Mrs. Hargraves tittered in a pretentious way as she turned to Edna.

'Oh, she hasn't changed a bit, Edna. Still the haughty lass we all know and love', she snorted ironically.

Sharon gave Annie a swift displeasured glimpse.

'Dinner is served', the butler announced standing aside, as

the guests moved into the formal the waiters pulled them out to be seated. Once settled, the servers started bringing out the first course.

'You have impeccable taste, Edna, in everything. Your fashion, manners, and charisma', Mr. Simmons flattered, preening Edna's self-esteem

'Why thank you, John', Edna crooned as she faintly blushed.

The guests ogled the food as it was placed on the widespread table, next to the eight brightly lit candles, which were flawlessly positioned as the centerpiece. While each appetizer was sighted, the dinner guests' mouths watered, noticing the mussels, clams, oysters, bruschetta, spinach dip, and a vegetable dish. They passed around the platters to one another with sizable eagerness. Sharon and Annie sat quietly with considerable dignity as they watched Mrs. Hargraves trowel the scrumptious food down her throat, opening her mouth wider than Sydney Harbor, making a 'yummy' sound as she swallowed the delights. Annie modestly leaned over to Sharon and whispered,

'No wonder she's the size of a hippo.'

Sharon replied, 'You shouldn't insult hippos like that.'

Both girls sniggered into their serviettes, pretending to wipe their mouths. The wine flowed as salads, sparkling cold duck, bread and stews, fruits, nuts, and chocolates were brought to the table.

'This was absolutely delectable. Most people fantasize about a life like this. Don't worry, Edna, I make sure I let people know all about your expensive tastes, what you wear, how big your house is. I like to play with people's illusions of having a splashy existence like this', Mrs. Hargraves exclaimed, somehow believing she was paying the hostess a compliment.

'Thank you, Muriel, but there's no need to promote our privileged statuses. I'm sure everyone in Richmond knows who we are and how we live', Edna said as she tried to water down the discourtesy.

Sharon sat across from Muriel, watching her belch then pat her tight thin lips with the serviette, thinking all the while, 'I could just slap her big fat pudgy face.'

They continued sitting at the table, the women sipping sherry and the men enjoying a glass of port in hand, chatting and catching up on the latest chin-wag.

'So, young ladies', Mr. Simmons directed his attention to Annie and Sharon. 'Where is this exciting holiday going to take both of you?'

'We're backpacking around Europe for six weeks', Sharon informed.

'Wow, that's very thrilling. Europe is a big place, which parts are you mainly trekking through?' he continued.

'We'll be visiting Paris, Amsterdam, Prague—you know all of the "must-see" cities', Sharon conversed. At this point, Annie quickly interrupted.

'We're also going to explore some other less-known places as well, like Romania, Transylvania, and Estonia, just to name a few.' She beamed with pleasure.

'Estonia? Never heard of it. And Transylvania? Isn't that where Dracula lives?' He darted his eyes around the table as the gathering started to laugh.

'That's only folklore, Mr. Simmons. One of the reasons I want to go there. I've been studying up on Norse mythology as an addition to my History degree', Annie said, dismissing his guileless remark.

'Well, it all sounds very interesting, Annie. I hope your

search for those legends and myths don't turn out to have any authentication to them.'

'They're only legends, Mr. Simmons. For example, did you know that the Viking stories and legends are recounted in many ancient written sources and scenes? They are depicted on a number of surviving Viking-age carvings in England, the Isle of Man, Norway, and Sweden. Here's another captivating story. People don't realize this, but the red color assimilated with royalty is the color of revenge.' She smiled, getting caught up with her knowledge of the mysterious.

'Really?' Mr. Simmons leaned forward as though he was endeavoring to catch a more enriched view of the story.

'Yes, well, the Black Prince's Ruby also has a remarkable past. The 170-carat rough-cut spinel made its first appearance in 1367 when Don Pedro "The Cruel", King of Castile, murdered the ruby's owner. Needing to be rescued from his enemies at the Battle of Nájera, Pedro gave the ruby to Edward, Prince of Wales, as payment for Edward's help. He wrapped the ruby in plain paper and sold it for five pounds. There are so many other stories, I could go on telling them all night.' Annie lounged back into her chair, pleased with the opportunity to share her facts with a captive audience.

'It's all very stimulating, Annie. Not many people are interested in that kind of history', Mr. Simmons concluded.

'Nobody realizes how many tales there are, would you like to hear another?'

'No, thank you, Annie, that's enough. It's getting late, and I'm sure our guests don't want to be experiencing any nightmares tonight.' Her father interrupted.

Sharon sat there dumbstruck, completely ignorant of her sister's passion for weird ghoulish stories.

'Alright, girls, it's time for you to head off to your rooms. Say good night to everyone', Warren initiated.

'Good night', the girls obediently conveyed. As they climbed the stairs to the landing, Sharon grabbed Annie's arm, stopping her from going any farther.

'What?' Annie exclaimed, surprised by her sister's forceful grip.

'Is that what you've been doing all this time in the library with that Liam bloke? Reading up on bizarre urban legends?' Sharon's eyes were wider than a saucer, and her lips clenched so tightly, they were turning white.

'No, Shaz, we just studied for exams and helped each other out with assignments. Why are you so freaked out?'

'Freaked out? Those legends and myths you've just been broadcasting at the dinner table all come from countries that we're going to visit on our trip. I had no idea that you had such a hunger for the macabre, Annie. Now I understand why you were so insistent on taking a detour from our original itinerary. So you can pursue your creepy obsession. Sometimes, I don't know who you really are. Good night, I'll see you in the morning.' Sharon loosened her grip on her sister's arm and headed up the stairs, two at a time, advancing on Annie's ascent before she could say another word

Annie closed the bedroom door behind her. She wandered up to her bed and flopped down onto it, feeling despondent.

Why does everyone disregard my curiosity with these legends?' she pondered. *'I know it's not everybody's cup of tea, but at least they could be polite enough to pretend they're inquisitive about it. In the future, I'm not going to include them, not going to convince them.*

I will coordinate my own destiny because trying to persuade them

16

is only a waste of time. I won't discuss anything about it at the farewell party tomorrow night either, she firmly concluded and rolled over onto her side, still dressed in her dinner attire, and fell asleep.

Sharon, on the other hand, promenaded around in her room, admiring her reflection in the mirror, still wearing her pink and white frock. Twirling around proudly, like a little girl modeling a fairy dress, she thought how captivating she looked. Unexpectedly, she came to an abrupt halt, her mind fixated on Annie's peculiarities.

'She's certainly an oddball', Sharon muttered to herself. Then she wondered whether agreeing to visit these out-of-the-way places would intensify Annie's hunger for the macabre. 'I just hope she doesn't go all freaky-deaky on me when we're so far away from home. She seems very captivated by it. I'll definitely have a chat with her before the party tomorrow night', she concluded. Removing the dinner dress, Sharon changed into her nightie and snuggled profoundly between the blankets, all the while her mind engrossed with thoughts of Annie and as slumber beckoned her; she plunged into a deep state of dreaming.

She wandered through a vast field of yellow flowers, lightly brushing their cheerful blossoms with her hand as she strolled casually amongst them, cheerfully lighthearted, and marveled at the stark contrast between the yellow acres and the pale-blue sky, which merged together in the distance. Appearing just ahead was a small patch of missing florets as though someone had forcibly plucked them out by the roots and as she approached the bare ground, she carefully examined the earth and observed that the naked patch was slightly rising and falling like it was alive and breathing. She stood for the longest time, mesmerized at the vision; and after it stopped moving, Sharon boldly kicked some of the naked dirt around with her foot. There, partially submerged in the ground, she viewed a pendant, old and covered in dirt. So Sharon cautiously removed the stones and loose soil from around it and picked it up, cradling it in her right hand as she watched the mud dirty her skin. The intricate engravings were worn, and even though the stone in the pendant was so tarnished, the gut of the jewel still lustered a bright glow, capturing the dazzling sun's rays that flickered from within its belly. Sharon held the pendant close to her face and instantly detected an aroma secreting from the nugget, and it smelt of stale blood. Still clutching the pendant in her right hand, she turned her palm downwards for a minute, revolted by the sour stench; and when she rotated her hand upwards, opening up her palm, the pendant's image had completely unbound itself from the damp earth. It shone as though it was brand new again, igniting the glowing belly even further as the pendant implied a fresh growth of strong origins from somewhere ancient and remote. As she held the pendant, she watched it fervently, and it gave her the impression that it was passionately reaching for the sunlight—robust, iridescent, and finally free—and then without any warning, it completely vanished, like it was never there in the first place, as though the whole experience had just been a visual joke. Sharon jolted awake, her eyes opening like car headlights that had just been switched on as the adrenaline coursed through her system, leaving her feeling disturbed. With fear penetrating her heart, her breathing became ragged and harsh, and she started feeling hot as the sweat trickled slowly down her neck, and her hands began to tremble. For some reason, she felt stressed and afraid; her head was spinning out of control, pushing all lucid thoughts into blackness as the mounting fear seized at her hands and legs, restraining them like prison shackles.

Calmness gradually shrouded Sharon's demeanor, and as she rolled over onto her side, snuggling into the pillow; she mumbled to herself, 'This all Annie's fault ... I wish she'd stop talking about those creepy legends of hers'

Two

Chapter 2

‿‿ᘒᕤᘒᕤ‿‿

W hile the sun quietly descended over the horizon, transmitting rays of golden and crimson radiance, increasing every moment in its brilliance, the party guests began to arrive. Firstly in small numbers, gradually increasing with the passing hour. As they entered the grand front entrance, with its domed ceiling and elegant chandelier hovering above the sweeping staircase, waiters greeted each person in a respectful manner, smiling as they offered flutes of champagne to arrivals. Housemaids removed hats and coats from guests and placed them in the cloakroom, while Warren and Edna welcomed everyone, distributing insincere pecks on their cheeks at the entryway of the parlor room. A small group of performers played relaxing jazz music while the guests socialized and networked, in a very composed manner, and it set a very tranquil atmosphere and had everyone anticipating the impending night of the farewell party.

The twins surveyed the guests, spying on them from the privacy of the landing in front of their bedrooms. They weren't in view of the incoming visitors, hidden behind a pillar, like two children peering down from an attic as they dissected each and every person.

'Oh look, Annie, there's Mr. and Mrs. Goodwin and their daughters Helen and Katie. Hasn't Katie gotten fat? She looks really awkward, the way she's standing all stooped over and disfigured like that', Sharon whispered in a judgmental manner.

'And that sickly yellow gown she's wearing doesn't do anything for her pudgy figure. You know I read somewhere that because yellow is the color of traffic lights and signs, it identifies caution all over the world? Maybe that's the message she's trying to express: watch out everyone, chunky chick approaching.' Both girls started to snigger.

'You're as mean as a snake in the grass', Annie muttered between smirks.

As they continued to inspect the crowd, they noticed the renowned Mr. and Mrs. Greer with their two sons, Jack and Tony, all dressed up to the nines in their tuxedos and bow ties.

'The Greer boys look rather dashing, don't you think, Shaz?' Annie queried. 'How long ago was it when you were dating Tony?' she continued.

'I don't know, maybe ten months ago, give or take', Sharon murmured, absorbed in viewing her old boyfriend's Viking-gold hair and ritzy clothes.

'He hasn't changed much in appearance, maybe become a bit more broad-shouldered and muscular', Annie promoted.

'Yeah, maybe he has, but I bet he's still an egotistical prick',

Sharon answered, unperturbed. 'Now there's something you don't see every day', Annie continued as she modestly pointed towards the door. The girls' eyes became simultaneously locked on the entryway like magnets. As they shared the same indulgence, their gazes were fixed on an exotically handsome man sauntering casually towards the posing waiters. His short brown hair he'd groomed so meticulously had a flowing quality like small waves on a liquid surface. A manful gritty stubble adorned his strong jaw, and as he broadly smiled, everyone became curious with delight at the vigor of his youth and anonymity. With a glass of champagne in hand, he coolly strolled into the parlor, briefly stopping to greet Edna and Warren, all the while glancing around at the magnificence of their home. Annie and Sharon stood there, motionless and flabbergasted.

'Who is that?' Sharon broke the silence between them. Annie just stood there for a moment, examining the gorgeous young man while scowling with careful eyes as he vanished further into the parlor to join the other guests; she believed there was something familiar about him. The way he walked about, his movements and gestures she seemed so acquainted with, and then it finally dawned on her.

'It's Liam ... who invited him?' she quietly confirmed, her voicing trailing off as if she was questioning herself.

'Are you okay?' Sharon touched Annie's arm, and she jumped, surprised with fear.

'Who invited Liam?' she repeated, facing Sharon.

'Oh, I kind of did. Mum wanted to know which friends you'd like to ask, and because you've been spending so much time with him in the library, I just assumed he'd be an obvious choice', Sharon justified.

22

'And you didn't think of mentioning it to me?' Annie was visibly upset.

'It's no big deal, Annie, he's your friend, he's here, and he's looking really hot. Who would've thought he'd scrub up so well anyway?'

'Why didn't Mum ask me who I wanted to invite?'

'Because she knew that you'd say no one ... that's why.' Sharon was beginning to become irritated.

'Oh, and by the way, don't start discussing your creepy curios to anyone tonight. You'll just come across as a weirdo.'

'What?' Annie said, still dismayed.

'Are you serious? You know, Annie, your Norse mythology crap.'

'Shut up, Sharon, I wasn't going to say a word about it anyway. I hate you at times, and my trust for you as a sister needs some serious questioning too', Annie miffed as she went into her bedroom, continuing getting ready for their splendid debut.

'Oh, stop grumbling and go put your big girl panties on', Sharon bluntly snapped back.

By the time they were organized, sounds of laughter, music, and continuous babble drifted up the staircase from the energetic parlor

Edna beckoned Tilly towards her and whispered a quiet word into her ear.

'Can you assemble the girls for me please, Tilly, I think the guests are ready to see them now.'

'Yes, Mrs. Karce, I will do it immediately', Tilly responded politely and made her way up the staircase, knocking on each of the girl's bedroom entries.

'Annie, Sharon, the guests are awaiting your arrival. Your

mother has asked if you could gather yourselves at the top of the staircase in about five minutes please', she initiated through the closed doors.

The party guests were ushered from the parlor into the grand entranceway and assembled themselves into a crowd five meters from the bottom of the staircase. Tilly gave three knocks on each bedroom door, signaling the girls to appear, and they instantaneously emerged from their rooms. Clasping each other's hand, Sharon and Annie moved gracefully together and posed at the top of the stairwell. The gathering sighed as they observed the two visions of beauty. Modeling the luxurious silk evening gowns and precious jewels, they displayed their character of wealth, sparking the imaginations of the guests. As they floated down the stairs, their comparable aqua-and-butter-lemon frocks accentuated their waistlines with the plunging necklines, displaying their rarely seen assets. With their long hair bundled up in a twisted topknot, all eyes were upon them as the girls dazzled past the onlookers and greeted their parents with smiles and adoring hugs. Everyone moved aside to let the girls pass, and like monarchs, they entered the parlor chamber, with the crowd following hot on their heels. The musicians continued to play while each person individually congratulated Annie and Sharon on their college success.

'It's wonderful to see your mother and father so happy and so proud of you both', one of the lady guests remarked.

'You look wonderful, that dress is absolutely stunning. The last time I saw you, you were only little girls—look at you now. You've developed into such desirable young ladies', 80-year-old Mr. Woods uttered, eyeing off the girls' elevated bosoms

Chapter 2

'Hello, Sharon, Annie, congratulations. You look wonderful tonight, I like your frocks, even though I think it's slightly ruined with all those jewels you're wearing. Less is more, you know', Helen Goodwin declared, cunningly motivated by her green-eyed agenda.

'Thank you, Helen, I think you and your sister look lovely too. Katie is the spitting image of a gigantic canary. I didn't know we were throwing a fancy dress party tonight, did you, Annie?' Sharon mused as she looked coolly at her sister.

Sharon stepped closer to Helen and whispered into her ear.

'Don't worry, sweetness, I'm not as needy and self-centered as you are, but your false flattery is suitably noted. You never know you might pick up a desperate nobleman tonight. Mr. Woods seems very enthusiastic.' As Sharon grabbed Annie's hand, whisking her away towards their elite group of friends, Annie gave Helen a cheesy grin.

The vicious rivalry between the two sets of sisters began as children when Mrs. Goodwin would bring Helen and Katie over for playdates. From an early age, Helen recognized the difference in attractiveness between herself and Sharon, so consequently, a strong competition developed. In the beginning, they would gossip about mutual friends and probe into cherished subjects in an effortlessly designed conversation, but as that stage passed, their friendship became laced with tension and conflict. At times, Sharon's random mind games would work as torture on Helen, elevating her fear towards the older friend as she became anxious with Sharon's declining logic and lack of self-control. It didn't help Helen's situation, who was already harboring feelings of insecurity and doubts of her own success as an emergent child in a highly competitive social scene. Sharon was mindful of this, so she deliberately irritated Helen's vulnerability. To gain a sense of power over Helen, Sharon took control of her distinctive toys that she'd bring over and would hide them or, worse, partially destroy them, therefore frightening her into doing what she wanted. Whilst the two younger siblings sided with their older sisters, resentment developed. Therefore since their mothers were ardent friends, not a word was spoken about the antagonism between them.

They weaved their way through the party crowd, greeting everyone as they passed until they reached the assembly of 'cool kids'.

'I saw you talking to Helen', Debbie said to Sharon.

'Yeah, she hasn't changed, still considers herself to be incredibly entertaining and wonderful', Sharon jeered. 'Anyway, I don't want to talk about her', she quickly added, turning her head around to scrutinize the other guests.

'There she is again, so typical.' Sharon continued observing Mrs. Hargraves monopolizing the buffet table, vigorously pushing food into her mouth, one delectable savory and sweetie after another.

'I swear that woman eats enough food to supply Ethiopia', she added, making the girls snigger. Annie viewed the overweight, gobbling Mrs. Hargraves, and that's when she noticed Liam, standing against the rear wall, staring at her. He beckoned Annie towards the opened concertina doors that led out to the water fountain courtyard. Without the other girls noticing, Annie slipped gently away and joined him on the shadowy porch.

'Hi, Liam, I barely recognized you tonight. You look like a completely different man', she emitted with a large smile.

'Well, I thought I'd surprise you, I'm not always the scruffy bloke you regularly saw on campus.' He grinned back, moving closer to Annie until his six-foot-two-inch statue was diligently poised over her, face-to-face. Annie immediately stepped back.

'You have a magnificent home. I suppose you and Sharon will inherit all of this one day.' He changed his focus, sensing Annie's reluctance.

'Oh yes, I suppose we will, but it's not that simple.'

'What do you mean?'

'You know, it's not as simple as waiting for Mama and Papa to pass away. There are circumstances attached to our inheritance', she spoke to him, turning around and strolling towards the balcony fence.

'Circumstances? I'm not sure what you mean?

'Conditions, Liam. Like we have to excel in our professions, not to bring dishonor to the family name, marry someone who is of equivalent wealth and has an immaculate social status, don't bring any litigation against a family member, no criminal record ... stuff like that.' 'What happens if you break any of these conditions?'

"We'll be written out of the estate inheritance and won't receive a penny from it.'

'That's a bit rough. You can't control destiny or fate. You're inexperienced in life, Annie, and it's only human nature to make mistakes. Obviously, your parents aren't very merciful.' 'That's the way it is. There's a lot of money and prominence involved. Our parents have drummed these conditions into us ever since we were young.' She turned around to find him standing right in front of her. Once again, he stood over her, so she slipped under his arm, dodging his worrying presence.

27

'Don't move away from me, Annie', Liam pleaded as he grabbed one of her arms.

'I like you very much. I'm going to be somebody one day. You'll be proud of me when I make my fortune. I feel that when we come together in the absence of reality, my world becomes magical. It's like my entire being fills with adoration, comfort, and light and it's all because of you.' He drew her towards him, and she felt his hard, erect manhood.

'Stop, Liam', she pleaded with him.

'What?' He seemed amazed that she wasn't sinking helplessly into his arms.

'Will you be my girl, Annie?' Feeling the strength of his grip on her upper arm, she nervously tried to wriggle free.

'Stop, you're hurting me', she begged.

'All this time, have you been stringing me along?' He stated, not letting go of her.

Realizing that he had control of her, she relented and gave him a hug, and as she looked over his shoulder, Annie detected Sharon watching them from inside the parlor.

'No, no Liam, I haven't been stringing you along. I like you too. It's just that ...' Liam loosened his grip.

'Do you really like me?' he asked, interrupting her sentence.

'Yes, of course, I do.' Annie broke free from him.

'Will you go out with me then? Before you go away?' He beamed.

'Oh, I can't ... we've got an engagement with my cousins. Sorry, maybe some other time', Annie said, quickly picking up the front of her gown. She hastily walked back into the parlor, thankful to be joining the other guests.

'You are the center of my world, Annie. I'm the only one who understands you and loves you', he shouted and as he stood there staring after her, overwhelming feelings of jealousy rose up into his heart. He was tormented over her rejection and finally acknowledged that Annie just saw him as an impoverished chump, teasing him and sucking him in with her beauty, charm, and elegance.

'What an idiot I've been. *All of her so-called friends are unreliable, and I'm the only one who she can completely trust*,' he mumbled to himself and swiftly jumped the courtyard railing, disappearing down the lantern-lit driveway.

Annie stood beside Sharon, her heart pounding in her mouth. She remained there like a statue for what seemed like an hour until Sharon snapped her out of her trance.

'Are you alright, Annie? You look like you've seen a ghost. What was that all about? You out there with Liam? Where is he anyway?' Sharon kept on with the plaguing questions.

'Yes, I'm okay. He just wanted to take me out on a date. It's no big deal, Shaz. I said no to him anyway. I don't think he took it very well. He's probably left the party and gone home.' Annie secretly wished he did.

'Well, I'm glad you said no. Mama and Papa wouldn't approve. He's beneath us, Annie. I tried to tell you that he had devious intentions, but you wouldn't listen.' Sharon beckoned a waiter to come fill her champagne glass and turned back to talk with her friends while Annie stood gawking out towards the open concertina doors.

'You shouldn't have invited him in the first place, Shaz', Annie said, quietly muttering under her breath.

A high-pitched resonating sound rang throughout the room as Warren Karce tapped a wine glass with his fork, gesturing for Sharon and Annie to join him, and the congregation hushed their chatter.

'Hello, everyone. For those who don't know me, I'm Warren Karce, father of two beautiful daughters, Sharon and Annie. We come together this evening to celebrate their success in completing their education and heading overseas for a much-needed holiday. Both girls have studied hard and diligently over the years. Sharon, achieving her degree in Medicine, and Annie, her degree in History. Tonight is one of the most difficult things I've ever had to do, saying farewell to my little girls and welcoming two fine young women. Both of them have been a gift from God to Edna and me. We'll always be grateful to have been given the honor of being their parents. May God continue to bless them and grant them safety, love, and happiness in their voyage and all the days of their lives. 'Oh okay, Bruce has just looked at his watch, which is the signal that he needs a drink, so ladies and gentlemen, please be upstanding and raise your glasses to Sharon and Annie.' Warren stepped to one side as the guests raised their glasses and gave a verbal expression of honor and goodwill towards the girls.

'To Sharon and Annie', the crowd voiced harmoniously.

As Annie stood beside her parents, facing the throng of people, she could've sworn she caught a fleeting glimpse of Liam's face partially hidden amongst the back row of the horde. She moved her head from one side to another, trying to get a better look, but the party dispersed and blended into a sea of moving figures, and she lost sight of him.

'Relax and enjoy the party, everyone', Warren yelled over the rising flurry of voices.

'Come on, Annie, let's dance', Sharon instructed.

The swarm of girls boogied together on the cleared dance floor, laughing and talking as they enjoyed the rest of the night into the early hours of the morning. On a few occasions, Tony Greer tried to interject and ask Sharon for a dance, and each time she'd decline his offer; but as the night wore on and Sharon drank more champagne, she relented and finally agreed to his persistent request. Annie retired to a quiet area of the parlor and watched Sharon and Tony dancing cheek to cheek as the music slowed down to a romantic cavort. Tony lifted his head slightly backward, and before Sharon realized his purpose, he kissed her firmly on the lips. Sharon melted into his arms, and after their lengthy embrace, she smiled warmly at him, and they strolled out to the fountain courtyard, hand in hand. Annie sat in the lounge, mystified by Sharon's indecisive nature. One minute she was criticizing Tony, and now she's all over him like white on rice. At this point, Debbie wandered over and assembled herself beside Annie.

'Are you okay, girlfriend?' she queried.

'Kinda', Annie answered in a dejected tone.

'What's going on, lovely? You should be as happy as a lark. You've got your big trip coming up, aren't you excited? Look at all the people that have come to farewell you and Sharon, you can't tell me that you're not cherished and loved', Debbie encouraged.

'I suppose. It's just that Sharon puzzles me. She's all over the place with her emotions. On one hand, she's slating Tony Greer, and now she's outside in the courtyard getting all lovey-dovey with him.'

'Are you jealous of Sharon?'

'No, not at all, Deb. She's my sister, but she does cloud my thoughts at times.'

'Look ... she's been drinking champagne all night. It's probably the grog that's making her so passionately affectionate towards him. That's all, Annie. Sharon's a big girl now, you have to stop comparing yourself to her. I know that you're twins and she can be very domineering at times, but start carving a life out for yourself. Separate your existence from her, and begin a new chapter. Otherwise, you'll morph into a mini Sharon if you're not careful ... Don't tell Sharon I said that, she'd kill me', Debbie joked and gave Annie a heartfelt cuddle before standing up and rejoining the others on the dance floor.

By the time her conversation with Debbie finished, Annie visually scanned the courtyard and noticed that Sharon and Tony had vanished. She stood up and went to the concertina doors, inspecting the veranda. No one was there, so with perplexing thoughts, she casually joined her friends and enjoyed the rest of the night. Around 3.00 a.m the party guests eventually thanked the hosts and made their way home while the waiters and waitresses began cleaning up the chaotic mess left behind.

'Where's Sharon?' Edna asked Annie as she went to kiss her parents good night.

'I'm not sure, Mama. The last time I saw her she was out on the parlor balcony with some of her girlfriends.' Annie flushed as she told her parents the small lie.

'She's probably in the gardens, Edna, don't worry about her so much. I'm sure she's alright. Sharon can take care of herself', Warren pacified his wife.

'Yes, well, let her know that she didn't say goodnight to us, and I'm not very happy about it', Edna continued with disappointment in her voice.

'I will Mama, Papa, good night, and thank you so much for the wonderful party tonight.' 'Good night, Annie', her parents replied as they began climbing the stairs to their bedroom. Annie gazed after them for a while then wandered instinctively back into the parlor, dodging the hastening waiters as she finally arrived in the courtyard. With hands clasped firmly on the railing, she stood there, her thoughts preoccupied with the earlier happenings that had transpired during the night. She stared into the shadowy gardens, inhaling deeply the intoxicating ladylike perfume that percolated the air from the combination of jasmine and orange blossoms. Closing her eyes as she gasped another yawning breath, she heard faint distant voices coming from within the obscure gardens. She leaned forward and peered in the direction of the verbal sounds; capturing a better look she saw two vague silhouettes, their figures linked together, holding each other's hands. With her eyes fixed on the couple, she witnessed them entwined in a warm embrace. Before the womanly figure started the long walk back to the manor, she handed the man an envelope, and as they both departed, she paused briefly to wave her Romeo goodbye. Annie instantly recognized the feminine shape walking towards her; it was Sharon, but who was the young man with her? His masculine outline didn't resemble Tony Greer; he was smaller in shape and didn't have the same elongated stride as Tony. Annie swiftly ran inside and up the winding staircase and stood in front of her bedroom door, waiting for Sharon to appear.

The large entrance door inched gently open, and Sharon quickly glanced around to see if anyone was nearby. Securing her safe return, she skulked up the flight of steps only to find Annie, unmoving, at the entrance of her room. Sharon stopped abruptly in her hasty steps when she saw Annie standing there, frozen in the dim light.

'Shit, Annie, you scared me', Sharon whispered starkly. Annie didn't say a word, waiting firmly for her sister's explanation.

'Well? Has the cat got your tongue?' Sharon continued.

'Where have you been? Mum and Dad asked about you, they wanted to know where you were. Mum's upset that you weren't here to say good night to them.' Annie spoke quietly in a low-pitched voice.

'I've been walking in the garden with Tony, it's no big deal.'

'I saw both of you, and that man wasn't Tony, Shaz.'

'Oh, and now you're an expert on depicting men from a distance, it was Tony okay?' Sharon said forcefully.

'What was the envelope you handed to him?' Annie kept grilling her sister.

'If you must know, little Miss Busybody, they're tickets I bought Tony for the theatre production Cat on a Hot Tin Roof. Do you know how hard it is to purchase those tickets? It's been sold out for months. I purchased them at a much higher price than usual. Got them from a scalper at Uni. That's why I had to keep it hush-hush. If Mum and Dad were to find out that I was spending my allowance on scalpers, they'd be pissed off. Happy now, Sherlock?'

'Why can't he buy the tickets himself? He's got the money and the contacts?'

'He's broke, okay? His parents have cut back on his monthly allowance. Now you have all the facts, you can go to bed a contented kitty.' Sharon entered her bedroom, closing the door behind her as quickly as she opened it.

Annie strolled into her room and sat down on the couch. It was only now, after all the mayhem was over, that she felt a sharp pain in her upper arm. She rolled back the sleeve of her gown and noticed a large bruise emerging, right where Liam had held on to her so tightly. Not only was it materializing into a blue and dark purple shape, but the contour was precisely the form of his hand.

'That's just great. I can't let anyone see this', she moaned with despair and promised to never have anything to do with Liam ... ever again.

Due to their enduring sheltered lives, both girls weren't very knowledgeable when it came to the topic of applied male and female relationships. Edna and Warren had ensured that their daughters remained untouched and pure for their pending husbands, and Warren made a devoted point of shielding both his girls from unintended visits by young men; in particular, he presented as overly protective towards his more sensitive youngest daughter Annie. Unbeknownst to her parents, Sharon had entertained some limited stealthy affairs over the years, sneaking out into the dark, cold nights to liaise with her latest boyfriend, quietly tiptoeing down the staircase with her shoes in hand, until she'd reached the large entrance door and opened it with diligent proficiency, the intoxicating adrenaline rush motivating her to gamble with chance time and time again. With a degree of discretion, they would hook up at expensive hotels, where they'd greet each other with passionate hugs and kisses, comfortable in their affections, while giggling and indulging in Cava champagne, clinking their flutes together in tribute to accomplishing another devious get-together.

Before her lover could speak, Sharon would place down her glass and turn towards him, pressing her breasts up against his chest, moving closer as her fingers fondle his crotch, cupping her hand around his balls and squeezed them gently until the handful develops into a hard and alluring cock. He would groan a little and would begin to feel lightheaded, and as Sharon slowly pulled her pale pink dress up over her head, he noticed that she wasn't wearing any panties and her soft pussy hair was as black as a raven. His hand touches it, gently inserting his fingers deep into her vagina, and instantly, he feels her warmth and wetness. She would tell her lover to wait a minute and take his hand, ushering him into the bedroom where she would lie on the bed, spreading her legs broadly while leaning back against the pillows and gestures for him to enter her. She would clutch the pillow with her hands as he breathes heavily, his hot gasps mounting with every plunge, his face rosy and energetic as their bodies slip against each other from the eluding sweat. Sharon would tremble and vibrate under her concubine's forceful skill of lovemaking, and she radiated when he launched his cries of ecstasy, violently climaxing until every drop of his cum was deposited inside of her.

'Go and clean yourself up', he abruptly whispered; and even though it was a command, Sharon obeyed, mechanically going into the bathroom, wiping herself off and within half an hour, they parted ways, resuming their separate lives ... until their next steamy connection. Annie, on the other hand, was the polar opposite of her sister. She was virginal and had never experienced the pleasures of a close intimate relationship. Her general coldness and lack of interest in physical affection from courting men were met with an aloofness that was frostier than a winter's day. After listening to her mother's warnings and descriptive portrayal of the consequences of having sex, intrusive thoughts continually plagued her mindset. Would her lover perceive her as inexperienced or frigid?

Chapter 2

The fear of getting pregnant and the anxiety about her performance prevented any arousal or desire from her. Even those romantic admirers that had spent hours chatting with her, selflessly drinking in her words, baring their hearts, and sharing their joys, dreams, and failures were continually rejected and were left feeling inadequate as their self-esteem was smacked into a pulp. And with their masculinity threatened, they would sometimes spiral into personal attacks against her, which did nothing to heighten her craving for a sexual relationship. So ultimately, at the age of 23, Annie was a virgin, emotionally trapped in the distorted image of her mother's interpretation of a healthy sensual relationship

Three

Chapter 3

The airport looked more like a hypermarket than the girls had expected. As they stood in the security line, they examined the sea of curious faces, a percentage of them bored while others looked excited. The tiles underfoot gleamed white, and everywhere, people were milling about. Some lounged on comfy chairs, inspecting the departure boards and checking their watches while the remaining holidaymakers vigorously consumed takeaway food and drinks.

'Now remember to call us once a week and let us know how things are going', Edna coached the girls as their luggage was being placed on the conveyor belt at the check-in counter.

'Yes, Mama, we will', they said concurrently.

'Listen to your mother, she knows what's best for you both', Warren added.

Chapter 3

'Yes, Papa, we know', again, they responded in a parallel tone.

'Okay, well, have a wonderful time. We love you, and we'll be waiting for your calls.' Their parents lodged a kiss on each of the girls' cheeks and waved goodbye as they entered the departure terminal.

'Goodbye, Mama and Papa', and they disappeared, blending through the multitude of bustling travelers.

'Finally, we get to do whatever we want', Sharon said, thrilled to be out of her parents' control.

'Yes, it's going to be fun, but behave yourself, Shaz. We don't need any trouble'. Annie interposed

'Oh, I'm sorry, I thought we left Mum back at the gates. Lighten up, Annie, otherwise you're going to make this trip as exciting as a wet blanket', Sharon dictated as she made a beeline for the exclusive jewelry and accessories boutique.

'Look at these exquisite rings, necklaces, and watches ... oh, and they've even got diamond bikinis. Now, these elegances are a symbol of exceptional taste and my glamorous lifestyle', Sharon radiated.

'Come on, if we spend all of our money here, we won't have any left for when we're overseas. Besides, I heard our gate number being called out over the loudspeaker. We've got twenty minutes before departure.' Annie hurried Sharon along, and they made their way towards the gate.

'Flight 733 from Sydney to Paris via Hong Kong will be boarding in approximately fifteen minutes from gate 58', the hostess's voice announced over the speaker.

'We're just going to make it, Shaz. How long is the flight again?' Annie buzzed as they got closer.

'It'll take about 27 hours and 35 minutes to be precise,

and that includes stopping over in Hong Kong for five and a half hours', Sharon informed her. The girls handed the flight attendant their boarding passes and were ushered to the business-class section closest to the front of the aircraft. As soon as they were seated, preflight drinks were offered to them by the air hostess. Sipping at their beverages, the girls considered the cabin and viewed a semicircle, fully stocked bar with hot and cold snacks and all the cocktails you could imagine. The seats had a width of 87 inches with full flatbed accommodation available complemented by soft velvety pillows to rest a weary head-on. As a result of their young sheltered lives, Annie and Sharon had never traveled out of Australia before. Edna was always busy entertaining her selected friends or involved in one distinguished community venture or another, and Warren was constantly engrossed with his CEO position in the prominent architecture firm. Any extended holidays the girls did experience were either at the famed Wellington Riding School where they would spend their days near the beach pony-riding, toasting marshmallows, and consuming chocolate-covered bananas around a bonfire or at the highly regarded holiday lodging institute the Cambridge School for Visual and Performing Arts, which offered expert educational summer camps in everything from art, film-making, and fashion to drama, directing, and music. Even though they enjoyed these extended vacations, they felt stifled with the disciplined schedules and jaded by the fact that they weren't allowed to behave more freely than usual and enjoy themselves.

'How exciting is this, Shaz? I can't believe that we're on our own without Mum and Dad looking over our shoulders', Annie shined.

Chapter 3

'Yes, we can finally be true to ourselves, doing what we want and being who we want to be', Sharon answered. Annie looked at her sister inquisitively, a little confused as to what she really meant by that statement. The aircraft was nearly ready for take-off. The girls sat there dumbfounded, ogling the good-looking men in their business suits who were busy arranging handheld briefcases and making themselves comfortable in their designated seats. A few of them, one at a time, turned around prudently and offered the girls a charming smile.

The air hostess began making her preflight announcement.

'Ladies and gentlemen, welcome onboard Flight 733 with service from Sydney to Paris via Hong Kong. We are currently 3rd in line for take-off and are expected to be in the air in approximately seven minutes. We ask that you please fasten your seatbelts at this time and secure all baggage underneath your seat or in the overhead compartments. We also ask that your seats and table trays are in the upright position for take-off. Please turn off all personal electronic devices, including laptops and cell phones. Smoking is prohibited for the duration of the flight. Thank you for choosing Australia Airlines. Enjoy your flight. We will now instruct you through the safety briefing.'

The girls looked at each other as they clutched their hands firmly together. The plane inched its way towards the take-off strip and, once it had arrived, turned and sat motionless for a few minutes as the air hostess finished her speech. Sharon and Annie heard the engine throttle stirring to a loud rumble, and the plane began to accelerate, increasing at an uncomfortable speed. Shortly after take-off, they felt a sinking sensation; while the flaps of the plane retracted and as the plane ascended in a steep climb, it glided through different

41

forms of clouds. Immediately after the 'fasten seat belt' sign was turned off, some passengers began maneuvering around the cabin, instinctively reaching for their phones or laptops, which were stored in the overhead compartments or, they sat on the meager stools around the semicircle bar, waiting to be served. Sharon reached down into her handbag and pulled an item out of it.

'I'm going to the ladies', she announced to Annie

'What have you got in your hand, Shaz?'

'You'll see.' Sharon stood up and made her way to the toilet and closed the door behind her. Annie inspected her sister's graceful figure, checking out her stylish olive-green pencil skirt, modest blouse, and cream high-heeled shoes as she glided down the aisle … and so did the men. Sharon was in the amenities for some time and when she did materialize, she had changed her blouse into a provocative off-the-shoulder number, which accentuated the fullness of her breasts. She ambled slowly back to her seat, providing the appreciative men with a prolonged gaze and an alluring smile.

'Where did you get that blouse?' Annie acted shocked when Sharon sat beside her. 'You know Mum and Dad wouldn't approve,' she continued

'Well, they're not here, are they?' Sharon goaded with an arrogant snigger in her voice.

'You look like a tart', Annie protested.

'Maybe so, but tarts are sweet, delectable, and tempting and that's me to a tee.' Flipping out her compact and viewing her reflection in the tiny mirror, Sharon puckered up and applied makeup to her enviable lips. Promptly, she got out of the seat and made her way towards the bar, placing herself on a stool in front of the countertop.

Chapter 3

'May I have a vodka and tonic, with a squeeze of lemon', she instructed as she poised her alluring figure on the chair. She didn't need to work hard or fight for the attention of the admiring gentlemen as, one by one, they casually strolled up to the bar next to her and ordered a drink.

Annie pulled a laptop out of its case and began exploring the route they would be taking throughout Europe. She glanced over at Sharon, who was sitting with all the refinements of a duchess, chatting and laughing with three men, with her drink in hand, delicately touching each of them on the arm as she giggled falsely at their pitiful attempts to flatter her. Annie refocused her attention to the trip ahead and visually mapped out their itinerary, making sure that it included all of the captivating towns and villages where her hunger in folklore would be at its most abundant. She charted her way along the Ural Mountains line, from the source of the Ural River down to the Greater Caucasus from the Caspian Sea to the Black Sea where she discovered that the landscape varied from desert to frozen coastlines, tall mountains to giant marshes. She read about the rich traditions of folk tales that derived from a number of Slavic myths and traditions and learned that Russian folk characters are very colorful, and they also betray ancient pagan roots. One particular legend which immersed her was the tale of the Baba Yaga, a witchlike old woman who lives in the forest in a house that rests on chicken legs and is surrounded by skulls and bones. Another story tells of the firebird, an enchanted creature with fiery plumage that is difficult to catch, therefore its capture or to pluck one of its feathers out is often the challenge facing any brave man who tries. Both the Baba Yaga and the firebird can either be good or bad, terrifying or benevolent, and they can bestow favorable or hostile enchantments on their prey; but above all, they must never ever be antagonized.

Another legend of the timbered mountains is that of La Llorona. Once a Spanish soldier married a beautiful woman, and they had two children whom the soldier loved very much. However, the soldier came from a rich family and his parents disapproved of his wife and threatened to disown him unless he married into prosperity. Not wishing to lose his inheritance, the soldier cast away his first wife and married a woman of affluence. His first wife was filled with a terrible jealous rage. To avenge herself against her unfaithful husband, she drowned their two children in the nearby river of the forest in the Tatras Mountains. The soldier was horrified when he learned about what she had done and tried to have her arrested. But his wife, driven insane by rage, jealousy, and guilt, escaped into the wild, timbered mountains where she roamed throughout the land, searching the waterways for her children. But she could not find them. Finally, in an agony of body and mind, she drowned herself in the river too. But her soul could not escape to heaven because of the weight of her terrible crime, so La Llorona's spirit still wanders the forest, her wailing echoing throughout the mountains and its valleys as she is condemned forever to search in vain for her children who she will never find, as they are no more.

'Hi there', a male voice unexpectedly sounded right beside her. Annie jumped back into her seat, startled by the sudden appearance of the gentleman.

'Oh, you startled me', she blurted out.

'Sorry about that, my name is Simon, what's yours?'

'Annie', she replied timidly.

'Nice to meet you, Annie. What's so interesting on that

computer of yours?'

'Oh nothing, just mapping out my trip is all', she replied as she closed the top-down, preventing him from viewing the topic she'd been reading.

'Is that your sister over there at the bar with all of those blokes?' He supposed, turning his head towards the roaring conversation.

'Yes, it is"

'How come you're not over there celebrating your forth-coming trip like she is?' He continued. 'I'm not like my sister.'

'I expect not. She seems very self-assured. I suppose she has every reason to be, she's gorgeous.'

'Then why aren't you over there with the other men?' Annie irked, curling up her mouth with distaste at Simon's tactlessness.

'Why should I when I have you all to myself, looking just as beautiful as your sister, and there's no competition?' Simon grinned, believing he was paying Annie a compliment.

'Piss off, will you?' she abruptly blurted out. 'I've got better things to do with my time than have a non-competitive chap like you trying to win my attention ... unsuccessfully I might add.'

'Okay. Wow, no wonder you're sitting here on your own. See you around then.' Simon stood up and went back to his seat. Sharon had witnessed the brief encounter between Annie and Simon and promptly swayed over to her sister.

'Who was that?' she spoke incoherently.

'Just some loser', Annie replied softly.

'Why don't you come over with me and I'll introduce you to my new friends?' Sharon persisted.

'No thanks, I'm busy looking at our course of direction

once we land in Europe. It looks like you're relishing in the male company over there, so go back and have another drink.' Annie reopened her laptop and commenced looking at the screen as she spoke.

'Ooooh, who's a nasty little miss then? Okay, it's your loss, but I hope you're not going to be this bitchy and difficult throughout the entire holiday.' Consequently, Sharon made her way back to her adoring followers and ordered another drink, laughing deceptively so as to irritate Annie.

By the time they had landed in Hong Kong, Sharon was entirely befuddled from the alcohol she'd consumed and was making plans with her male friends to meet up for dinner that night. As they arrived at the terminal, she staggered in her high-heeled shoes, bracing herself against one of the cooperative gentlemen.

'Okay, where do we go from here?' she hollered at the gathering.

'Come on, just follow me', one of the men indicated. Annie sauntered behind the group, watching her sister's every move.

They stepped onto the streets and a bustling arrangement of restaurants, eateries, pubs, and bars welcomed their astonished senses.

'Wow, this is great', Sharon expressed, sheltering her eyes from the unexpected display of harsh fluorescent street lighting.

There were people everywhere, rushing around from one place to another; and as the group meandered their way towards the preferred restaurants, they passed a myriad of street stalls selling blouses and old-fashioned clothes with bright retro patterns, tapered silk slacks, and floral prints, and trinkets. Tourists and local people alike scrutinized and haggled stridently over the trade price of the apparel while at the food stalls, seafood, noodles, and other treats were consumed with gusto by the infinite throng of tourists.

'Here we are, my favorite place to eat', the front-runner of the group announced.

It was a restaurant worthy of a six-star rating. The food was intelligent, humorous, and carefully thought out. The chef flawlessly married traditional and new-world Chinese cuisine, and each course was a one-bite wonder. Fresh plump oysters were served up with ginger and spring onion sauce, the flavors lingering in the mouth long enough for a smile to appear on the faces of the patrons. Next, they consumed smoked quail egg in crispy taro crust with a dollop of caviar, and as the creamy yolk broke in their mouths upon entry, the sweet crunch of the taro's snowflake crust offered a blunt peculiarity.

'You must come here often', Annie said, directing her query to the man sitting beside Sharon.

'Yes, I do, whenever there's a stopover in Hong Kong. It's the first place I make a dash for when I've got an insatiable appetite', he replied.

'Do you bring all of your new lady friends here?' Sharon spoke incoherently, adorning herself all over him.

'No', he reacted, gently moving her off his shoulder.

'It's a very nice place, but now we've finished our meal, don't you think we should be heading back to the airport terminal? Our plane leaves in two hours', Annie continued, secretly wanting to get Sharon on the plane as soon as possible before she passed out.

'Yes, let's get going, we'll pay for the meal, just as a thank-you for providing us with such lovely company tonight', he offered.

'We've got money' Annie objected.

'I insist', he replied.

'No, it's fine, look, here's my Mastercard', she said, drawing it out of her purse.

'Please let us pay. We'll split the bill between the five of us. Don't let this charming encounter end on a sour note, Annie', he implored.

'Well ... okay then, I suppose it'll be alright this time.' She grinned, succumbing to his invitation.

Back on the plane, Sharon began to feel the after-effects of drinking too much alcohol; and as the airplane leveled out after take-off, she made a speedy gallop for the toilets.

'Oh, I feel crook', she moaned to Annie upon returning.

'It's not a wonder, Shaz. You've consumed enough alcohol to host a wedding', Annie responded.

'Yeah, I know, and it's paying me back. I'm going to sleep for a while.' Sharon reclined her seat and placed a pillow under her head, and before you could say, Jack Frost, she was dead to the world. Annie stared out the insignificant portal window of the plane, and her mind began to drift back to the day when Liam had offered to buy her lunch as a treat.

'We've got two free periods after midday. Instead of pouring yourself over books in the library, how about I shout you lunch at the cafeteria. Then we can take a stroll through the campus grounds', he proposed.

'Okay, that sounds nice. Thank you', Annie approved

They moseyed into the canteen and stood at the counter, revising the menu together. 'What's taking your fancy, Annie? Besides me', Liam teased.

Annie gave him a nippy glance, dismissing what he'd just said.

'I'll have the orange chicken. What are you going to order?'

'I think I'll order the luxurious, saucy pizza—we can share if you like.'

They sat opposite to each other, at a table near the large window overlooking the Uni grounds as Liam began the conversation, hoping that the good experience would make them closer.

'This is great, Annie. You know I remember the first time I saw you. I was browsing the library, and I remembered that you were reading a book, then staring at the computer, your hair was a little bit messy as you kept running your fingers through it. You appeared worried, so I approached you and asked if everything was alright. When you looked up at me, your beautiful blue eyes pierced my heart like an arrow', he confessed, leaning in closer to the table with both arms resting on it.

'Oh, was I? Can't remember what I would've been worried about. What did I say?' she briefly replied.

'You just said hi. That's when I sat down beside you and asked what was so intriguing on your laptop. You said that you were reading about mythology and having difficulty with an upcoming exam.' He was present, focused, and fascinated by what she had to say, as he was interested in cultivating a relationship with her and seeing that connection last for the long haul. The waitress arrived and placed their food on the table. Annie sat quietly, inspecting the dish in front of her.

'So? What is the most embarrassing phase you ever went through?' Liam prodded, endeavoring to initiate the conversation again.

'Um ... I suppose it was when I wanted to be a drifter and not be regimented by the endless rules and limitations my parents and our nannies always commanded of me and Sharon. I'd search for clothes to dress up like a gypsy, you know, I'd cover my head with scarves and tie my hair up or braid it. I'd dress in bright calf-length skirts with short puffed sleeves and gold coins around my neck and walk around in bare feet', she briefed him.

'Ahh, so there's the beginning of your interest in European mythology and Romani culture. How old were you when this gypsy phase was fashionable?'

'I was probably ten or eleven years old.'

'That's a very impressionable age. I can imagine your parents didn't approve, being all high society and all', he quizzed.

'No, they didn't approve. They'd make me switch my clothing, but little did they know that I'd stash my gypsy clothes into a bag then ask to play outside in the estate grounds where I'd change back into them and pretend I was a carefree, wild child living in the forest.'

Liam laughed out loud.

'There's a little rebel inside of that prudish nature of yours.' Annie didn't appreciate him calling her prudish, so she finished up her meal without saying another word and pushed her plate away.

'Looks as though you've finished. Would you like to go for a walk?'

'I suppose so', she answered halfheartedly.

Strolling through the gardens, Liam surveyed Annie's womanly figure as she walked somewhat in front of him. He wanted to create memories with her that would last forever, something they could both share for years to come, so he tried to encourage Annie to indulge in the bold.

'I've been fantasizing about making you feel good. I thought that roses are too generic, so what can I do to be your knight in shining armor?' Annie turned around to answer him, and Liam rapidly kissed her decisively on the lips as he simultaneously clutched a generous amount of her buttocks drawing her into him.

Shocked at his brazenness, Annie slapped his face and ran back to the campus building, feeling like a cheap bimbo. Crying, she burst through the entrance doors of the Uni and made her way to the lockers, grabbing her purse and books, and escaped down the hallway to the library where she hid in a corner away from meddling judgment.

Recalling all of this and still gazing out of the airplane window, humiliation began to well up in her. She sniffed back the tears and looked at Sharon, who was still passed out on the seat next to her. That was when she felt the sharp throbbing pain again on her upper arm where Liam had grabbed her the night of their farewell party. She delicately rolled up her sleeve, and even though the deep purple bruise was disappearing, the contour of his hand was still unmistakably visible, as though someone had drawn an outline of it with a bright-red crayon, and it was angry looking. Carefully repositioning her sleeve back down, Annie questioned why the handprint wasn't fading like the rest of the injury. She began to agonize over the thought that she had become permanently branded, and Liam's determination might not come in the form of his physical self but of the unyielding mark he'd left behind. She tilted back her chair and snuggled into the pillow, eventually falling asleep to the murmur of the cruising airplane engines.

Over the intercom, the girls were awakened by the announcement that they would be landing at Paris in an hour, so they gathered their toiletries and headed for the bathroom to freshen up. Sharon came back looking completely resurrected from her drinking binge, and as she sat next to Annie, she squeezed her sister's hand tightly.

'Eeek, we're nearly there, little sis. Can't wait to absorb the sights and sounds of la Ville Lumière ... the city of light. We're staying at the La Maison Favart, right? Which room number have we got booked?' Annie busied herself, filling the purse with essential makeup, and made sure she had her wallet as she looked at the hotel coupon.

'We'll be staying in room 184. I hope it's as nice as the brochure pictures show.' Annie beamed.

'Why did you call Paris the city of light?' Annie queried.

'I can't believe you don't know that, Annie. I thought you'd be up on all of the info, after spending all your time at the library and after completing a History degree. Well, originally this nickname came not from the illumination of the city, but from Paris being the birthplace of the Age of Enlightenment. Paris played a leading role in Europe's sharing of education and ideas, being the home of countless writers, inventors, and philosophers. 'Here's some other fun facts. Did you know that the Eiffel Tower was supposed to be a temporary structure, intended to stand for 20 years after the 1889 World Fair? It's also believed that there is only one stop sign in the entire city, and here's something that's right up your alley for the weird and wonderful. There's a flat in Paris that was left unoccupied under lock and key for 70 years, but the rent was paid every month, and when the renter passed away, a painting by Boldini valued at more than $2 million was found inside. How about that, Annie? You're not the only one who's done some homework and don't worry, the hotel will be as magnificent and the room as extravagant as the brochure says', Sharon educated her sister. 'I knew about the Eiffel Tower and Paris's history with poets, painters, and philosophers, Shaz.'

'Okay, that's good. I was beginning to think that you might've cheated throughout your history course', Sharon taunted.

The girls continued to chat while the air hostess instructed for landing protocol to begin, and as they glided downwards into Paris, like two little children, they squeezed both of their faces up against the window, competing with each other to catch a glimpse of the most romantic city in the world. Those hours on the plane had felt like a week, and as they stepped out onto the tarmac, the diversified aromas of the Paris air smelt desirably sweet; so before checking into their motel room, Sharon and Annie decided to take a discovery excursion to see the sights of the elaborate metropolis. They perused the incredible shopping in the huge avenues, malls and small boutiques and eventually found themselves at the Boulevard Saint-Germain.

High-end party wear, elegant home décor accessories, and all the top luxury brands bewildered the sisters as they tried on endless sassy dresses, stylish shoes, and elegant purses, everything that made them look their best from head to toe. With their arms heavily loaded with bright-colored shopping bags, the girls exited the boutique, completely absorbed in their endless gossiping with each other when an oncoming passerby unexpectedly spilled their coffee on Sharon's clothes.

'Whoops', the stranger profusely apologized as they mutually tried wiping off the stain, while Annie stood there, astonished at what had just occurred.

'Didn't you see me? I was right in front of you', Sharon angrily blurted out.

'Pardon, madame, mes excuses.' The man expressed his regret for the mishap.

'That's alright, just watch where you're going in future.'

'Oui ... bonne journee.' The man saluted before quickly departing.

'He was cute' Annie indicated, trying to distract her sister's irritation from the hot coffee stain on her lemon blouse.

'I couldn't give a toss how cute he was ... look what the idiot did to my shirt', she whined.

As Annie endeavored to help her sister sponge the remaining liquid from her blouse, like a light bulb had switched on in Sharon's brain, she suddenly regarded her bag.

'You've got to be kidding me!' she yelled.

'What?' Annie stood there, amazed at Sharon's abrupt outburst.

'My wallet is gone ... that bastard stole it.'

'How could he do that, Shaz, he was flat-out wiping the coffee off your blouse', Annie revealed.

'Did you see anyone else hanging around while this was going on?' 'There were so many people walking past and glaring at the accident, I didn't take much notice', Annie implored. 'Well, he must've had a sneaky accomplice who pickpockets gullible tourists like me ... unbelievable. Now I'll have to cancel all of my credit cards. He got away with two hundred Euros as well ... What a great start to our holiday.'

'Don't worry, Shaz, when we get to our hotel, we'll take care of everything ... Come on, let's go.

54

Four

Chapter 4

⚬⚬⚬⚬

I t was 4.30 pm when the aloof hotel butler escorted them into room 184. The first thing that greeted them was the tall floor-to-ceiling windows, with its luxurious drapes of gold and crimson decorations; they provided a paramount view of the infamous city, shimmering and glistening in its colored lights like a Christmas tree. The farthest of the all-inclusive bay windows captured the angle of another hotel, across from the neighboring alleyway, but it didn't hinder their views; all they could see of the adjacent building was a section of its corner windows on the fourth, fifth, and sixth floors. Two king-sized beds with smooth Egyptian cotton sheets were adorned with a variety of pillow types, while champagne, chocolates, and flowers were assembled effortlessly on the dressing table between them.

The room was sensibly decorated and occupied modern

chattels, offering a pleasant stay and filling the room with a sophisticated atmosphere of peace and harmony.

The walk-in wardrobe provided the girls with a full-length mirror where high-quality fluffy robes hung motionlessly, and comfy slippers were placed directly beneath them as though an invisible person was already dressed up in the snuggly outfits. As the attentive and friendly porters brought in their luggage, Sharon perused the hotel's guidebook while Annie quickly grabbed her bags and began unpacking her delicate underwear and neatly pressed clothes.

'Ooooh, look, Annie, there's an alluring restaurant, encircled by gardens, that turns into a jazzy nightspot afterward. It's on the highest level of the hotel', she radiated eagerly.

'That's great, but aren't you going to unpack your things first?' her sister questioned.

'Yes I will, but now I'm going to have a shower and freshen up then cancel my credit cards.' So Sharon grabbed the fluffy robe and slippers and dawdled into the bathroom, closing the door behind her; she turned on the shower taps and started running the water.

'No worries, Shaz, I'm going to ring Mum and Dad. They'll be expecting our call to see if we've arrived safely', Annie responded loyally, and as she dialed the number on her mobile phone, she heard Sharon's untrained singing waffling from the bathroom. After a few minutes, the call was answered by their devoted household butler.

'Karce residence, William speaking', he spoke in a proficient manner.

'Oh hello, William, it's Annie, is Mum or Dad there please, we're in Paris, we arrived about 4.30pm.' Annie beamed, happy to hear his familiar voice.

Chapter 4

'Yes, Miss Annie, I will fetch your mother. Glad to know you've arrived safely at your destination. One moment please.' William placed the receiver down. Annie stood there for a few minutes, eager to listen to her mother's adoring voice.

'Hello? Annie dearest, is that you?' Her mother finally spoke.

'Hi, Mama, yes, it's me, we've made it to Paris. Can you believe it? Annie said with an illuminating voice.

'When did you arrive? How was your flight? What's Paris like?' Her mother blitzed her with questions. Annie laughed.

'Everything is great, Mama, looking forward to visiting the Conciergerie palace tomorrow. It was a prison during the Reign of Terror during the 14th century. Sharon just wants to shop' 'My inquisitive Annie, always on the search for more weird and quirky stories. Well, you girls be careful. I don't want you taking any unnecessary risks. Remember, you're in a different culture, and not everyone is as approachable as they are here at home', her mother warned. 'I know, Mama, we'll be careful. Just thought I'd call and let you know we're okay', Annie reassured her mother

'Where's Sharon? Can I talk with her for a moment?' Edna insisted.

'She's in the shower, Mama, singing in her dreadful tone-deaf voice. I'll get her to call you tonight.'

'Oh alright, but your father and I are entertaining the Hargraves, Simmons, and the Greers this evening, so if she doesn't catch us, tell her to call tomorrow', she instructed.

'Is Tony and his brother going to be there as well?' Annie probed.

'No, lovey, the Greer boys have gone overseas for a holiday, why?'

'Oh okay. Just curious. I didn't know they were going away,

when did they leave?'

'A couple of days after Sharon and yourself flew out of Sydney', Edna replied.

'That's odd because Sharon was talking to Tony the night of the party, and she never mentioned anything about them traveling overseas. We could've arranged a meeting with them somewhere. How is Papa?'

'He's alright, he's had this nuisance headache all afternoon, but we've got Dr. Bartlett calling in. Your father is resting at the moment. I'll let him know his beautiful daughters are safe and sound. Love you, dear, tell your sister to look out for my gentle little Annie. Remember, we want to hear from you once a week. Goodbye, precious, stay safe.' Edna hung up the phone.

Annie placed the mobile on the coffee table, studying it for a minute as Sharon finally appeared from the bathroom, wearing the robe and towel-drying her hair.

'Was that Mama?' she asked.

'Yes, I called while you were in the shower.' Annie reacted like she was in a trace.

'Didn't Mama want to talk to me?'

'I told her you were in the bathroom and that you'd probably call tonight, but they're entertaining friends, including the Greers. She said it would be better if you rang tomorrow. Did you know that Tony and his brother were taking a holiday overseas and flew out not long after us?' Annie explored.

'Typical Mama, always entertaining some friends. I swear she does it just to display her importance. What? Tony, overseas? No, I didn't know that.' Sharon put up a front.

'Are you sure? Because you spent a considerable amount of time with him at the party. He didn't mention an overseas holiday? I think that'd be high on someone's priority list to talk about', Annie searched.

'I said I didn't know, geez, Annie you can be a pain in the arse sometimes. What does it matter anyway? They're not interesting enough to bother with. Come on, stop obsessing over the Greer boys and start getting ready to go to the restaurant. I hope we meet some seductive gentlemen there tonight.' Sharon gleamed.

'I'm not obsessing, Shaz, I just think it's weird that he didn't say anything to you, that's all, and I'm not staying for the nightclub later on either. I just want something to eat and then come back here to relax.'

'You're as exciting as a sack of potatoes, Annie, let your hair down a bit, we're on holiday, and we're in Paris. Live a little. Maybe I should've brought Debbie with me instead of you', Sharon said as she darted an irritated glimpse at her sister.

'A sack of potatoes can be very exciting to someone who's starving, Sharon, and I don't appreciate you patronizing everything I say. I'm having a shower now', Annie huffed as she grabbed her toiletries bag and went into the bathroom, slamming the door behind her. 'Touchy', Sharon jeered after her.

Annie stood under the hot running water, still questioning Sharon's integrity towards her, while Sharon questioned Annie's reliability about having a good time. Once Annie came out of the bathroom, she entered the wardrobe and put on an elegant dress; and when she returned, Sharon went up to her, giving her a heartfelt cuddle.

'I don't want to fight, okay, little sis? I've taken the liberty to reserve a table for us at 8.00 pm, so in the meantime, let's open this complimentary bottle of champagne and toast to our exciting and joyous trip. There are chilled glasses in the bar fridge. Would you get them for me please, Annie?'

The obedient sister collected the glasses while Sharon opened the bottle. The cork exploded from the bottle, allowing the gold liquor to flow up the stem, foaming out of its opening. Sharon poured the champagne into their long flutes. They toasted each other, clinking their glasses together.

'To high spirits and a safe and happy holiday ... and exciting too', Sharon broadcasted.

They sat on the lounge chair, chatting and organizing the forthcoming expedition together. 'So after Paris, we head off towards Germany, Slovakia, and then Romania. Is that right, Annie?' Sharon questioned between sips of her beverage.

'Yep, and thanks for indulging me with my fascination with that area, Shaz. I'm really looking forward to actually seeing Transylvania—all of Romania in fact. It reads so interestingly on the Internet and in books.' Annie sat on the edge of her seat.

'What's so interesting about it? Come on, now's your chance to tell me, I'm all ears.' Sharon humored her sister.

'Romania is a southeastern European country known for the forested region of Transylvania, ringed by the Carpathian Mountains. Its preserved medieval towns include Sighisoara, and there are many fortified churches and castles, particularly the clifftop Bran Castle, which has been long associated with the Dracula legend. It actually exists, cool, huh?'

'You're so into this mythology stuff, you'll give yourself nightmares, Annie'

'It's part of history. I've been told that the town's folk are intriguing, and they're stuck in a time warp like they don't belong to the modern world. Their clothes wear the history of the area, it's kind of absorbed into them. Where else would you experience something like that?' Annie continued.

'Where does the story of Dracula actually come from ... how did it originate? I mean surely it's only a legend, right?' Sharon appeared sincerely curious.

'Well ... even though the legend of Dracula is purely a fictional character, Bram Stoker named his infamous oddity after a real person who happened to have a taste for blood. He was Vlad III, the Prince of Wallachia. Born in Transylvania as the second son of the nobleman Vlad II Dracul, he took the name Dracula, meaning son of Dracul, when he was initiated into a secret order of Christian knights known as the Order of the Dragon, hence in Romanian, Dracul means "dragon". 'He earned his place in history by impaling his enemies alive. He was into torture, mutilation, and mass murder. Though he didn't shy away from disembowelment, decapitation, boiling or skinning his victims alive, so after his tyranny, he was known as the 15th century Prince Vlad Dracul the III and was immortalized by Bram Stoker's gothic novel of Dracula, which was published in 1897. In 1931, archaeologists found a casket partially covered in a purple shroud embroidered with gold. The skeleton inside was covered with pieces of faded silk fabric with a raised pattern woven with gold and silver thread, similar to a shirt depicted in an old painting of Dracula. The casket also contained an ancient metal crown with turquoise stones and a ring, linked to those worn by the Order of the Dragon ... it was sewn into the shirtsleeve. So there you go, Shaz, you learn something new every day.' Annie sat there, content and satisfied with her mastery.

'That's just delightful', Sharon uttered apathetically, glancing at her watch.

'We've got half an hour before we head up to the restaurant. There's some cashews on the counter over there, can you get them for me, Annie? I'll refill your glass', she guided.

'Oh okay.' Annie got up out of her chair and went to the counter, clutching the foil bag of nuts. She walked back over to the lounge while Sharon handed her a full glass of champagne.

'Bottoms up, Annie.' The girls sipped the bubbling brew and eventually grabbed their handbags, making their way to the entrance and subsequently to the lift just down the hallway of the hotel floor.

When the lift access opened into the restaurant foyer, they entered; and as they were ushered to their awaiting table, the other patrons turned their heads as the gorgeous sisters strolled past.

'Everyone's looking at us', Annie said unnerved.

'I know, and why not? We're the best-looking women here', Sharon said, proud as a peacock.

While reading the extensive menu, a waiter approached their table.

'Mademoiselle, do you wish to look at the wine list?' he enunciated in a thick French accent. 'Just bring us the best champagne you have and two glasses', Sharon advised.

'Yes, Mademoiselle, right away.' And the waiter hurried off to retrieve the liquor.

'Shaz, we've already consumed a bottle of champagne, do you think it's wise that we have another one?' Annie objected.

'Will you stop with the babysitter attitude? We'll be fine, besides, I need to get chilled out before the nightclub starts. It's just a little Dutch courage is what I'm looking for, have you seen the suave men around here?' Sharon secretly spoke from behind the large menu. 'Here is your champagne,

Mademoiselle. Would you like me to pour? Oui?' He signaled. 'Oui, s'il vous plaît', Sharon replied.

'And your order? What will it be?' the waiter continued.

'For my entrée, I'll have a dozen naked oysters. For my main, I'll have the rock lobster served naturally with traditional dipping sauces. What will you have, Annie?'

Annie smiled up at the waiter.

'I'll have the warm olives in chili and thyme grissini, and for my main, I'll have pan-seared fresh salmon with béarnaise sauce please.' She closed the menu and gave it to the attentive waiter.

'Nice choice, little sis, I like your tastes', Sharon praised. 'Oh, and before you go, we'll both have the white chocolate and Malibu parfait for dessert. Je vous remercie.'

'Your French is really good, Shaz.' Annie was flabbergasted.

'Merci, ma soeur', Sharon responded.

'What does that mean?' 'I said, "Thank you, sister". See, you're not the only one with unexpected surprises' Sharon grinned.

After their meal, they sat chatting over yet another bottle of champagne Sharon had ordered. Although Annie participated in the beverage, she didn't drink as much of it as her sister.

'I'm going to the ladies', Annie informed Sharon.

'Okay, I'll fill your glass while you're gone.'

'Thanks, but after that one, I've had enough.' Annie smiled at her sister then headed for the amenities.

While she was absent, Sharon picked up the bottle and both their glasses, walking outside onto the balcony. The restaurant began to take on another façade with attendants closing the doors behind them as they rushed around, transforming it into a fancy nightclub. Young people drifted around the wide and lengthy terrace, with drinks in hand, chit-chatting to one another, and just as the terrace was being quarantined Annie returned, joining the premature festivities as the location converted from a sophisticated restaurant into a free-spirited discotheque atmosphere.

'Here, this is your glass', Sharon said as she handed Annie her drink.

'Thanks, where's the rest of the bottle, Shaz?'

'Oh, I polished that off. You said you didn't want any more, right?' Sharon began to boogie around when she heard the music playing and roughly an hour later, the staff reopened the doors. It was like another world when they walked in, with dry ice smoke swirling around on the dance floor in an array of blues, acid green, hot pinks, and gold; and as everyone arrived, with more people filling up the place from the restaurant lift, each person became hyped up and were ready to have a good time. Even though the scene was a hotspot for the locals, it was remarkably elegant by virtue of being fashionable and displayed a crowd acting proudly flamboyant and pretentious. The music got louder, pounding out a rhythmic beat that echoed through their bodies. The dance floor became a sea of bodies fusing together like a swarm of bees, and Annie and Sharon found themselves locked in the middle of the horde as they all simultaneously moshed up and down in an oversized mass of people.

'I'm not feeling very well. I'm going back to our room', Annie shouted in Sharon's ear.

'Okay. Be a party pooper. I'll see you in the morning', Sharon roared back.

Annie squeezed her way through the crowd and finally made it to the elevator doors. Before they closed, she turned around, trying to catch a glimpse of Sharon, but she'd become disbursed through the vortex of people, so she stepped aside, allowing more individuals to invade the premises, and eventually moved into the lift. When Annie entered their suite, she glanced at her watch; it was 2.00 am. The radiant city glow animated the room so brightly it allowed her to walk around without turning on any additional lights. Flinging her handbag against the coffee table, she slumped down on the lounge, kicking off her shoes, and pondered about the ideas she had planned for the upcoming days. After a while, Annie stood up and strolled over to the large windows, gazing out over the memorable city; and as her eyes moved around analyzing the horizon, something captured her attention in the adjacent hotel building. She moved closer to the glass, achieving a better look, and what she saw was a shadowy figure, just standing there at the corner window of the fourth floor, glaring right back at her. It didn't move, its body facing openly in her direction, the dark shape asserting its vigilant cold stare and apparent display of dominance over her. A powerful feeling of terror ascended, starting from her shaking hands and heart racing, her fingers began numbing, the rising trepidation penetrating outwardly from deep within her skin. She quickly closed the drapes and, for a few minutes, deliberated with who or what this manifestation could be. But before she dismissed it completely, she took one last peep to determine whether it was real or not; however, when she did, it wasn't on the fourth floor any longer. It stood in the exact same position, on the sixth floor, its glare still fixated on her.

'Who the hell is that? How could he move so quickly up two levels?' Annie mumbled to herself. She didn't dare take another look; instead, she dashed hastily to the bathroom and closed the door.

'I'll have another shower and sober up. It must be the champagne, and I don't usually drink, especially imported stuff. Yep, that's what it is, the grog.' She tried convincing herself and as she undressed; her upper arm began to throb again. Upon examining it, Liam's discolored handprint flushed intensely like it was a new injury. She allowed the hot water to run over her entire body for more than fifteen minutes, all the while crying uncontrollably as she recalled the night Liam grabbed her arm forcefully and the unwholesome apparition she had just experienced. Stepping out of the shower, Annie dressed into her nightgown and slipped into bed. She deliberately faced the curtain-shielded window, still unsettled; and after a long time, she eventually fell asleep. Around 6.30 am, Sharon stumbled into their hotel suite, looking unkempt and exhausted, with shoes in hand. She noticed Annie sound asleep on the king-sized bed farthest away from the windows.

Placing her belongings down on the floor, she made her way to the restroom where she ran a shower and hopped in, washing off any indication of the provocative night before. Making herself a cup of tea, she opened the blinds, permitting the sun's rays to infiltrate the room. Sitting on the couch, sipping the tea, Annie began to stir and sat up in bed, rubbing her eyes. 'Morning, Shaz, how was your night? When did you get back?' she said.

'I walked in half an hour ago, had a shower, and now I'm having a cup of tea', Sharon answered mechanically, not really attentive to the verbal exchange.

'Wow, you had a big night then. Did you meet anybody?' Annie threw back the covers and sauntered over to the kitchenette, boiling the jug.

'Yes, a few nice people, going to meet up with them later on this afternoon', Sharon murmured.

'But what about our plans to explore the Paris attractions today?' Annie whined

'Not interested. Look, I'm buggered, so you do your own thing while I get some much-needed sleep', she groaned, placing down the cup and sauntered over to the bed, pulling back the covers.

'You're supposed to call Mum, Sharon', Annie reminded her.

'You spoke to her yesterday ... nope not going to ... she knows we're alright. Oh, can you close those drapes please, sis? I'll be fine this afternoon. Just give me a few hours.' So she placed her head on the pillow.

'Shaz, before you go to sleep after I came back from the nightclub last night, I saw a man watching me from that building across the alleyway. He just stood there glaring at me, and he was wearing a black coat and broad-brimmed hat.' Annie tried to enlighten her sister. 'What? It's probably your imagination again, Annie. Who'd be watching us? We don't know anyone here. Now be quiet so I can get some sleep', Sharon retaliated.

Annie walked cautiously over to the window, initially not wanting to look in the direction of where she saw the disturbing menace; but as she drew the curtains shut, she robotically glimpsed over at the hotel and with the rose-colored sunbeams flickering on the corner of the building. There wasn't even the slightest hint of the man's existence.

Once dressed, Annie made her way down to the foyer with a tourist brochure in hand. She asked the hotel porter for directions to the nearest art gallery and traveled by bus, down the boulevard, soaking up all the unusual sights and sounds, finally arriving at the Musée d'Orsay, which is set on the bank of the River Seine. Popular with art enthusiasts, Annie marveled at the art and sculptures from the period of 1848 to 1915, featuring works by big names such as Delacroix, Monet, and Renoir. She revered how the gallery was set in a converted train station where visitors could admire the stunning beaux-arts architecture and the huge original turn of the 20th-century hanging clock.

After fully appreciating the infamous colonnade, she jumped on another bus, which took her to the Centre Pompidou, whose reputation was fascinating as it stocked most of Europe's modern and contemporary art, displaying all methods of media from video to sculpture, the 20th-century movement of modern art, and the revolutionary fragmented and abstract paintings by Pablo Picasso and George Braque. The morning went by so quickly, and as Annie looked up at the large clock in the Conciergerie, she decided it was time to grab a bite to eat, so she positioned herself at a rustic wooden table with a red-and-white chequered tablecloth and ordered lunch. As she ate her smoked herrings with warm potato salad, she studied the assembly of people who were getting about their daily business, relentlessly alternating from one side of the busy street to another. Sipping at the coffee cup, she watched a bus that had just pulled up on the side of the road, allowing its passengers to disembark. At least a dozen people scurried off the stationary vehicle, scrambling to get out of each other's way before racing off in the direction of their important engagements. She smiled as a frustrated mother struggled to control her disobedient toddler, all the while it was obvious that the child was determined to escape her parent's grip. The mother stood unmoving for a second, attempting to regain her composure; and as she stepped onward from the bus, she revealed a man who had been standing right behind her. Annie's mouth plunged open when she distinctly recognized the man's face as he looked around the hustling area, trying to acquire his bearings; it was Liam, she was sure of it. The man turned to his right, disappearing amongst the crowd with Annie hot on his heels. She could see him in the distance, and every so often, he would halt, look down at some literature he held in his hand, then hurry off again. These sporadic rests enabled Annie to advance ground between them until she'd followed him to the La Fontaine aux Lions fountain, its cast-iron cauldron and magnificent rigid lions with water pouring from their mouths. The man stopped and calmly sat on the fringe of the water's border, inspecting his watch. This was Annie's chance to confront Liam and ask what the hell was he doing in Paris, and just as she was advancing towards him, a young woman cut her off and threw herself into the arms of the anticipating gentleman. Annie stood steadfast in her tracks, conspicuously glaring at who she presumed was Liam; and as the couple made their way past her, embraced in each other's affection, she disgracefully realized that the gentleman was only a resemblance of him.

'I'm going crazy', she muttered, slowly positioning herself on the edge of the fountain, resting from the flood of anxiety that had swamped her body. By the time she had returned to the hotel and entered the floor of their suite, she could hear music and laughter penetrating from behind room 184's entrance.

'Don't tell me Sharon's entertaining', she thought as she despairingly opened the door.

'Here she is', her sister announced, walking up to her and grabbing Annie's hand, pulling her towards the gathering.

'Darling, these are the lovely people I met last night', Sharon broadcasted with the vigor of an excited puppy. Annie stood there, smiling, and nodded hello to everyone, all the while thinking Sharon didn't mirror a woman who had staggered in at 6.00 a.m. drunk as a skunk. 'So? How was your day? What did you see?' Sharon recited sarcastically.

'It was nice, thanks, but I'm really drained'. Annie moaned.

'Don't be silly, here, let me pour you a glass of champagne', Sharon affirmed, moving over to the bar and fixing Annie a drink.

'Here you go', she said, handing her the glass.

'This is Alex, Barry, Sonia, Jessie, Pierre, and James', Sharon introduced everyone.

'Hi, nice to meet you all.'

'Now let's party', Sharon yelled, holding her champagne glass high in the air.

The night wore on, and the music got louder, and so did the conversation with everyone fervently joyful, either dancing around the room or shouting over each other, trying to catch somebody's attention. Each time Annie finished her drink, Sharon would give her flute a top-up until she couldn't consume any more alcohol, so while no one was looking, she concealed her glass under the couch and drifted towards the walk-in robe, shutting the door behind her; she crumbled onto the floor from exhaustion and fell asleep, and that's where she woke up the next morning.

Walking out of the closet, Annie looked around and observed Sharon asleep on the bed with Alex lying next to her with his arm draped across her lifeless body. Positioned on the other bed was Sonia and Jessie while Barry, Pierre, and James were nowhere to be seen; so she opened up the drapes to let the sunshine drench the murky, alcohol-saturated room. One by one, Sharon and her playmates awoke and made themselves a cup of coffee.

'Awww, will someone close those blinds?' Sharon nitpicked.

'We're going now, thanks for the great night, you really know how to party, Sharon', Alex and the others said after finishing their coffees and offered their goodbyes as they exited the suite.

'Shaz, you've really done nothing but drink and party since we've arrived ... you're lowering your morals, and you're acting like a tramp. Mum and Dad would be mortified! You haven't spent any quality time with me at all ... you pick up these strangers and allow them to come into our suite ... you don't know who they are. You're beginning to scare me', Annie opposed.

'Not now, Annie, put a cork in it, will you? We'll be spending the next couple of days together. I'd rather stay in today and just chill out. Why don't you do the same? We'll order room service', Sharon grumbled and pulled the covers back over her head.

Annie agreed with Sharon's request as she did feel somewhat weary from the previous day's events, so while her sister slept, Annie wandered about listlessly, essentially bored and melancholic that she was squandering a perfectly marvelous day in the most exhilarating city that ever was.

Five

Chapter 5

~ ✿✿✿ ~

T
he overnight express from Paris to Moscow was ready
to depart at 6.00 am, so the girls were up bright and
early to catch the high-speed train. They hustled
about and positioned themselves in first class, on the wide
and plush seats, which provided plenty of room to stretch out
confined legs, whereas the friendly staff delivered guidelines
on how to access the first-class lounge, which provided food
and drinks. Conversation wasn't discouraged, but it was made
very clear by the signs posted on the train à grande vitesse
walls, that it should be maintained in a discreet manner and
restricted, which suited Sharon just fine as she had spent
the last two days traipsing around Paris with Annie talking
incessantly about art, culture, and other mind-numbing points
of curiosity.

As the train thrusted out of the terminal and commenced
moving gradually at first, pursuing the lengthy labyrinth

journey towards its final destination, the girls settled in, Sharon pulling out her luxury travel sleep mask with its carry pouch and earplugs and placed the cover over her eyes, subsequently jabbing the plugs into her ears. Annie watched momentarily as Sharon nestled back into the seat, placing a blanket over herself, so she bent down to the hand luggage and plucked out her laptop and a paperback book. She attempted to engage in her continuing interest with the anticipated destinations they had yet to discover, but as she stared out the window, she became hypnotized by the passing landscapes.

Conifer-coated mountains set the scene for Hansel and Gretel–style villages, which were punctuated by dozens of mostly small lakes formed by retreating glaciers during the last ice age. Annie smiled to herself as she thought how much they resembled watery islands dotting the inland landscape. By the time she started concentrating on her computer, it was midday. Sharon was sound asleep, swooned by the cadenced flowing of the train. Annie stood up and wandered in the direction of where the first-class dining lounge would be, and when she arrived, it was crammed with voyagers. She visually skimmed the carriage, and in the farthest right-hand corner, she saw a stylish lady, around the same age as her mum, sitting at a table on her own, so she made her way towards the solitary woman.

'Hello, my name is Annie. I didn't realize there'd be so many people here. May I take a seat at your table please?' she questioned in her utmost courteous manner.

The lady looked up and smiled.

'Of course, my dear, I don't mind at all. My name is Lilly.' She held out her hand as a gesture of goodwill. Lilly was a somewhat fragile-looking woman with a punkish blonde hairstyle. Her mouth was large, her nose upturned, but her facial expressions were of someone cultivated and intelligent. The only thing Annie found intimidating about her was the fact she wore huge dark sunglasses and they blotted out her eyes. In contrast, Lilly's attire was sharp, refined, and urbane; her jacket's lapel was slightly encrusted with rhinestones, accompanied with white pearls, which hung loosely around her neck. They sat quietly together for a while, reading the menu.

'So, Annie, are you on holiday? Where are you from?' Lilly inquired in her strong German accent as she placed the catalog on the table.

'I'm from Australia, and yes, my sister and I are on holiday. We've just finished our degrees and are taking a break for six weeks', Annie informed her

'Good for you. Sounds like a well-deserved break then. Are you stopping over in Germany?' 'No, we're going straight through to Moscow then heading to Romania', she enlightened her new friend as they ordered their food.

'That's a long trip, what's in Romania for you, Annie?'

'Just curious about the mythology there, I'd like to visit the preserved medieval towns and take an excursion through their castles. I've been interested in the area since I was a little girl.' 'Do you believe in legends and folktales?' 'There is a lot of history behind them, it's a country that was once harsh and full of mystery, and because of the oppression of life, the Romanian people created tales of monsters and heroes to give them hope and understanding. Plus, I think it provided them some entertainment around a fire on a cold winter's night.' Annie chuckled.

'Yes, well, you be very cautious about prying into folklore.

It's been known to bewitch those who invest time in their curiosities', Lilly advised, and after she consumed the food, she unswervingly stood up, bidding Annie goodbye and a safe trip.

Annie remained at the table for some time, reflecting on what Lilly had counseled, and finally concluded that she was just a superstitious old lady. Gradually standing up, she headed back to her designated seat, and when Annie arrived there, Sharon was nowhere to be seen. Feeling confused, she positioned herself down on the chair and continued to gaze out the window. Half an hour had passed, and Sharon was still missing.

I wonder where she could be, maybe she's gone to have lunch, but I didn't pass her on the way back,' she said, rationalizing to herself out loud. And just as she was about to ask one of the concierges if they'd seen her sister, Sharon sauntered up the aisle from the opposite direction of the dining car.

'Where were you?' Annie queried as Sharon sat down.

'Nowhere, I just wanted to check out the other end of the train. I was hoping there might have been a bar, but there isn't, so that's a bummer.'

'Fair dinkum, Shaz, that's all you think about is alcohol … and men', Annie said, extremely displeased.

'Well, I don't have any intentions ending up a tedious old spinster like you, Annie.' Sharon exhaled with contempt and placed her sleeping mask back over her eyes and plugged her ears, shutting out any further discussions.

The next stopover was Munich, with the train conductor announcing that it would be allotted at the station for approximately five minutes. Leisurely, the TGV pulled in, finally coming to a halt; and as the doors opened, an assembly of people scrambled off the train, covering the platform, hauling their suitcases behind them. Annie inspected the miscellaneous people from her window, and as the train began to pull away from the station, there stood Liam, fixed in the middle of the bustling crowd, scornfully watching her with a malevolent grin on his face. Her heart began to pound wildly, and the hairs on her arm stood to attention as a force of chills ran down her spine. She turned her head, straining to get a better view of him as the train advanced farther away, but she lost sight of him within seconds. Feeling the overwhelming distress rising up in her entire body, she abruptly disturbed Sharon's siesta, terrifying her with a sudden shake.

'What? What?' Sharon uttered out noisily, ripping off her sleeping mask.

The other passengers gazed at the sisters with apprehension, a few motioning a pointer finger up to their lips, emulating a *'Be quiet'* gesture.

'What's so important that you've woken me with such a fright?' Sharon continued as she sat upright in her chair.

'I saw him. I saw Liam. He was on the platform at the station just staring at me with this wicked sneer on his face', Annie proclaimed.

'Liam? Why the hell would he be here in Europe, and besides how could he afford an overseas trip? Didn't you say the guy was penniless?' Sharon alleged, trying to calm her sister, who was trembling and as white as a ghost

'I'm telling you, Shaz, I definitely saw him.'

'Look, you're in a foreign country, and anybody can resemble someone else especially when you're tired. I haven't seen you rest since we've boarded this train. It's possibly a placebo hallucination or delusion you've experienced from lack of sleep. Here, take my mask, shut your eyes, and forget all about it, okay?' Sharon patted Annie's arm with compassion.

Before Annie settled in for a catnap, Sharon whispered into her ear,

'Lovey, you've got to repel that monster you're feeling from within. Now forget all about what's just happened and go to sleep.' Sharon reclined back in the chair and surveyed her sister with concern.

Feeling marginally hesitant, Annie finally settled down to sleep, but even though the eye mask provided her with a somewhat dark sanctuary, as the time passed, the sensation of the incident's weight grew, and it became savage and impenetrable. Images of the shadowy figure in Paris and Liam's evil stare kept appearing sporadically in her mind combined with the resonating sounds of Lilly's warning and Sharon's patronizing undercurrent of resentment. Beads of sweat began developing on her brow as the fear of losing her mind or dying infiltrated her intellect, climaxing to an unacquainted feeling of detachment towards herself. Pulling off the mask, she became dizzy, unsteady, and lightheaded, with surging terror that was both complex and persuasive. Fear of the thing she might know but was desperately trying to ignore. Helplessness from not being able to induce rationality and make any logic out of the synchronized happenings she had been suffering. She looked over at Sharon, who was immersed in a magazine.

'Shaz, I don't feel so great', she uttered gently.

'Why, what's the matter with you now, Annie?' Sharon asked, gradually looking up from the literature.

'Not sure, just feeling dizzy and a bit panicky.'

'As I said before, you haven't had any rest, and I think this trip has been, to some extent, intense for you. I'll go and get us a cup of tea and some biscuits, okay? Just calm yourself and wait here. I'll be back in a jiffy.' Sharon smiled. Placing down her magazine, she headed towards the dining car.

Once again, Annie fixed her gaze on the fleeting picturesque countryside, and her mind reflected back to the virtuous community of Richmond Province. The simplistic life and the enjoyment she experienced from her socialite leisure activities, like fashionable communal gatherings, which had diverted her attention from any serious tasks and sheltered her from the ugly extremes of the world. Things were impulsive and spirited, and there weren't any psychological consequences involved. She felt as though she'd been egotistical towards filling her days with endless engagements, hospitable requests with her parents enduring love and guidance; and right now, she'd give anything to be back there. Sharon reappeared, struggling to balance the piping hot cups of tea and biscuits with the propulsion of the train. 'Here you go, Annie', she indicated, offering her one of the mugs.

'You'll feel better once you've got some hot tea into you', she continued.

'Thanks, Shaz', Annie said, taking a mouthful of the steaming beverage.

'What's got you so restless, Annie?'

'Just stuff, I feel as though I'm losing it', she answered, disgruntled.

'You know what it is? You're feeling melancholy, that's all. Once we get to Bucharest, that spark of curiosity will ignite and you'll be in control again', Sharon comforted.

'I suppose so, this train trip must be taking its toll on me. How much longer have we got, Shaz?'

Chapter 5

'Once we've stopped in Munich, it's another fourteen hours after that, I'm afraid. Have your cup of tea, relax, and get some shut-eye. You can hang on to my sleep mask, alright?' Sharon looked content. So Annie did as her sister instructed, and within half an hour, she was asleep; she didn't even wake when the train pulled into Munich.

Sharon began wandering the train like a vagrant without a specific reason or destination, pausing systematically to text or view messages on her mobile phone. She found an empty seat two carriages away from where Annie was sleeping and sat down, contemplating the approaching journey and whether her sister was rationally adequate to continue, but her mind rambled back to their childhood that instantly brought about an emotional state of pain.

She sat quietly, glowering at her dress and picking at its edges, thinking about the rejection she had received as a child, influenced by her parent's biases when quarrels established between Annie and herself. Even though her sister was only two hours younger, their parents considered Annie as the darling little one and cherished her as such. She'd always been Daddy's little girl, and Mama had just followed suit. Sharon always felt wounded by this, and the persistent rejection she'd receive, mismanaged her instinctive need to belong. She would brood over past hurts; the memories replayed over and over in her mind, which simply increased her distress, heightening her trauma levels, and it eventually converted into an obsession with her. Somewhere in a book, she had read that the road to wisdom is flagged with pain and suffering. Well, as far as she was concerned, there are two kinds of pain: the kind that makes you strong and the kind that causes worthless suffering. Sharon had no patience for worthless things.

She meandered back to her designated chair and joined Annie, sleeping the rest of the afternoon and into the night. By the time the girls awoke, the morning was glowing and well underway as the casting sunbeams radiated in every direction, illuminating the town of Bucharest. They gathered their luggage from the train and stepped into the old town; its vibrant thoroughfares were full of life with small streets and a big variety of buildings, where so many people were moving this way and that in such a dynamic, animated expanse. Annie looked about and immediately recognized the splendor of 17th- and 18th-century Orthodox churches and the graceful, charming villas that were tucked away in quiet corners. Annie flagged a taxi, and after cramming their luggage into the boot, they hopped in and gave directions for the awaiting hotel. They drove along looking out the window, and at every turn of a corner, there were museums, parks, trendy cafes, and drinking gardens. The taxi traveled down a leafy neighborhood, and after it pulled up at the address, they entered the hotel and witnessed this regal, old-world building, in its former glory dating back from 1893. The marble columns and carved wooden staircase recalled its original features including period furnishings and an exclusively decorated, elegant lobby. Annie stepped up to the reception desk while Sharon explored the foyer.

'Yes, madam, your name please', the concierge gestured.

'Annie and Sharon Karce.'

'Here you are, you'll be staying in suite 49. Just use the lift, and it's on the third floor, the porters will bring your bags to the apartment', the smartly dressed employee said, passing Annie the keys.

'Thank you, sir. Come on, Shaz, we have to take the lift.'

Chapter 5

When they arrived in their room, Annie was flabbergasted with the French neoclassicism origins, which included direct copies of Greek and Roman decorations and furniture. The orthodox beauty of the oak-paneling incorporated arches, pillars, and caryatids within a geometric framework took her breath away. The paintings that hung suspended on the walls were accomplished in opaque watercolors and classical sideboard tables, which were flanked by scroll-footed pedestals supplemented both the beds. To complete the 18th-century magnificence, gilded furniture and ornaments fastidiously bejeweled the apartment and a mediocre-sized griffin maintained its upright position in the adjacent corner. As Sharon gauged the room, she walked directly up to the griffin sculpture.

'What is this ugly-looking animal thingy', she vexed with some repulsion.

'It's a griffin', Annie educated her.

'And what is it supposed to represent? Your worst nightmare?'

'No, Shaz, actually it's a legendary creature, and it's perceived as a powerful and majestic animal. The head and wings of an eagle represent "the king of birds" while the body, tail, and hind legs of a lion symbolizes "the king of beasts". During the Persian Empire, it was seen as a protector from evil, witchcraft, and slander.'

'Well, can I put a sheet over it? It's creeping me out', Sharon tested.

'No, you can't. That will stop any positive strengths radiating from it', Annie said, perturbed. 'Whatever. Your distortion with this mythology junk really needs examining. You're possessed with this shit', Sharon condemned.

'Maybe so, but that's why we're here. After I've experienced the philosophies and traditions of this area, I'll be more informed and able to discuss the evidence with my history students. That's my main objective, Shaz. Come on, let's quickly change and go check out the local sights', Annie recommended, trying to change Sharon's attitude.

They stepped out of the hotel and wandered the streets of Bucharest and instantly noticed Romania's capital buzzing with its unconventional summer gardens. Entering a gate of an emerald oasis, which was hidden behind a villa, they followed the footpath and encountered a green canopy of trees. Beatniks swung in hammocks while bohemian sequence lights and wooden counters festooned the terrace. The girls sat down at a table and ordered their lunch. Annie chose the cheese platter while Sharon requested the butterfish with green rice and lemon, and they relished the encouraging banter with each other, socializing in the impromptu setting with a bottle of wine. The following days in Bucharest were enjoyable, and their mutual contentment towards each other intermingled like a hand in glove. Annie called home once a week, at her mother's scheduled request, but each time, she was informed that their father's well-being was slowly deteriorating.

'We should cut our holiday short and go home if Papa isn't getting any better', Annie complied.

'Look, he's got the best physicians money can buy. I'm sure they'll figure out what's wrong, and besides, Mama is there with him. We've only got four short weeks and then our holiday will be over and it'll be back into the slog of working. This is a once-in-a-lifetime opportunity for us, Annie', Sharon persuaded.

Chapter 5

They frequented the sunshiny garden bars every day, banqueting there for both lunch and dinner, complimenting their meals with copious amounts of alcohol. Sharon was repetitively collecting new friends while Annie just went along with the experience.

'What's on your itinerary tomorrow, Sharon?' Annie queried as she strained to interrupt one of Sharon's incessant conversations with a stranger.

'What? Oh, I think I'm going to hang out with my friends. Didn't you say that we might go on a day trip to that beach tomorrow, Julie?' Sharon responded to Annie but had turned towards the lady sitting alongside her, aiming the question at Julie, ignoring Annie.

'Yes, we can do that. Would you like to join us, Annie?' Julie suggested.

'Thank you, but I have my own plans. I've booked a day tour visiting Transylvania and Bran Castle. I'm really looking forward to it', Annie acknowledged.

'Okay, but you're more than welcome to come with us if you change your mind', Julie continued.

'Annie won't change her mind, she's infatuated with ghoulish stories. It's the main reason why we're here. It'll eventually drive her crazy', Sharon criticized.

'Really? Be vigilant, Annie, some say that they're only stories while others believe they are true. Some argue that because these legends have been repeated so many times over the centuries that they've forged an existence of their own.' Julie smiled

'Ooooh, you better be on your toes Annie, you never know, you might finally meet that disfigured bogeyman you've been searching for all these years', Sharon mocked as the rest of the group heckled along, envisaging the thought.

The following morning, Annie was up early and equipped herself for the day's excursion. As she was leaving the suite, she regarded Sharon, who was quietly snoozing in bed.

'Bye, Shaz, I'm leaving now.'

'Mmm', Sharon groaned in a lethargic manner

Annie stood there for a moment before closing the door behind her and then subsequently headed off towards the train station with a haversack secured tightly over her shoulder. The journey to Transylvania would take five hours, so Annie relaxed and enjoyed the transient scenery. Once at Brasov station, Annie walked out into the community and witnessed one of the most charming villages she'd ever seen. Dotted with centuries-old medieval Saxon cottages, the cobblestone streets were an animated combination of cows mooing, horses pulling carts, and grungy geese waddling about, all contributing to the idealists; peasant image of the town. Old men sat lifeless in the dim shadows of a few giant trees as the air bubbled with birds whistling and farm animals chained up in excrement-strewn backyards.

A small group of tourists gathered next to a bus, where the conductor was announcing the approaching tour to Bran Castle. Annie handed the man her ticket and sat up at the front of the bus, inspecting the other tourists as they embarked. After half an hour of the bus weaving its way through a twisting road, around the last bend, it finally revealed the eerie structure of Bran Castle as it hovered high on its stony perch, clinging to the craggy mountain like a vulture watching its prey. The towering stone walls and red columns only enhanced its unnatural reclusive façade, and the castle's silhouette firmly accomplished its center stage to the dramatic backdrop, the Carpathian Mountains. The tourists disembarked and followed their guide, up the unyielding pathways into the fortress where gothic furnishings and well-preserved rooms and chambers detailed the scenes of ghastly legends. The chaperon led them through many of its immaculate, elaborate rooms still adorned with original luxuriant décor while he constantly immersed his visitors with unpleasant stories, conjuring up visions of howling wolves and bats with human blood dripping from their gluttonous little fangs, pulsating around, against an unnerving full moon.

As the group moved along, the chaperon explained how the castle concealed secret interlacing passageways within its walls and has led to rooms that have only been discovered recently due to the castle undergoing restoration work.

'You never know, there still might be chambers that are yet to be discovered', he joked. Annie loitered back from the group, absorbed in probing every nook and cranny of each room. She nudged at wooden and stone carvings that were fixed against walls or fireplaces, hoping to reveal an undisclosed passage as the group moved into Vlad III, the Prince of Wallachia's bedroom. The other sightseers had departed by the time she caught up, so Annie had the opportunity to explore, in detail, the four-poster bed and the thick, elaborately carved wooden canopy. She sat on the bed at first then casually positioned herself in the middle of it, gazing up at the undercarriage of the bedhead, examining the intricate artifacts... and that's when she caught sight of it. A trivial carving of a rat's head, no bigger than a chickpea, its beady compacted eyes staring right back at her. She thought it odd as most animal carvings on gothic furnishings were of dragons, horses, or lions' heads.

Her curiosity made her reach up and poke the nose of the rodent's head with her fingernail, then she poked the eyes and heard something open from below the enormous bed. Annie climbed off the mattress and surveyed beneath it. A wooden panel had opened, and when she heard the voices of another group of tourists about to enter the room, she slipped under the canopied bed. She could see their shoes milling around, close to where she was hiding; so in fear of being caught, Annie crawled through the opened panel and found herself on a small landing, which supported the top of a narrow vertical spiraling staircase. She scaled down the dusty steps until she reached a dark wood-paneled room, and once her eyes adjusted to the shadowy chamber and using her mobile phone's light, she glimpsed in the corner of

the room a primitive desk with an imposing chair thrusted precisely under it. Brushing away years of accrued cobwebs out of her face, Annie walked over and stood at the desk, eventually dragging the hefty chair out and sitting down on it.

'This must have been the prince's confidential underground study or something', she muttered to herself.

Unknowingly, amongst the blackness, dozens of watchful little rat eyes were inspecting her, not understanding who this unusual being was or what she was doing in their abode. All around, she could hear them squeaking, hissing, and chattering, chomping and grinding their sharp teeth with provocation towards her presence. Opening the drawers of the table, she blew away centries of filth while rummaging around for something like trinkets, documents, or relics of some kind. The second draw wouldn't close properly, so Annie gave it a robust thrust and instantly heard a firm thump sound on the floor, so she promptly looked down onto the ground underneath it. There among the rat droppings, dirt, and cobwebs an old rubicund metal case rested, the size of a matchbox.

Annie reached down and picked it up, staring in wonderment at first before she delicately opened it to expose a pendant with a deep-red stone approximately five centimeters in diameter. The surface of the nugget appeared blistered as though someone had once thrown it into a ferocious fire, but in the middle of the stone lustered a bright-yellow glow resembling the gem capturing the sun flickering within its belly. The chain was handmade with an intricate vintage design crafted in silver and had an incandescent luster that reflected light even in the dark-greyish room.

'It's so beautiful' Annie thought, spellbound by the gem's allure.

Suddenly comprehending that she had to be back with her group, she quickly jostled the pendant into her pocket, closed its gestation box, and placed it smoothly back where she believed its hiding spot had been. Ascending the circling staircase, Annie emerged from the opened panel and gently closed it; and like a ghost, she waited until no one was around to finally crawl out from beneath the four-poster bed. Brushing off the dust and cobwebs from her clothes, she reunited with her group as they boarded the bus for their return trip to Brasov. Annie merged with the queue and established herself at the back of the coach, all the while, her hand positioned firmly upon the pocket where the hijacked pendant was secretly hoarded. The final leg of the trip home was long and strenuous, and she erratically drew the pendant out to shrewdly gaze upon it, again and again, still captivated by its beauty; but each time she took a peek, her upper arm would begin to ache. She rolled up her sleeve, and even though the bruising and red mark from where Liam had grabbed her were absent, it still delivered soreness as though the injury was there to remind her of Liam's threat. Arriving at their home base, Annie walked into the suite, only to find that Sharon was absent. A note and a bottle of wine rested on the sideboard table next to her bed. Placing the backpack on the sofa, she casually wandered over and picked up the note, and it read:

Dearest Annie, as I mentioned, I've decided to stop over with Julie and friends for a couple of days, we'll be holidaying at a resort near Vadu Beach. It's one of the last pristine beaches on the Black Sea, and I must visit there before we go home. Enjoy the wine I bought for you as a peace offering. Call me if anything arises. Take care, and I'll see you by the end of the week. Lots of love, Sharon.

Annie placed the note back on the table and dejectedly sat down on her bed, utterly bewildered that Sharon could just take a mini trip without a word of warning.

'*I thought she said that they were only going for the day*', she cursed, unpacking her things and wandering into the bathroom to take a shower and once she had finished, she decisively opened the bottle of wine, filled the glass, and fashioned a toast to herself.

'Here's to you, Annie, and a great unsociable holiday with Sharon', she expressed as she raised her flute then guzzled the entire quantity.

Wandering pointlessly around the suite, swilling wine from the bottle, she functioned as though she was lost, feeling void of any true emotions, and concluded that her heart was entering a cold, frozen place where she couldn't feel anything at all … so lonely.

88

Chapter 5

It was 11.00 pm when Annie finally went to bed. She had tucked the pendant away securely, wrapping it carefully in one of her handkerchiefs, and placing it in the corner of the dresser. Resting her head on the pillow, she drifted off to that transitional period between wakefulness and sleep, envisaging her day's activities in her mind's eye and the glory of discovering the mysterious pendant. She rolled over onto one side, and that's when she heard it ... a systematic, gullet whirring clicking sound.

It started off slow at first then got progressively faster and slightly higher in pitch towards the end and repeated the cycle. Bolting swiftly upright, she turned on the light and stared in the direction of where the noise was transmitting from, but she couldn't see anything, so she switched off the lamp and positioned herself back down to sleep ... and then she heard it for a second time, the methodical, gurgling clicking sound. Hoping to catch it this time, she flashed her mobile phone torch towards the sound and there it sat, all bundled up in the corner of the room, a withered-up hairless creature with a big mouth and feet, an unnatural elongated head, its sunken eyes intensely fixed on her with a deathly stare. Annie instantly began screaming as the creature scuttled up the wall like a large spider climbing its web, erratically turning its bizarre, convulsive skull around to ogle at her again. She immediately snatched up the hotel phone and, amidst the obscure dark, she called the reception desk for help.

'Help me, please help me, there's a strange creature in my room, and I need somebody here quickly', she cried.

Subsequently, a muscular hotel attendant knocked on the door then immediately advanced into the room, because Annie was still wretchedly crying, huddled up in bed with four pillows enclosing her. He turned on the light.

'What's the problem, miss?' the hefty attendant questioned.

'There was this ugly terrifying creature climbing the walls in here. It was just there', she said, pointing her shaking hand at the corner of the room while the man poked around the apartment, inspecting all conceivable spaces.

'I can't find anything, miss, I've checked everywhere, and you're the only one here', he reassured, glancing at the empty bottle of wine that was sitting on the coffee table.

'You've undoubtedly had a big day, and I bet you've been to visit Dracula's castle today ... am I right?' he continued.

'Yes', Annie replied meekly.

'Well, that's it then, the creepy castle and its stories have ignited your imagination, and it's come back to haunt you. Get some sleep, miss, everything is alright. Try and rest your mind', he encouraged, turning off the light and closing the door behind him.

Annie just lay there, unresponsive, sniffing away the tears, blankets pulled tightly up to her chin with pillows surrounding her like a fortress, her gaze eternally static towards the corner of the room where she last saw the insidious goblin.

She remained there hypnotized, eyes like saucers, transfixed in that position all night until the rays of the sun's saving grace penetrated through the curtains and brought saneness back into her mind and realism. Weary and apathetic, Annie skulked out of bed and made herself a cup of coffee. She wanted to call Sharon but knew in her heart, she would only reprimand her for going to Bran Castle in the first place and blame her fanciful interests in the associated creepy legends and tales, so she resisted and decided to entomb the sickness of the night's lingering visions deep within her soul. Sharon

Chapter 5

will never know about the cherished pendant either. It was going to be her secret to keep.

Six

Chapter 6

Edna balanced the bowl of hot chicken soup on a tray along with a piece of wholemeal toast and freshly squeezed orange juice. She placed it skillfully down on the plate table in front of Warren.

'How are you feeling today?' Edna queried.

'No too bad, thanks, dearest', Warren replied, digging his spoon into the soup.

'I think those strong painkillers are helping. Have you heard from the girls?' he continued. 'Yes, they're fine. Having the time of their lives, although I've only spoken to Annie, I haven't even heard from Sharon. She's such a trustworthy daughter, our Annie, she's very worried about you and how things are going here', Edna acknowledged.

'Well, the next time you speak with her, tell her that I'm fine and not to be concerned. I just want them to enjoy their break away. They'll be home in a few weeks anyway', Warren appealed to his wife.

Edna and Warren had been married for 45 years. They met during a garden event at Edna's parents' manor, and the moment Warren laid eyes on her, he was besotted. She looked diminutive and fragile, like a porcelain doll, standing beside her mother in a pink formal dress crafted in luxurious silk and taffeta, so charmingly exquisite in the full skirt and fitted bodice gown, trimmed flawlessly with pearls and precious gems. As the festive day established itself, Warren gathered up the nerve to approach the figurine-like girl; and once he struck up a conversation with her, she emerged as an overprotected child, immature in her expressions and general chit-chat. It was obvious that her parents gave her everything she wanted and that they believed Edna should not endure any type of problems at all. They made every decision for her whenever challenging situations arose, so her predestined adulthood evolved within a well-ordered and sophisticated discipline. Warren was a self-aware young man, and he considered that his courtship regarding Edna should be done with a serious and mature attitude. He wanted her family to approve of him, as his ultimate objective was marriage, so he eventually asked her parents for the honor to court their daughter, and they complied. They would hang out with her group of refined and polished friends since he was ardent to learn more about her personality and how she interacted with other people as well as her interests in starting a family and her beliefs on the significance of family principles. After two years of courtship, Warren proposed, and they were married at the St Andrews cathedral in Richmond Province with hundreds of people attending, including celebrities and the district's socialites.

The media was a large presence on their wedding day as the celebration was extravagant, and her family wasn't shy about showing off their wealth. Upon arrival at the reception, guests were ushered to their tables where personalized tote bags awaited each patron with mini bottles of champagne and a gift certificate to a favorite local coffee shop. Each lady guest was given a corsage as they walked through the reception doors, and everyone remarked on how lovely the auditorium looked with strings of twinkle lights, dishes full of fruit purees, lavender sprigs, and citrus twists decorating the tables. Warren and Edna appreciated their lives together and took the time to enjoy special moments, celebrating their milestones and life cycle events with the memories that were created by such occasions, strengthening their bond. Their tenderness and respect for each other deepened as they valued the other's opinion, and it assisted them during the more challenging moments in life, with the closeness that developed, contributing to their long-lasting marriage.

'Your test results should be available in a couple of days. I'll be relieved when we find out what's really going on with these persistent headaches of yours', Edna confessed.

'Yes, well, we'll know soon enough, I suppose', Warren sighed.

'Just rest up now and don't burden yourself with any problems.' Edna stood up from the chair, and as she was exiting the door, she turned and blew Warren a kiss.

'I love you, darling, don't hesitate to call Tilly if you need anything.' She closed the door and made her way down the sweeping staircase.

Entering the sunlit parlor, Edna gathered up her embroidery

and sat on the luxurious sofa to commence her reputable handiwork. The indoor plants that adorned the room offered a feeling of comfort and serenity. Her needlework had been an essential part of her elite upbringing, and the objects that she crafted were often intended as gifts to her friends or for the Country Women's Association, but they also duplicated as visual symbols of her skills while also offering a mental oasis, evoking calm emotions and an optimistic outlook.

It was 4.00 p.m. when the doctor made his visit to the manor house, William ushering him in and announcing his arrival as he entered the parlor.

'Oh hello, Dr. Bartlett, how are you? Thanks for coming, I hope you're bringing good news about Warren's tests, Edna said as she placed down her stitching.

'I'm not at liberty to discuss it here, Edna, could we please come up to Warren's room and I'll enlighten you on the results? I need your husband present', he briefed her in a dismal tone. 'Yes, certainly, please follow me', she said, concerned with the doctor's behavior.

'Warren, darling, Doctor Bartlett is here to see you, he has some information about your test results.' She smiled. Warren sat up in bed and adjusted his pillow and blankets.

'Hello, Doctor, so what are the findings?'

'Okay ... your tests show that you have a malignant tumor on the frontal lobe of your brain. Before you ask any questions, please let me explain what the symptoms will be if the tumor is allowed to progress', he instructed as he watched Edna's expression anguish with grief.

'You are already experiencing some of these indicators, Warren, with the morning headaches and occasional vomiting. As time advances, you will have changes in your behavior with cognitive impairment and a clumsy, uncoordinated gait. You may also experience impaired speech, lack of recognition, and seizures', he informed.

'Oh my god', Edna howled, crumpling onto the chair beside Warren's sickbed.

'Is it operable?' Warren asked in a calm voice.

'Yes, that was my next question, Warren. Are you willing to undergo surgery?'

'Of course, he is', Edna interrupted.

'Shush, please, dear', Warren advised. 'When can the surgery be done?' He continued.

'Well, because you've been on blood thinners for a while, we'll have to take you off them for about five days, so any time after that', Dr. Bartlett said.

'We must call the girls', Edna interposed.

'No, Edna, why? It will only upset them, and besides, I don't want them here while I'm having the surgery ... it will only cause distress. Let them finish their holiday, and we'll deal with the issue once they're back home', Warren protested.

'Starting from today, you will stop taking the warfarin tablets, and I'll check on you during the following week', the doctor detailed.

'Thank you, Dr. Bartlett', Warren continued. 'Tilly will show you out', Edna furthered.

As Dr. Bartlett exited the bedroom, Edna turned her attention towards Warren.

'This is absolutely shocking, I can't believe it's happening to us', she whined.

'That's life, dearest, we just have to face the problem at hand. Doctor Bartlett knows what he's doing, and we will definitely get through this.' Warren eased his wife's concerns.

Chapter 6

Edna went back downstairs and informed the house staff of the doctor's conclusions. She made it very clear that she wished for them to attend to Warren's every need and asked Tilly to do hourly checks on her husband, just to safeguard that he was comfortable and didn't require anything. Walking slowly into the parlor, she picked up the embroidery, wishing to recommence the stitching; but instead, she just sat there frozen. Her eyes riveted out the window, anticipating the impending weeks and the looming obstacles that had just transpired. *'I don't know how to tell the girls, and I'm afraid of how they'll react'*, she admitted to herself. *'It's going to be a strenuous couple of weeks'*, she continued.

Annie laid down on the bed, visualizing the occurrence of the previous night. She reached over, pulling open the dresser drawer, and grasped the pendant, unwrapping it from the shielding handkerchief. Rolling over onto her back, she studied the jewel from back to front, admiring the intensity of the radiant bonfire that intimately seared from inside it. She considered wearing the vintage necklace but decided to get it scrubbed up, freeing its inherent beauty as there was residual murky filth and tiny cobwebs still fused within the elaborate chain, so she roamed into the bathroom and began washing it, and that's when she heard a knock at their hotel room door.

'Yes, who is it?' she yelled from the bathroom with her hands still in the washbasin. The knocking persisted. So in a huff, Annie dried her hands and went to answer the bothersome visitor.

'Yes, what do you want?' she blurted out, exasperated as she swung the door open, but nobody was there. Protruding her head just outside the entrance, she looked up and down the corridor in both directions, but there wasn't a soul in sight. Bewildered, she closed the door and began walking towards the bathroom when the thumping started again; although this time, it was violent and threatening. She instantly reopened the door and stepped out into the hallway and saw a shadowy individual looming at the end of the passage, its silhouette figure ominous in presence, wearing a black hooded cloak that was lowered over the person's face. 'Who are you? What do you want?' she yelled at the sinister being. It answered in an intense, bad-tempered voice.

'I am watching you', it snarled and then scurried off, disappearing around the intersection of the corridor. Annie ran after the creepy brute, chasing it up until the juncture, but it had vanished. She stood there paralyzed for a moment, a million feelings racing through her body; but ultimately, the hallucination had left her disoriented, creating a fervor of vulnerability and weakness, subconsciously making her question her own mind and rationale. Wretchedly, she walked back down the corridor and into her apartment, finally reentering the bathroom. She went over to the washbasin and witnessed that the water with the submerged pendant had turned pitch-black like someone had just poured a container of liquid ink into it. 'Are you kidding me?' she asked herself. 'I've got to get out of this apartment', she announced, so after she plucked the necklace from its obscure watery grave, she wiped it dry and hurled it onto the bed. But even with the pigment from the black water staining and carbonizing the majority of its glint, the belly of the stone continued to blaze lustrously. Annie chose to revisit the bohemian drinking garden where she and Sharon had lunched on their first day in Bucharest, even assembling herself at the table they relaxed at on that day. The waiter moseyed up to her table with a menu in his hand.

'Would you like to order anything, madam?'

'I might just have a drink at the moment', she replied.

'Oh, pardon me, miss, is your name Annie? I think there has been something left here for you by your sister ... Sharon, isn't it?' he suddenly recollected.

'How do you know us?' she probed suspiciously.

'Your sister left a detailed explanation of you, plus you both look exactly the same—well, not quite exactly but very alike', he explained, a little uncomfortable with Annie's mistrust. He hurried back into the café and returned, carrying a bottle of wine.

'Here you are, Miss Annie. Sharon has asked me to apologize for her absence and said that you'd forgive her if I was to give you this exclusive bottle of wine.' He smiled as Annie inspected the bottle.

'It looks nice, may I have a glass?' she conceded.

'I'll fetch you a tumbler and a bucket of ice right away.' So the waiter hurried off, retrieving the desired items.

For the entire midafternoon, Annie sat in the summer garden, sipping on the bottle of wine and indulging in the cafe's exceptional food, and by the time she returned to the hotel suite, it was twilight. The hours spent at the summer garden had put her mind at ease after those terrifying encounters, and she was actually looking forward to Sharon's return. Entering the apartment, she observed that the chambermaids had been in and tidied the room, including making the beds but Annie strolled directly into the bathroom and while she was at the basin, she remembered throwing the pendant onto the bed, leaving it exposed for anyone to see.

Turning rapidly, she made a beeline towards the mattress, and there it rested, in the exact same position where it had settled; the black discoloration that formerly marked the gem was completely gone, and elusively placed beside it was a note. Picking it up, she read the untidy pen-crafted warning the message provided.

This pendant is not a souvenir for you to take. It will cause bad luck, illness, or death to you or a loved one. Wickedness and evil will reproduce in your life. Put it back from where it came before it's too late.

Abruptly, she rejected the note, throwing it onto the floor, and stepped away from the bed, all the while glaring at the pendant as it shrewdly lay there, the intense blaze in its gut-eyeing her right back. Retrieving her monogrammed handkerchief, she picked up the pendant and the note, wrapping them in the linen hankie, and rushed out the door and down the hallway, abandoning the package in a garbage bin that was assembled in the corner of the vestibule. She closed the lid and walked back to the suite as the bundled pendant lay disposed of in the bottom of the bin, sheathed in the hankie with the distinctive trademark 'A Karce' facing upwards. All of the oppressive phantoms came flooding back, saturating her intellect with vivid manifestations, the heightened level of arousal made her sharply engrossed with questioning her stability and the deteriorating soundness of her perception, beckoning feelings of isolation and distress. She wandered up to the imposing griffin that was mounted in the corner of the room and stood there, looking into its eyes. Finally, she asked the sculpture.

'Why aren't you protecting me?'

Inaudibly, she slinked into bed, pulling the covers up over her chest; and as the night advanced she remained alert, watchful, and attentive for any further visions to materialize. Hours had passed and slumber flooded her troubled mind, so she turned off the lamp and began to fall asleep; then without delay, she heard a scraping noise, fitfully accompanied with a hideous, evil cackle. Switching the light back on, she witnessed an emaciated old man, hairless and bluish in color with pointed elf-like ears and a curious extension from the top of its head, his bright reddish eyes immovable on her with a hungry stare and an evil smile that deceived all innocence.

She began yelling at the creature, 'Fuck off, fuck off, fuck off', over and over again until the goblin spontaneously vanished through the wall. But before it did, it morphed into a wolf, exposing its bloodstained fangs as it gradually perished. Still gripped in the terror that had just happened, Annie, unmoving like a statuette, sat upright in bed for what seemed like half the night until she warily lay back down hauling the blankets over her head and entombed herself underneath the coverings, but as she shrouded her body, she muttered only one solitary frightened verdict ...

'The only way out is inward.'

The following afternoon, Sharon breezed into the apartment, humming her favorite song without a care in the world. She placed her bags at the entrance near the doorway and scanned the area, noticing that the only evidence of Annie's attendance within the room was a pile of disheveled blankets on her bed and pillows scattered beneath and on top.

'Annie, are you here?' she called, walking into the bathroom; but she couldn't detect her sister anywhere, so she decided to undress and have a shower. Eventually, Sharon emerged and boiled the kettle to make a cup of tea; and as the jug steamed away, she wandered over to Annie's bed, studying the unkempt disarray. She began tidying up the divan, straightening some of the sheets, and pulling out the pillows from underneath the blankets, and that's when she noticed a protruding bulge that lingered farther down, towards the bottom of the bed. Tossing back the entire overlay, there lay Annie, eyes staring vacantly, her long dark hair clumped and gnarled, drenched with vomit, her face grey tinged and mouth gaping open with blue-colored lips, indicating that the life that once dwelled within her was gone.

Annie had died alone.

Sharon jumped back from the bed, clasping her hand rapidly over her mouth, attempting to silence the shriek; her eyes neurotically fixated on her little sister's corpse. In thorough shock and her mind racing with a million convoluted feelings, she finally moved towards the lifeless body and pulled the covers back over her as she couldn't deal with the expression of agonizing torment that was frozen on Annie's face. Overwhelming fear consumed Sharon, and she became irrational, pacing repetitively about the room, utterly terrified of the constricted feelings that were escalating within; her shaking hands were having difficulty keeping still. Amidst her trepidation, she suddenly heard a rustling noise outside the room. Gingerly, Sharon went to the door, opening it softly and through a narrow opening, she watched a busy housekeeper emptying the garbage bin at the end of the corridor, the same bin where Annie had ditched the pendant and its accompanying note. She closed the door and foolishly predicted that no one would've seen her return to the room this evening, so in her intensified responsiveness, she began thinking illogical thoughts, planning an escape before anyone else found her sister. Frantically, Sharon began

Chapter 6

packing all her belongings, stuffing them desperately into bags and rushing around the apartment, collecting anything that would associate her to the death; then as though a light bulb had switched on in her brain, she abruptly stopped. Suddenly comprehending that everyone knew Annie and herself had been traveling together and had simultaneously reserved the room, she collapsed down on the couch and began to cry. Things were becoming more complicated, and she didn't know how to deal with the imminent problems that were plaguing her, so she reached for the phone and made a despairing call. It rang five times before the recipient answered.

'Hi, it's me', she spoke softly.

'Hi, what's up?' the voice on the end of the receiver asked.

'It's Annie ... she's dead', replied Sharon, sniffing back the tears.

'What? How? This wasn't supposed to happen.'

'I know it wasn't, I don't know what to do, please tell me what to do', she pleaded.

'Okay, okay, just leave your stuff there because you've been away for a couple of days, and as far as anyone knows you haven't come back. Make sure that you empty the contents of your purse once you've left the hotel, just keep your wallet and passport, okay? Meet me at my place as soon as you can', the voice instructed.

'Alright', she obeyed. Sharon placed the phone down then went about rearranging her possessions back to where they had been initially and quickly grabbed her bag, and as she was exiting the door, she turned around towards Annie and delivered one final remark to her sister.

'Goodbye, sweetheart, rest in peace', she declared and then

hung a **Do Not Disturb** sign on the handle of the door; then she fanatically vanished down the hallway.

Once outside the hotel, Sharon hastened to the train station, but before she boarded the next departure, she cautiously looked around the platform, scouting the area, and quickly emptied the full contents of her bag into a dust bin, only preserving her wallet and passport, exactly what the voice on the phone told her to do. Then she stepped onto the adjoining carriage as it began its slow departure out of Bucharest.

The hours leading up to Annie's death, she had rested silently under the covers, absorbed in her eavesdropping, and immediately hyperventilated at every sound, whether it was real or not. Beneath the warm secure crypt she had fashioned for herself, she began drifting off to sleep when she heard the door of the apartment open and close. Peeking through the blankets she witnessed an intruder, dressed in a black cloak with the hood hanging over its face, and instantly recognized it as the same menacing individual from the hallway incident the time before. And as it mutely walked around the apartment, Annie kept ghostly quiet. The tormentor moved from one end of the room to the other, picking up and inspecting items then placing them back in their original position, until it loitered at the end of her bed. Paralyzed with fear and as her wheezing became strenuous, Annie fought to draw a breath under the concealment of the blankets, realizing the escalating need to gag. The bed started to vibrate as the intimidator placed both hands on the bottom-corner bedposts and convulsed it sadistically, knowing that its prey was camouflaged there, stricken with relentless panic. And as it began to speak with its harsh raspy voice, sounding like gravel in its throat, it amplified up, conveying his intentions.

'You bitch who thinks she's so essential and powerful with all your money and prestige. I am always watching you', it growled and raised the bottom end of the bed into the air, dropping it down with an unexpected crash, again and again. She clutched her previously injured arm as it began throbbing from the impact. Annie trembled violently, not uttering a sound, and as the tyrant skulked out the door, leaving her twitching around, her body convulsed from the onset of the irregular heart palpitations she was suffering combined with a choking seizure as the vomit penetrated up, erupting out of her mouth, eventually asphyxiating her. As she lay there dying, her final thoughts were of her parents and sister and how much she treasured them with all her heart and soul, and with one last breath, she whispered *'I love you'* and then departed.

On the train, Sharon tied her long hair up in a chignon then wrapped a scarf over her head. Next, she put on oversized dark sunglasses, hoping that if anybody on the train was interrogated by the police, the commuters wouldn't be able to identify her description. She sat there for two and three-quarter hours, her face perpetually siding towards the window, all the while mentally recreating the haunting visions of Annie's fossilized expression of terror on her sweet face. The next stop was her departure, and when the train docked, she inconspicuously disembarked, walking rapidly towards the address where the individual on the telephone resided. Arriving at the entrance, she pounded frantically on the door until the occupant of the villa opened it, but before entering the premises, she immediately removed her sunglasses and headscarf and torpidly stood in the doorway as the resident finally appeared. Sharon unpredictably hesitated and just stared at the occupant with absolute shame of the scandal they had just executed. Stepping into the house, she flung her arms around the individual's neck and sobbed uncontrollably, uttering one simple remark.

'Oh, Liam, what have we done?'

Seven

Chapter 7

W illiam carried the hospital bag out to the awaiting
car and deposited them in the boot while the
remaining domestic staff lined up to advocate
their well-wishes and support for Warren's forthcoming
operation.

'All the best, Mr. Karce, I'm sure everything will go
smoothly', William said in his high social class accent.

'Thank you, William, thank you, everyone. I will see you
soon', Warren replied with optimism, waving to them all as he
and Edna entered the back seat of their chauffeur-driven car.

As the vehicle ambled along the circular driveway towards
the gates, Warren turned to Edna. 'Have you heard from the
girls recently?' he enquired.

'No, dear, not of late', she answered.

'It's not like Annie to forget to call us, she's very attentive
with instructions. Have you tried calling them?' Warren

continued.

'Yes, I asked William to call both their phones a couple of times over the last few days, but he said the calls went straight to the message bank. He did leave a voicemail each time though.' 'Okay, well, if we don't receive any communication from them soon, then I want you to follow it up', he ordered.

'How? What would you want me to do?' Edna requested.

'Call Garry Jenkins, he's a private detective and a friend of mine. You'll find his number in my directory, which is stored in the top drawer of my desk.'

'Do you really think we need a private detective? It seems a little extreme, they're probably having so much fun that time has just slipped away and they've forgotten, that's all, dear. Please don't burden yourself before the operation. I will take care of it as soon as I can. At the moment, you are my main concern.'

Once at the hospital, Warren and Edna reached the clinical area where an identity band was placed on Warren's left wrist with all of his printed information on it. They followed the nurse to the reserved bed and instructed Warren that there will be a fasting period before the operation. She also warned that his bed may be moved when they return to the ward so the nursing staff can observe him more closely immediately after surgery.

'You're his wife?' the nurse asked, addressing Edna.

'Yes, I am.'

'Okay, that's great. Can you please keep an eye on his comfort and call me if you need anything? His operation is scheduled for 8.00 a.m. tomorrow,' the nurse continued.

Edna complied, and as Warren slipped into a hospital gown, she unpacked his belongings and sat beside him as he arranged himself into the bed.

'Remember what I asked of you, dear. If you don't hear from the girls, please call Garry', he reiterated.

Edna nodded with approval and sat for the rest of the afternoon, embracing Warren's hand, all the while speculating what was taking place with her two daughters. Not adapted to worries, Edna felt overawed with the current problematic situations she was facing and hoped that everything that was about to unfold would turn out fine, as she wasn't resilient enough to combat the impending challenges.

Later that evening back at the manor, Edna asked William to call the girls, and he did so without delay; but equally, their phones rang out, directly converting to their voicemails.

'Hello, Miss Annie, Miss Sharon. It's William calling. Your parents are very concerned that you haven't contacted them for some time. Could you return this call as soon as possible? Thank you', he proficiently versed.

'Did you get through to them?' Edna probed as she entered the studio.

'No, madam. Once again, it went straight to their voicemails. I did leave another message on each of their phones. I'm sure they are well', he responded.

'Warren has asked me to contact a private detective if we don't hear from them soon. I think it's a little severe. If you don't mind me asking, do you believe that's a good idea?'

'If Mr. Karce has made that request, then I believe it should be carried through. I know it's been six days, but in saying that, I'm sure everything is alright. Please madam, you have enough to worry about with Mr. Karce undergoing surgery tomorrow morning. You must rest, madam', William coached.

'Yes, yes, you are right. I must focus on Warren. Good night,

William, and thank you for your guidance', she replied and made her way leisurely up the staircase towards the bedroom and shut the door.

The following morning, Warren lay in bed, anticipating his surgery, as Edna sat beside him and while the wards man came to trundle him away, he turned to his wife and questioned, 'Did you try calling the girls again last night? Were you able to reach them? You didn't tell them of my surgical procedure, did you?' Edna deliberated over his question for a moment and lied straight to his face.

'Yes, dear, I was able to speak with Annie. Both the girls are doing well, and just as I had predicted, they're having the time of their lives and had overlooked calling and no, I didn't mention anything about your surgery. Every little thing is fine, darling. Don't worry and just get better', she fabricated, kissing him before he was taken away.

Edna lingered in the hospital waiting room for the seven hours it took the surgery to be completed, and once it was over, the surgeon approached her with a solemn expression on his face. She stood up straight away and walked towards him.

'So how did it go?' she tested impatiently.

'Well the tumor has been removed, but there has been significant impairment to the frontal lobe but that's not my main concern. He lost a lot of blood and his blood pressure is extremely low, so he's been taken to our intensive care unit for closer observation and monitoring. He's receiving a transfusion as we speak', the doctor educated.

'Okay? So when he does recover, what will the long-term effects of the damage to his frontal lobe tell us?', she investigated, running her fingers through her hair with apprehension.

'He will experience speech problems, changes in his personality, poor coordination, difficulties with impulse control, and trouble planning anything and sticking to a schedule. I'm so sorry to have to tell you this, Edna. We are doing the best we can for him.' The doctor placed his hand on her shoulder as a sign of comfort and encouragement.

'Thank you, Doctor, for your support. Can I see him now?' she answered faintly.

'No, I'm sorry, not at this time. We have to stabilize him first, and as soon as that happens, one of the nurses will come and fetch you, but that could take some time. I do recommend that you go home and rest. Come back in the morning, and if there are any immediate changes in the interim, the hospital will let you know.' The doctor gave Edna a feeble smile and slowly headed towards the ICU ward; with his head hung low, he removed his surgical cap, departing through the elevator doors. Edna gathered her purse, and while she was driven home, her speculation was loaded with feelings of guilt from misleading Warren about the girls and the uneasiness of truly not knowing what was happening with them; and with her husband's diminishing health, she was terribly burdened. Their perfect life was turning into a challenging dilemma. Once home, Edna sauntered into the parlor, not uttering a word, and with all the domestic staff's eyes upon her, she walked over to the sofa and sat down, her gaze static as she looked fixedly out the window, and remained there until she eventually fell asleep.

'Edna, Edna, where are you? It's lunchtime', a faint voice

amplified from within her profound dream.

'I'm here, Margery, and I'm coming right now', she yelled back as she jumped off the home-crafted swing that dangled under a broad canopied sycamore tree.

'Come on, lassie, you'll be late for lunch and you know how much your mama dislikes it when you're not there at the table before she is. Look at your dress, Edna, it's all tatty', Margery reprimanded.

'I know, Margery, I'm sorry. Can you help me put on a new dress?' Edna begged her domestic nanny.

'Yes, yes, but we must hurry', Margery granted as she took the young girl's hand and made their way to Edna's bedroom; and as they were exiting, they could hear the butler announcing that lunch was being served. Edna hurried to the table and seated herself just in the nick of time as her parents simultaneously entered the dining room and greeted her with a kiss on the cheek.

'Hello, dear, you look pretty', Edna's mother endorsed.

'Thank you, mama', she responded. Her father sat at the head of the table, while her mother assembled herself next to Edna, and he primarily helped himself to the best items available while the rest of the family waited until his plate was full; then they eventually served themselves.

'So, what have you been doing this morning, Edna?' her father quizzed while pouring himself a glass of red wine.

'I've just been playing outside on the swing', she answered.

'You be careful on that swing, dearest, we don't want you hurting yourself', He persisted.

'I won't, Father. I've been invited to Jenny's place to play. Can I go?' Edna pleaded.

'Don't you have homework to do?' her mother interjected.

'I suppose, but I'd really like to go.'

'Jenny is a nice enough girl, but she's very impartial to your feelings, and I don't want you feeling uncomfortable', her father responded, trying to discourage his daughter from any involvement that may result in her fostering uneasiness.

'I like her, and I'd—' Edna began to answer, but her mother interrupted before she could say another word.

'Your father has spoken, Edna, and I agree with him', she revealed.

'When you've finished your homework this afternoon, I want to see the completed assignment', her father added, not respecting his daughter's right to have any private thoughts and feelings.

'We love and care about you so much, Edna, and your needs are always going to be our highest priority.' Her mother continued, patting her daughter's leg under the table.

Edna knew that they loved her and they only desired the best for her, but for an eleven-year-old girl, their overprotective nurturing left her feeling smothered and muted, and she relentlessly dreamed of the day she could escape this hyperattentive existence.

'What about Saturday? Can I go and play with Jenny then?' She continued with her ambition. 'No, Edna, Saturday I've booked you in for an etiquette lesson with Mrs. Bunbury. She'll be here at 11.00 am sharp' Her mother conveyed, frustrated with her daughter's perseverance. Edna excused herself from the table and ambled up the staircase, disheartened with their refusal to spend time with her friend, so she entered her bedroom and collapsed down onto the bed, and began to cry.

'Mrs. Karce', a tender voice beckoned as William gently woke her from the dream.

'Yes, yes. Oh, William, it's you. What is it?' she muttered, attempting to clear the cries from her voice and wiping faint tears from her eyes.

'You've been sitting here all night. I thought you'd want to freshen up before breakfast, madam', William stated, apprehensive about her welfare.

'Thank you, William.' Edna stood up and made her way towards the staircase and climbed it wearily with despondency in her heart, and by the time she returned for breakfast, it was nearly midday. William approached her in a subtle manner to deliver some important news. 'Madam, I have something to tell you', he said in a discreet fashion.

'Yes, William', Edna verbally acknowledged, not viewing him as she buttered her toast.

'A phone call came through late last night. It was Sharon. She wanted me to inform you that they are doing fine. She also apologized for not contacting you earlier and said that because their trip has been so eventful, time had just slipped away.'

Edna unexpectedly looked up at William.

'How did she sound? You didn't mention anything about Warren's operation?' she challenged.

'No, madam, it's not my place to do so. Sharon sounded fine, but I detected a slight limitation in her voice', William confessed.

'What do you mean by limitation?'

'Nothing to be concerned about, madam, she just sounded like she was in a hurry and couldn't talk for long. She did mention that Annie is very well and enjoying her stopovers to those villages of folklore curiosities.' He tacked on a pleasing undertone to sidetrack Edna from his previous comment.

'Okay, that's good, thank you, William. Did she say where they are and when they'll call again?' Edna was pacified.

'No, madam, I didn't ask where they were, but Sharon said that they wouldn't leave it so long to call next time', he fibbed so as not to promote any more upset.

Edna finally finished the meal and gathered her belongings, departing through the manor entrance towards the waiting car and headed to the hospital; and when she arrived, their family doctor was waiting for her.

'Hello, Dr. Bartlett', Edna greeted.

'Hello, Edna, could you follow me please?' He replied in an earnest tone and escorted her into a private consultation room, closing the door behind them.

'Please take a seat' He beckoned, positioning himself behind the desk, opening up Warren's medical file as he sat down.

'Edna, Warren hasn't responded as well as we would've predicted. Through our imaging tests, it's been revealed that he continues to bleed in the frontal lobe, and there is swelling to his optic nerves. He's experienced a few seizures during the night, but we have been controlling those with anticonvulsants. He remains in intensive care until we can manage his symptoms.'

'Is he conscious?' Edna questioned.

'Yes, but he lapses in and out of consciousness.'

'Will there be any long-term effects of the continuous bleeding?'

'Other than the previous extended effects that the surgeon educated you on after the operation, there is a possibility that he could be permanently blind, but it's early days as yet. Rest assured that we are doing everything we possibly can to minimize this threat.'

'Thank you, Dr. Bartlett, can I see him now?' she appealed.

'Of course, you can, right this way, Edna.'

She followed him up the corridor and into the lift where they both stood silently until it reached the fifth floor. Directly stepping out into the ward, Edna promptly recognized her husband lying in the second bed from the nurse's station, his head swathed in bandages like a half-wrapped mummy and intravenous lines extending out of him every which way.

She cautiously walked up to his bed and gently kissed him on the lips, and to her surprise, he acknowledged her presence.

'Edna, is that you?' he asked in a deep, hoarse voice.

'Yes, dear, it's me', she replied.

'Have you heard anything from the girls?' was his first request.

'Sharon called last night. They're both doing well and are looking forward to coming home', she briefed.

'So you spoke with her?'

'No, lovey, William took the call and informed me of their conversation when I woke this morning', she confirmed.

'Have you tried calling them back?' A tone of uneasiness was elevating in his voice.

'No, I haven't. Warren, please don't worry yourself, they are fine. Sharon said that they'll call back as soon as they're able to. Just concentrate on getting better', she encouraged.

'I don't feel like they're fine. I have this bad impression that there's some kind of trouble. Ring Gary Jenkins for a consult', he uttered huskily as his voice trailed off.

'Ssshh now, everything will be okay', Edna tried calming her husband as she could see that he was becoming increasingly distressed, and then without any warning Warren began shaking frantically, setting off the monitors' alarm systems. Doctors and nurses dashed to his bedside, pushing Edna to one side as they attempted to control Warren's unexpected seizure. 'I thought he was on anticonvulsive medication for this?' Edna cried as one of the nurses escorted her away from the partitioned cubicle.

'He is, we just have to keep him under observation. The doctors know what to do. Why don't you grab a cup of coffee, and we'll come and get you when things have settled down?' The nurse comforted her.

Edna stood frozen in place, inaudibly listening to the anxious turmoil that was emitting from behind the curtains until the nurse diverted her to the elevator, and together they walked to the café. Sitting abnormally composed in the waiting room, Edna stared at the ground when the doctor finally approached her.

'Mrs. Karce. We have controlled the seizure, but every time he experiences these, it does more damage to his neurological system. He can't get distressed. We need your permission to put him into a medically induced coma. The purpose of this is to ensure the protection and control of the pressure dynamics of his brain. The high compression caused by the swelling can starve his brain of oxygen, and the swollen brain tissue can injure it further by pushing against the inside of the skull. The coma will slow down the brain's metabolism and will minimize the swelling and inflammation of the brain. This is the only way we can protect him from any further impairment', the doctor tutored.

'Whatever needs to be done to save my husband' Was all Edna could muster to say, the words clutching in her throat.

'Okay, could you please sign these forms, and we will

go ahead with the procedure?' The doctor presented the documents for Edna to view.

Like an android, she signed the authorizations without even reading any of the disclosures or coverages, and as soon as she placed the pen down onto the clipboard, she stood up and listlessly walked towards the exit doors of the hospital, accessing her chauffeur-driven car and drove away.

William met her at the entrance of their manor and shepherded Edna to the sunlit parlor and was observant of her indifferent persona.

'Are you alright, madam?' He probed as he assisted Edna to her favorite chair.

'Warren's desk in the study ... in the top drawer there's a directory. Could you bring it to me?'

'Yes, immediately, madam.' William hurried to the study and found the directory where she had initiated it would be and returned, offering it to her.

Opening up the handbook, she found the number and reached for the phone, and called Gary Jenkins.

'Hello, Mr. Jenkins? It's Edna Karce, Warren Karce's wife. I was wondering if I could make an appointment for you to visit our estate? At your earliest convenience would be appreciated.'

'Yes, Mrs. Karce. Would tomorrow morning suit you, say around 9.00 a.m.? What's it in regards to?' He spoke with a deep bristly voice.

'My daughters ... I'll fill you in when you get here' She spoke directly.

'See you tomorrow then.' Simultaneously, they tersely hung up the receiver.

The following morning, William responded to the doorbell

and beheld a tall thin man, wearing a black suit and tie and a black wide-brimmed boater hat. As he entered the foyer, Mr. Jenkins casually removed the hat, and upon doing so, the butler witnessed that his head was as long as his body. His oblong face was widest at the forehead and narrowed towards the chin with his dark-brown eyes widespread and his hair smoothed and greased back with an excess of liniment.

Mr. Jenkins was a responsive man and was up for any challenge that life could throw his way as the excitement and uncertainty of demanding situations made him feel alive, and his hunger for adventure provided him with a vital spark that made him potentially treacherous. 'This way, Mr. Jenkins', William marshaled him into the parlor where Edna was quietly submerged in her needlepoint.

'Madam, Mr. Jenkins is here to see you' He broadcasted.

'Hello, Mr. Jenkins.' Edna stood up to greet him, shaking his hand.

'Please call me Gary. How's Warren these days?' he enquired.

'Not so well. He's in hospital at the moment in an induced coma after having a tumor removed.' Edna sounded drained.

'Oh, I'm so sorry to hear that, Mrs. Karce.'

'Yes, it's been a terrible time, but let's talk about the issue at hand, shall we? The reason we need your services.' She ricocheted the conversation away from Warren's health problems. 'This meeting today is at Warren's request. He is worried about our daughters. They have gone overseas for a holiday, and even though we've asked them to call us once a week, the duration between phone calls is becoming longer. My eldest daughter Sharon did call two nights ago and said that everything was fine, but she didn't let us know where they were, and she sounded evasive.' Edna's voice quavered.

'So you spoke with her personally?' The private detective asked as he jotted down points in his notebook.

'No, my butler William took the call. He just relayed his impressions of the conversation to me. I wasn't here to take the call as I was at the hospital with Warren' She said defensibly. 'Where is William now? I would like to speak with him please.'

Edna rang her call bell, and William appeared in the parlor like a missile.

'William, Mr. Jenkins would like to talk to you about the phone call with Sharon the other night', Edna instructed.

'So you spoke with Sharon, is that correct?'

'Yes, sir, I did', William answered in a conformed manner.

'Tell me, Mrs. Karce said that you felt as though Sharon was evasive? What made you think that?'

'She sounded like she was confused and in a hurry or something. Like she didn't have time to go into detail about their trip when I asked how it was going', William presented nervously. 'Is that a normal response from Sharon, I mean does she always come across as elusive?' Gary continued.

'Sharon is a very talkative girl, she always has an opinion about everything, and so for her to be evasive is not in her usual character, Mr. Jenkins. Also, when I have asked William to call the girls on a number of other occasions, on my behalf, it's been going straight to their voicemails and it's not like Annie to decline a phone call, especially when it's from home', Edna intervened.

'Okay, so what is it you need me to do?' he asked.

'I believe they are supposed to be in Romania at this time. I would appreciate you flying over there and tracking them down and, when you do find them, please ask them to come home immediately as their father is in an awful state. I need their support.'

'I'll book a flight for this evening. I'd like to affirm my costs before I go if that's acceptable?' he confidently announced.

'Yes, that's fine', Edna said in a peeved way as she directed William to leave them with a flick of her hand. Gary waited until the butler had completely left the room before he began. 'One hundred dollars an hour plus expenses. I need two thousand dollars upfront for expenditures.' Edna instantly rose up from the sofa and walked into the adjoining room, leaving Mr. Jenkins for five minutes while she retrieved the cash from the private domiciliary safe, which existed behind a remarkable Picasso classic Three Women at the Spring 1921. She returned with the money and handed it to him.

'Let me know immediately when you have any information. I will make myself available for your every call. Under the circumstances, Warren won't know if I'm at the hospital or not, and I am very fatigued, so I will try to be here in the manor for the duration of your trip. When you require extra money, let me know and I will transfer it from Warren's headquarters. Bring my girls home please, Mr. Jenkins and everything will be satisfactory.' Edna walked with Mr. Jenkins to the main entrance and bid him a safe journey before ascending the staircase to retire for the day.

Back at the hospital, the medical staff placed Warren in an induced coma and kept a vigilant watch over him. They conducted neurological tests at his bedside every hour, checking the reaction of his pupils, the movement of his arms and legs, and his response to brief painful stimuli; and because of the potential for further brain damage, the intensivist doctor was responsible for any daily medical treatment of his patient's brain injury. The registered nurses called Warren's home frequently, informing Edna of his progress and the care that was being administered, and it gave her a fabricated sense of reprieve knowing that he was in good hands, while she centralized her time and energy on receiving her daughters home safe and sound. Edna savored the day when she could throw her arms around them again and they could mutually support one another, ensuring Warren's return and caring for him as a family should. But sadly, her uncharted resilience would be tested with the callous anguish that was about to be unleashed.

Eight

Chapter 8

It's been nearly 36 hours since you found Annie's body. I'll send one of my connections to go back to the hotel suite and collect some of your necessary things. Make a list of what you can't do without and they'll get them for you', Liam briefed Sharon.

'Would the hotel staff have found her by now?' He continued.

'No, I don't think so, I left a **Do Not Disturb** sign hanging on the doorknob of the room. I'll grab the stuff myself. It'll be suspicious if someone else enters our room.' She devoted her confidence in him.

'Good. As soon as you return with your belongings, we will vacate, but in the meantime, we have to change our appearance. When I was out this afternoon, I took the liberty of buying some peroxide and old clothes, just to disguise us and make sure that we leave no trace of our presence here.' Liam picked up the phone to make a call to his associate; his motivation was like a hound dog on a scent.

'Go in and cut your hair really short and bleach it with this dye. Then put on these peasant clothes, and before you know it, we'll have just disappeared ... poof ... like a puff of smoke in the air. Now you see us ... now you don't.' He chuckled as he mocked a vanishing act with his hands.

Sharon went into the bathroom and cut her hair short as a barber's number four style, then bleached it until it was as white as snow. She undressed from her expensive fashionable attire and put on the farmworker clothes that Liam had provided. As she analyzed the clothes she was wearing in the mirror, contemplating their strategy, Liam threw a straw hat towards her and signaled that she wear it as he busied himself replicating the exact bumpkin disguise. Unexpectedly, Sharon had a realization.

'Liam, I'm not going with you' She confessed.

'What? Why not? Now that Annie is dead, this is our new plan, we have to run' He pleaded. 'No, it isn't. We were supposed to send Annie crazy, get her committed, and blame it on those creepy obsessions she treasured so much, not kill her. If I run, it'll look like I'm guilty. and how do I solely inherit the estate's fortune if I'm imprisoned? I'm going to put on my original clothes and head back and explain that I've just returned from a few days' outing at the beach. You won't be associated with any of this if we aren't seen together. I'll make out that I had found her the way she is and act devastated. I'm going to leave now Liam, and I suggest you get moving on as well. I will contact you when everything settles down, okay?'

'For your information, Sharon, I didn't touch Annie in any way. She just croaked, and what about your hair?' He questioned.

'Maybe you didn't, but when they find her, they'll probably do a postmortem, and about my hairstyle is all part of my new beatnik surfer look, I'm into diversity' She triumphed, orbiting a full circle in a sensual mode for Liam to admire with the original clothes she had arrived in. 'Hey, don't forget the other half of the money you owe me. If I don't hear from you, I'll come searching' He cautioned as he winked at her while she swiftly exited the door.

Sharon slinked into the hotel foyer and craftily made her way to their hotel room. The **Do Not Disturb** sign still hung from the doorknob where she had left it, and upon entering the apartment, the stench of death punched her awareness like a solid slap in the face. Placing the fringe of her blouse up to her nose and mouth, hindering the pungent odor, she moved towards Annie's bed and flung back the covers, exposing her sister's decaying carcass.

As a medical student, Sharon recognized that rigor mortis was well established as Annie's top layer of skin was loose and, due to ruptured blisters, her exterior had a sheen to it; additionally, the gases that were trapped within the corpse was causing her to bloat, and the body was doubling in size. Sharon stepped forward, carefully placing her hand on Annie's cheek, and as she moved in closer, wanting to say something to her sister, Annie's eyes jerked and shifted their stony gaze upon Sharon, as though she was intently observing her with treacherous scrutiny. With instantaneous terror, Sharon shrieked and hurdled rearward, stumbling and falling back onto the adjacent bed with her eyes static on the body. She quickly realized that Annie's eyes hadn't moved as they were sunken and dehydrated with no texture or volume in them at all; they were both withered and hollow ... it had only been her guilty imagination. Sharon began to cry, and slowly picking herself up off the bed, she reached for the in-house phone and called reception.

'Hello, it's Sharon Karce here, room 49. Can you send someone in a hurry, please it's an emergency' She sniveled through her tears. Putting down the receiver, she poised herself gallantly on the lounge, her mind deliberating on what parts of her fictitious story she was going to communicate to the authorities, then suddenly a loud knocking commenced at the suite door.

'Yes, come in' She yelled at the entry without attempting to move off the lounge chair.

Sharon could hear the fiddling of keys while someone rummaged around for the correct one before they opened the door, and two burly hotel supervisors entered.

'What's the problem, miss?' One of them stated as they cringed at the stench that permeated their nostrils.

'There, she's there', Sharon whimpered as she pointed to Annie's bed, wiping her eyes dry with a hankie.

The men walked over to the bed and instantly convulsed at the condition of the body and the manifestation of panic on Annie's congealed face.

'Is this your sister? When did you find her like this?' The primary supervisor asked as the other man was on his internal radio to the director and explained their discovery. Within minutes, the hotel manager appeared in the room, assessing the status quo.

'I've called the police, and they're on their way. Don't touch anything' He proclaimed.

At this point, Sharon felt an upwelling of anxiety intensifying within her and bolted upright from the lounge and began pacing the room, wailing in a frenzied manner. A female supervisor had been called in, so as soon as she arrived, she advanced towards Sharon, placing her arm around her shoulder, endeavoring to console the weepy sister.

'Stop, don't touch me, leave me alone', Sharon unashamedly criticized her attempts, shoving the lady's arm off.

The hotel staff remained in the suite until the police arrived then departed once the manager directed them to do so.

'Don't go too far away, I will be interviewing everyone who was involved in the discovery', The detective cautioned in his Romani accent. He wandered up to Sharon, who was still agitated and crying.

'This is your sister? What's both of your names?' He probed coldly as he stood directly in front of her.

'I'm Sharon Karce, and that's my sister Annie Karce. We're on holiday from Australia' She offered a little more information to comply as an agreeable partaker.

'So tell me your account of what happened' He continued.

'I've just come back from a few days at the beach with some friends I met at the summer garden down the road from here. I walked in and smelt this disgusting odor, and there she was, just lying there under the covers.'

'Was she covered up when you came in?' He persisted to cross-examine.

'Yes, she was covered. I pulled them back to see what was under there, and that's when I saw her, with that look on her face' She said in her unrelenting sniveling.

'Then what did you do?' The detective pressed

'I called management immediately, what else would I do?' She studied him with an inquisitive look of apprehension.

127

'Don't you believe me?' Sharon roared at the detective.

'It's not that I don't believe you, Miss Karce, I'm only asking some routine questions.' The detective was puzzled by her hostile reaction.

By this time, the paramedics had just arrived and were engaging in the task of swathing Annie into a body bag while forensics took photos of the corpse and the crime scene. Sharon peered over the surrounding detectives shielding physical obstruction.

'Where are you taking her?' She hollered.

'She's going to the morgue for the coroner to do a post-mortem. The manager told me that you had long black hair when you left here for your beach getaway. Why have you changed your hairstyle, Miss Karce?' He enquired, redirecting Sharon's attention back to the questioning at hand.

'I'm on holiday, and I wanted a change, that's all.' Sharon wasn't dealing with the pressure the detective was placing on her.

'Okay, well, that's about all, I will need you to accompany me to the police station for a written statement, Miss Karce.'

'When?' she asked.

'Right now, Miss Karce, can you go with this police officer?' He directed her towards the awaiting constable.

They held Sharon in the station's interviewing room for two hours, asking intrusive questions like why did they travel to Romania? Was anyone else commuting with them? Why did Sharon go to the beach resort without Annie, and why wouldn't they do their sightseeing together considering they were single women in a foreign country, it'd be a lot safer, wouldn't it? What were the 'friends' names that Sharon stayed with at the resort? Did she call Annie at some point while she was away? Continuing on, there was one last demand from the detective.

"Don't leave Bucharest for any reason."

It seemed as though the debriefing would never end, and by the time Sharon returned to the hotel, she was immediately interjected by the manager as she entered the foyer.

'Hello, Miss Karce, I am so sorry for your loss. I just want to let you know that at the advice of the police, we have taken the liberty to move some of your necessary belongings to another suite as your original one is now a crime scene. You're now staying in room 67.

It's one floor higher, I hope you don't mind.' The manager smiled a cheesy grin as he handed the keys to her new apartment.

'Okay, thank you.' Sharon complied and took the lift up to the acquired level, and upon entering the room, she rapidly noticed it was the exact same design as the one before. Her purse and luggage were positioned on the bed, the suitcase unlocked, with clothes spilling out over the side, a sign that the police had inspected the contents before tossing it back in. Removing the bags and placing them on the couch, she lay down exhausted from the day's trauma and wondered where Liam would be right now; her thoughts meditating on the fact that he wasn't the one being exposed to the police investigation. As far as they knew, he didn't even exist. The more she thought about it, she felt increasingly irritated with Liam's impeccable guiltless situation and how he could easily dispute having anything to do with or even knowing Annie and herself. So before she allowed her mind to magnify an unlikely assumption and grow fervently out of control, she decided to take in some fresh air and maybe wander to one of the summer gardens for a bite to eat; and besides, the duplicated apartment was starting to freak her out anyway, envisaging Annie still lying there in the bed. The whole scenario was like something out of the twilight zone. As she strolled the streets, her senses were filled with the sounds of pumping music, people talking and laughing from the endless array of restaurants, bars, and eccentric shops; but as she meandered along, she also witnessed the struggles of life on the bustling streets. The sun was setting when Sharon eventually found a secluded pathway leading to an isolated drinking garden where she sat down and ordered dinner. Even though the images of Annie's death lurked in the back of her mind, she felt more tranquil and enjoyed a bottle of champagne as she listened to the relaxing jazz music that channeled through the restaurant's oasis speakers.

While Sharon ate her spaghetti marinara, she put down her cutlery to sip another mouthful of the champagne when she saw a tall thin man, dressed in a black suit and a broad-brimmed hat, leaning on the corner of a building slightly down the street, approximately 20 meters away, just standing there watching her every move. The brim of his hat was pulled down over his eyes, just enough so he could analyze her when he tilted his head back a little, but Sharon could distinguish that his face was elongated and pale. She queried in her mind why he'd be gawking at her, and then she remembered Annie mentioning something about a man staring at her from the adjacent building that night in Paris, and he seemed to be wearing the exact same outfit she had described. Sharon stood up confidently from her seat and, with a brisk walk, paced towards the stranger; but as she got closer, he turned abruptly around the corner he was standing at and vanished out of sight, and by the time she reached the junction of the alleyway, he was nowhere to be seen. Unmoving at the bend, she inspected the lane for a few moments then gradually turned around and walked back to the restaurant, but when she returned to the table, her handbag was lying on the ground with its entire contents sprawled out all over the floor. Picking up the bag, she replaced the scattered items back into her purse and discarded the remains of her unwanted dinner as she rapidly paid the waiter and left. Walking back to the hotel, feeling absolutely concerned at what was going on, her phone began ringing. Plucking it from her jeans pocket, hesitating to view the screen; it was Liam, so she promptly answered the call.

'Hi, Liam, what's happening?'

'Nothing, I just wanted to know how things were going. Have you deposited my money yet?' he grilled.

'Oh, everything is just peachy keen ... and yes, I transferred the remaining $125,000 into your account this morning', she snapped back.

'You sound pissed off, are you okay?' He continued.

'Everything is up to shit, Liam. It's alright for you. You're not the one who's being investigated by the police or have this creepy bogeyman shadowing you.'

'What do you mean creepy bogeyman?'

'I was having dinner at this restaurant, and I saw him checking me out from a distance. I went to confront him, and he took off' She enlightened.

'Hey, everything will be okay. We knew that we'd cop a bit of heat over this. That bloke is probably a copper keeping tabs on you. I'm only a phone call away if you need anything. Just stay cool, Shaz.' He tried calming her.

'I don't know what fairyland you're skipping through right

now, but everything isn't okay' She erupted back, and then she heard Liam giggle, which prompted them both to laugh. 'Where are you anyway?' Sharon continued.

'I can't tell you over the phone' He said awkwardly.

'Oh, why not? So you don't get caught? This is bullshit. Why am I the only one in the spotlight? Tormenting Annie was my idea, but you supplied the drugs to do it, Liam Cartwright.'

'Settle, petal, I have a plan, and you're included. I'll wait for you. Be in touch soon.' Liam rudely ended the call, unexpectedly hanging up in Sharon's ear.

With grumpiness, Sharon tucked the phone into her pocket and reinstated her walk back to the hotel, ignorant of the knowledge that the tall thin man was watching her yet again and had overheard the entire conversation, even observing the common amusement shared between the caller and herself. Arriving at the hotel suite, she decided to tidy up her tousled suitcase, and as she pulled out the crumpled clothes, something plunged to the floor beside her. Bending down to pick it up, right away she noticed Annie's monogrammed hankie enfolded around a heavy object; and upon opening it, there was the gothic pendant, with its scalded exterior and the bright-yellow glow still burning ardently from within along with the escorting piece of paper Annie had thrown in the garbage bin days before. But this time, the untidy inscription on the note read differently.

This pendant is yours to keep. Because of your malevolent ways, wickedness, evil, and bad luck will reproduce in your life You and your loved ones are ordained for decay

'What the fuck?' Sharon screamed and threw the pendant and its note across the room.

Sitting on the lounge, she felt exhausted from the endless

irritating problems that kept encircling her; and as she considered the circumstances at hand, Sharon finally walked over to the discarded pendant, gathered it up, and made the well-founded decision to surrender it to the police, so she made the call.

'Where did you find this pendant again?' The detective probed as Sharon sat in the living room area of the suite.

'I told you, it was in my luggage, all crumpled up with my clothes, in the mess your police officers left behind. What is that pendant anyway?'

'It's a primordial artifact from Prince Vlad of Wallachia's anthology of jewels. It was cataloged with the Romanian's museum collection many decades ago, but mysteriously vanished and was reported stolen, it's a priceless cultural heirloom and here it is ... in your possession Miss Karce. Do you know it has a powerful curse attached to it? The legend connected to the ruby pendant says that each time someone acquires the jewel, it activates the bad energy that is infused within, deliberate negative thoughts and actions become attached to it, so the nastier the deed, the more dramatic and long-lasting the effects of the curse. Unfortunately, anyone who has had it amongst their belongings is predestined for carnage.' The detective artfully smirked as he regarded the pendant that Sharon had given him.

'And you believe in that crap?' Sharon rebuked any such nonsense.

'Whoever left you the note certainly does' He said, with amusement.

'Where would your sister have acquired this?' The police continued his inquisition.

'Annie went to Bran Castle the day I left for the beach resort.

Maybe she found it there ... or in an artifacts shop ... I don't know. What about the threatening note? The person that left it must have murdered Annie ... there's a transparent clue, Detective, because I sure as hell didn't kill her.' Sharon was becoming bald-faced with her verbal comebacks.

'I'm taking the jewel and returning it to the curator of the museum. By the way, we've recently obtained CCTV footage of you entering the hotel, approximately 37 hours before you discovered your sister's body. Why did you lie about that? The last time Annie was seen alive was at the café where she ordered a meal and was given a bottle of wine that you had instructed the waiter to supply her, with your apologies ... of course. Is that correct?' The detective showed no respect for Sharon, as he never made eye contact with her and kept writing things down on a notepad as he spoke.

'Yes, I left the wine, so what?'

'And when you initially alerted the hotel staff of your sister's death, why did you say that it was the first time you'd been there after your trip? Obviously, you had returned earlier.'

'Okay, I was there the afternoon before, but I couldn't find Annie, I mean she wasn't just blatantly sitting on the lounge reading a magazine, sipping on a cup of coffee. It was the odor that led me to find her all covered up in bed the second time I was there.'

'Where did you go after the first time you had been to the suite and then left?' He kept plaguing her with questions.

'I went back to get my blouse from my friend, that's all. Are you going to charge me with anything? Do I need to get a lawyer? If not, I've had enough, I want this to stop now' She demanded.

'Yes, we have finished here, but I will be questioning you

again, Miss Karce. One more thing: who was the friend you retrieved the blouse from?' He advised.

'Julie ... and I'm sure you will be pestering me again' She replied, forcefully pushing her way past an associate police officer and stood firmly at the door, opening it and motioning for them to leave.

After the police officers departed, Sharon collapsed onto the bed and began to weep desolately. She pondered about calling home and letting them know of the horrid circumstances she was in but then decided against it as she began to fear that her parents would blame her entirely... the estate's inheritance would never be hers.

I'll make the scheduled call tomorrow morning, just to let them know that everything is okay' She mumbled to herself.

Liam traveled 838 kms by train to the border of Hungary and Slovakia and settled in a transitory flat where he hoped to find safety from the looming problems that were about to collapse his accustomed existence. His mind was conflicted, having difficulty staying in the present moment, as it was one step ahead of him, always anticipating what may transpire, and he was perplexed over his probable future as well as dwelling in the events that had just emerged. His judgments were his most noxious enemy at this point, and he had to act in the moment that he found himself in. He'd created this situation by his actions, and there was no way that he could think himself into a rich, whole, and dignified life anymore, and he had to do something about it. He'd changed his appearance by cutting his hair and tinting it black, and the beard that he was beginning to grow was flourishing ... It was time for a different strategic awareness, so Liam decided to occupy the backpacker hostel for a period of a couple of days, and then he was going to break free without Sharon. Stepping out into the streets, Liam cautiously regarded the laneway before roaming towards the marketplace to purchase some food and persisted to scan the urban surroundings, nervously guarded and skeptical; he constantly favored the left side of his body by frequently glancing over his shoulder. While at a produce stand, he quickly paid for his items, and as he turned to head home, he detected a tall thin man casually pretending to browse the marketplace but occasionally glancing sideways in Liam's direction. Without delay, Liam rushed into the hustling crowd, shifting and zigzagging his passage through the horde of people until he lost sight of the threatening oddity; and once he was securely within the flat, Liam packed his meager belongings into a backpack and waited until midnight. Adorned in a dark hoodie pulled completely over his head, he covertly escaped, fleeing down a twisting alleyway, hoping that he'd be erased from anyone's memory ... but Gary Jenkins saw him move out and was hot on his heels as they both vanished into the murky, nocturnal atmosphere.

The following morning Sharon called home.

'Hello, William, it's Sharon. How are you? Can I speak with Mama or Papa?' She expressed in a cheerful manner.

'I'm sorry, Miss Karce, but both your parents are out at this time' He perjured.

'Oh okay, just let them know that Annie and I are well, we're enjoying our holiday and look forward to coming home soon. Tell them not to worry, we are fine' She misled.

'Yes, miss, I will do that.' William concluded the discussion and placed down the receiver with unease in his heart. Meandering around the apartment, Sharon felt a sudden escalation of restlessness and meditated on why both her parents would

136

be unavailable at this time of day. *'It was 11.00 pm here, so that would mean it'd be 8.00 am in Australia. It seemed very odd that both of them would be out, they'd normally be partaking in breakfast right now,'* She alleged.

With her mind burdened with so many complications, she took comfort in the belief that she at least still had Liam to depend upon and set her focus on his everlasting support, until she fell asleep. Early the next day, there was a zealous knock at her door.

'Yes, who is it?' She yelled while putting on her robe.

'Bucharest police, Miss Karce' One of the officers voiced through the closed access.

'Just a minute, what do you want now?' She hurled open the door as she articulated her disgust with their boldness for waking her up at 5.00 a.m.

'Come with us down to the station' They ordered.

'Can I get dressed first? Do you have more questions for me to answer?'

'Just get dressed, Miss' They duplicated without any reaction in their voices.

Down at the station, Sharon was escorted to the interviewing room and sat there for ten minutes while the detective and his colleagues studied her through a reciprocal mirror.

'Does she look like she could commit murder, Detective?' One of his associates remarked in their native language.

'She certainly has a lot of resentment or a grievance to carry. Who would have thought that Australian women could be so haughty?' He answered, and with that comment, he advanced into the room.

'Good morning, Miss Karce' He addressed her impolitely.

'What's so good about it? You wake me up at 5.00 a.m. and

drag me down here to this stink hole' She protested.

'Yes, well, I have some more questions to ask you ... oh, and to tell you that your sister's toxicology report has come back from the coroner' He briefed her while offhandedly shuffling around with his papers.

'Yes? And? So what did Annie die of?' Her voice was firm and sharp.

'It's amusing to see how accordingly delicate you are to what I'm about to reveal.' The detective remarked

Sharon slumped back into the chair, folding her arms in front of her with a mark of disrespect and defiance.

'Yes, go on', She pushed.

'Your sister Annie was poisoned. The cause of death was ultimately from asphyxiation, but that was due to the amount of poison she had in her bloodstream.' He visually surveyed her for a reaction.

'What? What do you mean she was poisoned?'

'You know, poisoned, as in she ingested a harmful substance that eventually killed her.'

'Ha, you're a real smarty-pants. It was probably an accident. You don't know what you're consuming in this repulsive country of yours' Sharon grunted.

'Now, Miss Karce, there is no need for bigoted comments. It couldn't have been an isolated accident because it's been determined that your sister had been consuming this poison over an extended period of time. It was entrenched in her fleshy tissue and organs. It seems like a planned action by someone. Do you know anything about this?'

'How would I know about poisons?' She continued her objection.

'I believe that you have just finished a degree in Medicine, is that truthful?' Sharon didn't answer.

'So you'd have an excellent idea on how toxins work in the human body?'

Again Sharon didn't answer.

'I have received more CCTV footage on the afternoon of your first visit back from the beach, returning to the train station and emptying your handbag in a bin there. Why did you do that, Miss Karce?' Sharon still didn't answer.

'Well ... we've located and combed through the rubbish from that bin on that exact afternoon, and we found a syringe. Did that come out of your bag?' The detective kept a manifested stare on her while the corner of his mouth turned slightly upwards, emulating a sneer.

'Oh, for Christ's sake, that could've been anyone's ... there's that many drifters lurking around here, and they all look like junkies.' She finally broke her silence.

'Okay. We also repossessed the bottle of wine, and its cork, you provided for your sister at the café that day. Our forensic team have been working persistently throughout the night, and they have concluded that there's a small straight perforation in the cork, like a needle mark, and both the syringe and the wine bottle have been tested and contain residual particles of the exact poisons that killed Annie.' He intently ogled at her.

Once again, Sharon didn't answer, but the previous glow that colored her face had completely drained away, leaving her looking pasty white.

'I suppose I don't have to clarify what poison was used ... or do you want me to explain how it affected your sister?'

'I want a lawyer' Was all she could muster up to say.

'We found a cocktail of lysergic acid, diethylamide, phencyclidine, and peyote in the syringe, the cork, and the discarded bottle of wine. This would've caused your sister to have drastic changes to her sensory perception including powerful visual and audible hallucinations. Annie's destructive episodes on this lethal concoction triggered her to experience paranoia, high anxiety, nausea, and vomiting, and the long-term illness would've induced psychological disorders like schizophrenia and posttraumatic stress—'

'Stop it!' She bawled.

'Why, Sharon? You have a medical degree. You would have known how these drugs affected Annie. Where did you obtain them? You couldn't get them through customs. Are you working alone, or is someone else involved in this? Where did you go after you emptied your handbag at the train station?' The detective pressured harder.

I was working alone and I went nowhere' She lied, hopeful that Liam would somehow come and rescue her, sooner or later.

'Okay. Well, you're going to be accused of the entire crime of murder in the first degree, and you'll be looking down the barrel of a life sentence unless you tell me who else is involved. You're not brazen enough to carry this out in a foreign country ... alone.'

Sharon drooped her head, looking down at her hands as she squeezed them forcefully together under the table and didn't say a word for some time.

'Fine ... I'm not copping to this alone ... his name is Liam Cartwright' She admitted.

'How do you know this man?'

'He was a chemistry student at the University that Annie and I attended. He loved Annie, he was fanatical about her, but she had very little time for him.'

'So a rejected man with a grudge to bear? What was his incentive to harm her ... was it money? I mean you say he loved Annie, he wouldn't want her exploited?' The detective prodded.

'I was going to pay him $250,000 out of my trust fund, which matured when Annie and I turned 23 years old. The endowment was paid into our nominated accounts not long after we graduated from University' She informed him.

'What about yourself? What was your motive to kill your sister?

'I didn't kill her ... She wasn't supposed to die. I just wanted her institutionalized so I could solely inherit my family's estate once Mama and Papa passed on.'

'How does that work, Sharon? Firstly, let's get something straight ... you did kill Annie, and I imagine that if she was still alive, half of that estate money would have gone to her anyway, even if she had been committed' He interrogated concisely.

'No, it doesn't work like that ... There's a solid clause in my parents' testament that has a list of conditions, and it states if either of us breaches just one of them, that individual won't receive a penny.' Sharon was cool, calm, and collected as she spoke.

'Alright then ... that's all I want to identify at this point. I am charging you with conspiracy to manslaughter at this time of the investigation.' The detective switched off his tape recorder and turned to the escorting police officer guarding the doorway.

'Take Miss Karce away and proceed with fingerprinting and a swab for DNA testing.' He stood up from the table as the police officer handcuffed Sharon and steered her away towards the jail cells.

'What about my lawyer?' She shrieked at the detective.

'You'll be appointed one' The detective replied without reacting to her panic and secured the implicating folder of information that was placed in front of him

'This is total bullshit, get your hands off me. I'm Sharon Karce, and I demand to be treated like a lady. I'm an aristocrat', She yapped at the escorting police officer.

'You're no lady, miss' He whispered standing next to her as they waited for the holding cell gate to open, and upon hearing the forceful bang of the immense door anchoring its deadbolt behind her, Sharon roared out a bloodcurdling scream.

Nine

Chapter 9

Gary Jenkins made a phone call to the Karce residence as Edna was offered the receiver from William, she responded with desolation in her voice.

'Yes, Mr. Jenkins.'

'Hello, Mrs. Karce. I have some troubling news. There is something going on with your daughters here. They're still in Romania. I have sighted Sharon, but not Annie as yet, and I believe they are traveling with a young man by the name of Liam Cartwright. I'm unable to get any clear information from the police as they're very protective on what the issues are and haven't taken too kindly to the fact that I'm a private detective. The law is very different in Romania, Mrs. Karce, the government has joined the retreat from rule of law so that means that they are exempt from the code that all people are deserving of a fair justice system. Police evidence is highly cloaked, and violence is still a problem. Also, the hotel staff where your daughters are staying aren't cooperating either in fear of police retribution. I am on the trail of this Liam Cartwright and hope to obtain information from him regarding your daughters' He communicated.

'Liam Cartwright? That name rings a bell. I think he was a friend of Annie's while she was at University. I even invited him to the girls' farewell party. She informed him.

'Okay, that's great advice I can use to approach him. I'll call again when I have more evidence. How's Warren by the way?' He was concerned about his old friend.

'Not doing so well', Edna confided.

'I understand that you're under a lot of stress at the moment, Mrs. Karce, but be assured that I will do everything in my power to see that your daughters return home safely' He reassured her.

'Thank you, Gary, your courageous efforts are much needed.' Edna expressed her appreciation and then hung up the phone. She turned around from the writing desk and saw William standing there, watching with considerable unease for the lady of the manor.

'Are you alright, madam? Do you need anything?' he asked.

'No, thank you, William, I have to get ready and head down to the hospital and be with Warren. Can you ask Nick to bring the car around to the front of the manor?' She answered. 'Yes, madam', William confirmed, and once Edna was organized, she left. Sitting beside Warren's hospital bed, she maintained a protective watch over him, as every time she visited, his once strong physical existence was slowly wasting away. The rapid deterioration of his body and excessive depletion of his strength and muscle mass left him looking haggard and diminutive.

Chapter 9

'What is happening to my husband?' she asked a nurse.

'He's suffering from cachexia, Mrs. Karce, as a result of him being in an induced coma, although his decline is slightly faster than any other patients in his condition.'

'Aren't you feeding him through that intravenous tube?' Edna pointed at the injecting line running into Warren's arm.

'Yes, we are, but because he isn't active, his extended immobility is increasing his accelerated weight loss. I'm so sorry that this is distressing you, Mrs. Karce' The nurse attempted to support her.

'Of course, it's distressing. He's my husband, and he looks like he's dying right in front of my eyes. I understand that he'd lose some weight, but this fast deterioration of his appearance isn't normal. It's as though a treacherous entity has invaded his body and it's devouring him', She revealed.

The nurse stood there, astounded at what Edna had just verbally bared. Very few thoughts ever filled Edna's mind with fear and dread, but the sight of Warren lying there, his bloodless face skinny and skeletal looking, provoked disconcerting terror for the future. She had unending wakeful nights wondering what it would be like living her life without her chivalrous man, and it released devastating panic and pain. It was like her body and consciousness had expanded into a mysterious chasm of the unknown, giving her an irrational sensation that everything was outlandish and was pushing realism far beyond her comfort zone. She wanted to run away, hunting to avoid the situation that would change everything in everyday life, and the stress hampered her logic, contributing to this persistent feeling of insecurity and dispassion. Feeling a sickness mounting up in her stomach, Edna roamed back to the entry of the hospital and departed; functioning in an automated manner, she got into the car and positioned herself in the rear seat, all the while steadily composed like a guarded, subdued mouse. Once arriving at the dynasty manor, Edna listlessly ascended the staircase and went into her bedroom, where she bolted the door and retired her fatigued body in a large fireside chair. Nothing seemed to comfort her; she perceived her world as a dark place with no apparent hope for things ever-improving, so she lingered in the chair, with her eyes riveted out the window, she remained there for the entire day and night.

The evening sun spotlighted the passageway where Gary Jenkins had tirelessly stalked Liam to a remote, historical village at the base of the Tatras Mountains. The 13th-century German settlement founded a momentous Gothic church and a newly established University, and as Gary shadowed Liam, he witnessed him skulk into a dilapidated cottage, briefly stopping on the doorsteps to defensively survey the laneway before he swiftly entered through its shabby entrance. Huddling into an alcove of a deserted house, Gary heaved up the collar of his duffle coat, the thick, coarse woolen material pleasantly warming his neck, and diligently persevered the incoming darkness as he waited for another sighting of Liam. He stood there firm as a chiseled rock and skillfully extended his long arm down into the cavernous pocket of the jacket, seizing his mobile phone and initiating a call to Edna.

'Hello, Karce residence', William answered.

'William, it's Gary Jenkins, may I speak with Edna please?' Gary requested.

'I'm sorry, Mr. Jenkins, but Mrs. Karce is indisposed at the moment.'

146

'Alright, well, can you inform her that I'm in Slovakia and I'll call again in a few days?' He uttered softly, and as he disengaged from the chat, he observed a light glimmering from a minuscule window on the uppermost level of the dilapidated cottage. Liam's face appeared at the window, grimacing his expression to inspect the outside surroundings, and once he was pleased there was no one about, he withdrew from the porthole and turned out the light. Gary Jenkins had the patience of a saint, and he'd accomplished his determination through years working in law enforcement, acquiring the necessary skills for finding creative ways to pursue leads, and he possessed the vital talent of being able to convince people into revealing sensitive information that delved into extremely tough situations.

He'd never been married, and even though his appearance was unusual, Gary was an outstanding person with a nature gentler than a lamb. His problem-solving abilities for making quick decisions cultivated unraveling cases a breeze, and he never missed the important clues that were necessary for getting to the root of that investigation ... even the smallest ones. The night-watch hours dragged on for Gary, but once it reached 3.00 am, he detected Liam exiting the cottage and skulked down the laneway, heading in the opposite direction from where he was monitoring him. Following Liam around the township, he watched him scavenge through unwanted objects that were discarded outside people's cottages, picking up unused items and examining them; and if he was keen on it, he'd place the recyclables in a sack that hung over his shoulder, hoping to make some money selling them to traders whose paths he'd cross on the roadway from time to time. Like a floating apparition, Gary tracked Liam for

147

half a kilometer, maintaining a sheltered distance where he wouldn't be exposed, and as he saw Liam duck around the corner of a chateau and not wanting to misplace his suspect, Gary accelerated his stride. He marginally increased his distance on Liam and rapidly turned the identical corner, effectively coming tersely face-to-face with his suspicious assailant, their bodies colliding together; and as they gawked into each other's eyes in a soundless gesture, Gary felt a cold sensation penetrating his gut, and then all of a sudden a rush of searing pain coursed its way throughout his body. He lunged blindly at Liam, struggling to remove the knife out of his attacker's hand, but Liam repetitively plunged the dagger into him, amplifying the damage by twisting the knife each time within his victim's intestines. Gary stared at his hands as their physiques separated, and they came away dark and sticky with the blood spurting out like a hose. He grabbed at the pain as if that would stop it; then collapsing onto his knees, he subsequently crumbled into a heap on the steely cold pavement and just lay there, his life receding away while Liam rummaged through Gary's pockets and then escaped down the bleary pathway. Temporarily glimpsing back at the crime scene, Liam detected that his shoes were leaving distinctive tracks, conspicuously publicizing the direction of his retreat, so he rapidly kicked them off and shunted them into one of the hessian sacks he'd pilfered earlier on that morning. Soaked in blood, Liam returned to his decrepit hideout and proceeded to strip off the grisly evidence from his body, tossing his crimson-stained outfit into the fireplace and stood there completely naked, watching blankly as the proof of his corruption burned into a pile of ashes.

He'd become defective of any compassion, and as he stared

148

at the red and orange flames licking at the discarded garments, Liam blocked out his feelings; and with a deprived sense of meaning or worth for his life, he apathetically strolled into the bathroom and washed away the depravities of Gary's merciless slaying. Standing at the washbasin, his bulky hands clenched firmly on the sink, Liam contemplated his reflection in the mirror as an emotional prowling force sheathed him, robbing him of his joy, confidence, and hope. The big dreams and goals and the affluent life that he'd once craved for felt less of a certainty, and he began to spiral from a self-assured state of mind to one of burden and hardship. Motionless at the basin, engrossed in his judgments, Liam heard an acquainted voice from behind him.

'Hi, comrade, why are you standing there stark naked, and what are you burning in the fireplace? It smells awful.'

'Oh hi, Jock, I'm burning my clothes', Liam replied coldly, turning around to notice his companion.

'Why? What have you done?' Jock questioned.

'I killed that strange bloke who's been stalking me, and he followed me here.' Liam walked over to his backpack and hauled out a jacket and a pair of long faded jeans, dressing as he spoke.

'What? Please say that this is some kind of a joke you're playing, Liam.' Jock buckled at the knees and promptly sat down on the frayed lounge chair behind him, clasping his hands around his forehead as though an unexpected migraine had just occurred.

'No joke, mate. I know that he's been trailing me in regards to Annie's death. I had a quick look at his identification while he was on the ground, and he was a private detective. I reckon the Karce family sent him over here to find out what was happening with Sharon and Annie. I'll never let them catch me.'

'Friend, I've already helped you out heaps, setting you up with somewhere to stay and obtaining the chemical ingredients for those brews you wanted, now with this murder you've just committed, I can't help you any longer. The police will be searching, and I can't have you here. I'll get kicked out of University if I'm found tangled up in this. You've got to go right now ... there's not a moment to lose', Jock voiced as he stood up and walked over to the closet.

'Here's a sleeping bag, take it and head into the mountains, it'll be harder for them to find you up there. Once you're over them, you'll be in Poland. Good luck, my friend' He continued. Liam seized the sleeping bag and tucked it under his arm while Jock rummaged through his pantry, snatching cans of soup and beans and a map, as he also provided Liam with extra warm jumpers, and the two young men sturdily embraced each other before Liam escaped through the door of the cottage. Jock peeked out the window as he watched his comrade journey up the road towards the preternatural intimidating Tatras Mountains; and as Liam disappeared into the distance, Jock uttered to himself, *'Safe travels, Liam, you're going to need all the luck you can get.'*

The day was welcoming a pleasant ambiance as Liam trailed on, glancing up occasionally at the majestic mountain peaks that were touching the turquoise sky. He noted that the blood-soaked shoes were still concealed in the hessian bag, so while on the ruthless secluded track, he pitched them far into a dense grassy meadow. Achieving to reach the high plateau by nightfall, he prepared a campsite, all the while anticipating the forthcoming struggles he was about to face while visually dissecting the thick forests of conifers and the steep rising of corrugated highlands ahead of him. After scoffing into a cold tin of greatly desired beans, he glided into the sleeping bag; and as he lay there, gazing up at the impressive stars, tiny splashes of ice brushed against his face as it began to sleet.

The dark night not only transported freezing-cold winds across the long broad fields but it bore intensified resonances of wild animals, echoing sounds of low grumbles and moans, and the noise of snapping teeth. Liam didn't get any sleep that night, so in the early hours of the morning, he studied the map that Jock had given him and decided to take the road less traveled, suspicious of his presence being identified by hikers. He took a path up the soaring landscape and advanced into the dense woodland, and just as he entered, Liam decisively navigated left of the track, creating his own route through the thick scrub over the treacherous mountains.

It was still early in the morning when a crowd of townsfolk congregated on the bend of the chateau where Gary's lifeless body lay in a pool of cherry-red blood, his face bleached of color and with a manifestation of torture eternally petrified on his expression. Hearing the sound of a policeman's whistle propelling loudly, desperately trying to alert his associates of the encounter, Jock wandered out of his cottage and with his hands in his jean pockets, he coolly roamed towards the commotion; and once he had pushed his way through the gathering, his eyes feasted on Liam's despicable brutality. Scrambling to inwardly grasp what his friend had done, an unexpected urgency of fretfulness heaved up in his body, recognizing that he still possessed the mobile phone with the communiqué between Liam and himself. Determined not to become linked with the corruption, Jock secretly parted company from the crowd and migrated out of town into the countryside. He walked the rural tracks for an hour with the vision of Gary's spread-out carcass magnified in his thoughts; and as he passed a remote farmhouse, he detected an old water shaft that looked as though it was submerged deep into the ground. Jock leaped over the boundary fence and hastily moved towards the well, stooping down to pick up a rock as he advanced; and once he'd reached the stone wall, he inspected the gorge of the cavern, flinging the rock down to measure its depth.

Listening to the ricochets of the falling rock, he duplicated the same with his phone and waited until he heard the indistinct splash as it plunged into the bottomless muddy water; and without hesitancy, Jock sprinted back to the fence and proceeded homeward into town. When he finally reached his household, the police were doorknocking, struggling to ascertain from the locals if they'd seen any foreigners that may have passed through over the last couple of days.

'Hello, Jock!' A police officer greeted. 'We had a grisly murder here early this morning. It's not a common thing for this town. Did you see any strangers traveling through, you know, someone who was alone and didn't look like they were vacationing?' He continued.

'No, Constable, I haven't. I've been studying for my exams, so I haven't been out much', Jock lied as his eyes darted about, observing the locals casually analyzing him.

'Okay, where have you been this morning then?' The officer demanded.

'I've been going stir-crazy just staring at books and four

walls, so I went for a walk to get some air, that's all.' He persuaded.

'What time did you leave for your walk? You must have left early. Didn't you notice the crowd gathering on the corner up there?'

'I wasn't sure what was going on, and I didn't feel like getting tangled up with local chit-chat. I just needed to clear my head from studying.'

'Alright then, but if you see anything unusual, let us know immediately.'

'Not a problem, Officer.' Jock smiled and then advanced to open the door to his cottage where he vanished behind it and concealed himself in the shanty for a long period of time. The police shielded the area where Gary Jenkins's body lay while the forensic squad foraged for clues to his murder with the first sign being evidence of a chaotic scuffle as some of his belongings were scattered around him, except for his wallet, which had been taken out then accurately placed back in his coat pocket as it revealed bloodstained fingerprints on the exterior. Large drops of blood and soaked, burgundy-marked shoe prints trailed down the alleyway and this formed a pattern, originating the direction of Liam's escape route, thus helping police to reconstruct the crime. Deposited in Gary's right-hand palm was a fistful of Liam's brown hair, and upon examination, the police found that it had been removed forcefully as the roots of the chunk of locks were still connected and evident. This collaborated with their first suggestion of a powerful struggle, so all of the clues they were collecting became the proof that was needed to help them solve the crime. Their hunt for the perpetrator would take the police expedition farther into the wilderness than they would have anticipated in their wildest dreams.

A piercing-cold wind gusted as Liam trekked up the ascending landscape, which radically altered as he progressed along, totally unrecognizable in terms of its primitive nature; and with the fog removing any trace of the sun's warming rays, his hands and feet were numbing, developing into obstinate, icy attachments. Liam sat down on a moss-covered log to recuperate the loss of feeling in his extremities, and while he kneaded them vigorously, he noticed that not one bird was singing and the forest was as soundless as a boneyard. The thick canopy of the forest only added to the vagueness of which was the precise track to continue along, and as he considered his destiny, the darkness pressed in on him from all sides, and he began to hyperventilate, sucking in the bitterly cold air more rapidly; and every so often, he caught the desolate chorus howls of the inherent wolverines who occupied and governed the woodland. Liam slid down off the mossy log and sank his bottom into the wet undisturbed ground as he frantically heaved out the sleeping bag from its cover then enfolded it around his upper body whilst unfastening the backpack; he lurched in and snatched his last can of beans. He started to deliberate where his next meal would come from as his fundamental survival skills were pathetic, and he didn't have any prior knowledge of how to trap or forage for sustenance in the wild, so therefore these thoughts developed into a serious concern for him. Liam nestled into his sleeping bag and sheltered himself against the fallen tree as he identified that a few days without food would accelerate his fatigue and weakness, and with this state of mind, his feelings eddied out of control. Trembling in the shadows, his body agonized with the pain that had emerged over the last couple of days from the depressing arctic conditions; and as he drifted into an exhausted sleep, he comprehended that his efforts of escape were futile. It was midmorning when Liam woke, and as the feebleness of daylight struggled to infiltrate the forest, he stood up, saturated from the overnight snow and felt his toes prickle with pain as the sensation felt like they were red-hot. At great risk of losing his vitality, he began looking around on the vegetation for any kind of nourishment, grabbing mushrooms, berries, and even the unplanned grasshopper and snail, heaping them into his mouth. Crunching away at the foul-tasting breakfast, he resurrected his journey; and as he walked, he could hear the squelch of wet socks and boots and the crunching of the frozen ground beneath his feet. Slipping and slithering on the frigid terrain from time to time, Liam ultimately felt a severe pain radiating from the upper side of his leg. As he inspected it, he witnessed a twig protruding from his thigh. He attempted to remove it, but immediately, the branch snapped off at the entry of the wound, leaving him reeling in agony with blood erupting from the amplified laceration. He just lay there gaping up at the boundless awning of the forest, and before he knew it, he began hallucinating from the poisons in the mushrooms and insects that he'd consumed earlier. A breeze began to draft through, and as Liam looked up at the tall trees, their limbs swayed leisurely about, and the more he fixated on them, they triggered into extended hands with long spindly fingers reaching down to wrestle him. He bolted upright, screaming at the woody hands to leave him alone, and rapidly felt the searing pain of the injury, and while he grabbed at his leg to stop the throbbing, he became aware of a squirming sensation as hundreds of maggots obsessively feasted away at his leg.

With complete revulsion, Liam slapped at the worms with a passion, only to intensify his pain and suffering as he shrieked even louder. The piercing scream resonated throughout the secluded forest, which didn't alert anyone else; it merely announced to the wolves of his whereabouts. Powerless to rationally control the pain, he hurled himself backward onto the ground, instantly passing out, only to awaken hours later to the echoes of a distant banshee-type wailing, which didn't stop. His nostrils were chock full with the odor of wet putrefying leaf matter, which was scattered all around him, and he quickly realized that between every deplorable wailing moan, the creature moved unbelievably fast, as it seemed to advance quickly in his direction with each outpouring of torment. He waited a few minutes, his heart flogging itself in his throat like a pulsating drum, nervously anticipating the next haunting scream ... and that's when he saw it. Shrouded in white, the apparition floated tactfully above the ground and hovered in place, its fiery eyes piercing the shadowy expression as it scowled at the desperate man lying ten feet in front of it before suddenly launching itself towards him and attaching its extended yawning mouth onto his, drinking the life from his stranded body and leaving his consumed corpse behind ... forsaken and abandoned just like a portion of the decaying forest.

Even before the sun's earliest rays peeped over the skyline, the police gathered in the town square and prepared their expanded search for the wanted assassin of Gary Jenkins. They had previously uncovered the hessian bag, which concealed the blood-marked shoes in them, so with the support of their sniffer dogs, the police initiated a detailed pursuit into the harsh and rugged plateaus. The team had formerly analyzed the local weather before heading out and predicted that a storm would be closing in en route with their search, so as experienced mountaineers, the police equipped themselves with warm clothing, whistles. and torches as those supplies would be invaluable to attract attention once they had captured the assailant.

The tracking hounds dashed ahead with long overextended strides, while a handful of equestrian officers careered after them, following their loud booming voices as they scuttled up the track into the tablelands, the canines' endurance for sticking to Liam's scent and trailing it over such a long distance and rough terrain was remarkable. Relentlessly, the hunting team shadowed the distant howling of the dogs for hours, twisting and turning along the brutal track, until they noticed the predicted ice storm brewing in the distance. The area by now was already perilous and caused the slippery ground to be an additional hazard, potentially affecting the horses, so the squad decided to call back the dogs and group together until the storm passed. As the blizzard advanced, it appeared more dissolute than any in living memory as the rain, dense like grenades, destroyed everything in its path, punishing the discarded. The evening darkness and the damp-smelling air threatened to provide them with adequate shelter beneath whatever refuge they sought, so while the storm assaulted them, it was collectively decided to camp the night before advancing with the pursuit. The following morning, the squad recommenced their search; and even though the storm had washed away all traces of Liam's course, the smell from his shoes relinked the sniffer dogs to his scent, where they instantly continued along the track with a disorganized approach. Steadily escalating up the mountainside and into the forest, it became heartlessly quiet, with only the vibration of the horses' hooves clomping against the bedrocks as they traipsed deeper into the backwoods. Prudently examining the ground as they trotted along, they eventually received the critically awaited baying of a hound dog, desperately summoning them farther into the immensity of the forest; and as the bellowing got closer, the team took a left turn off the accustomed track and entered into the profoundly dewy wildwoods. With every imminent step, the sour stench of demise penetrated their nostrils, even making the horses occasionally rear up and retreat backward with repulsion; and as they pushed away low dangling branches and turned the last cluster of obscuring bushes, there sat one of the dogs, obediently locked in an upright posture, accurately seated next to the suspect. The police dismounted from their horses and slowly ambled over to the distorted body, trying to visually comprehend what had occurred to the gnarled leftovers. As they scoured the immediate area for clues, they couldn't help notice that the entire body had been eaten away, the bones fragmented and dispersed everywhere, leaving only a consumed blood-spattered skeleton with not a morsel of flesh on it, while Liam's entire head was just lying there, unharmed, abandoned and staring.

'What do you think happened here, Sergeant?' One of the constables probed as he held a scarf up to his nose.

'Looks like a pack of wolves have had a banquet on him, I'd say. There are tracks all around here. Must have been seven or eight of them. Look here, his belongings have been torn to shreds ... even his mobile phone's been gnawed into tiny pieces.'

'Yeah, but what about the head? It hasn't been touched?'

'Wolves don't eat every edible portion of a carcass' The sergeant educated the young officer as he circled Liam's remains, inspecting the horrific torment the deceased must have suffered. 'Take a look at the expression on his face.' As the officers stood around, glaring at the head, riveted by his grey-tinged face and mouth gaping wide open with its blue colored lips, they detected in his fossilized eyes the manifestation of agonizing torment and thought that maybe he didn't perish from wolves devouring him, maybe he died from some other terror.

'Do you think this is our guy?' The constable persisted to query.

'Yeah, it's our guy, look at his hair. It's the same color and texture we found in the murder victim's hand. Look here, there's a bald patch where the chunk of hair was torn out. This is the guy for sure, but forensics will make that positive identification. Bag him up, boys, we're heading back' The sergeant instructed.

'I wonder who he was' One of the assisting officers said.

'Don't know, but he's not a local. He was probably a drifter who thought he could burgle money from that poor bastard he killed back in the village.'

Wearing protective gloves, the constables guardedly picked up the littered skeleton parts as the sergeant took photos of the gravesite and partially ingested bones, and each time they'd place the head in its own distinctive bag, it would plummet out, revolving onto the ground, always with its face oscillating upwards, exposing his incessant tormented look—the exact same look that plagued Annie before she died.

'Careful, men, we don't want forensics accusing us of damaging the corpse's head' The sergeant shouted. Securing the body bags onto the saddles, they eventually mounted their horses and began the long voyage back down the mountain; but every so often, they'd hear a thump on the ground, only to realize that the head had fallen out yet again, just resting there with its face fronting upwards, reminding them of its existence.

'This thing is possessed' The constable remarked as he picked up Liam's head by the hair and shoved it back into the bag.

'Just make sure the bag is accurately sealed, Constable' The sergeant commanded as he turned around and propped himself on the back of his horse to address the subordinate officer. It was sundown the following day by the time the squadron reached the village police station, and as the other officers untidied the body bags, transporting them into the evidence room, the young officer responsible for bringing the skull immediately noticed that the sack was empty again. He examined the bag and established that the opening was strongly fastened, but upon further investigation, he discovered a threadbare hole in the bottom of the satchel. Before attracting any attention to the situation, he fretfully hurdled back onto his horse and galloped away in the direction from which they came, circling back and forth, reviewing his steps, while back at the station the sergeant held a routine itinerary assessment, and that's when he realized the young officer was absent.

'Where's Constable Nowak?' He questioned, exasperated by the officer's recklessness.

'I thought he was outside with his horse' One of the

160

squad members replied, and just as he was finishing his assumption, they saw Nowak standing anxiously in the doorway, perspiration flowing down his face. They stared at him for some kind of reaction and that's when he finally admitted to his carelessness.

'It's gone, the head is missing. I tried searching for it, but it completely vanished.'

'You simpleton. That head was the only proof we needed to link the cadaver to the murder', the sergeant exclaimed, slapping his hand up solidly against his brow.

'Now, what are we going to do?' He continued

Ten

Chapter 10

Bounded by four walls, there was nothing else to do but gawk at them. Sharon studied the timeworn paint that had started to chip away and the scribbly grooves left by other inmates, anything to pass time, as she felt like insanity was slowly motioning her to enter into its sphere of influence. The holding cell was typical. Six by eight feet with two metal bed trays, which were bolted to the wall, a sink, and a toilet. A small window allowed sunlight to filter through, but it didn't eliminate the murky atmosphere of the chamber; and as Sharon lay on the cold hard bed, with only a flimsy blanket separating her body from its steely block, she heard the footsteps of someone approaching. Sitting upright, she glided her lethargic body onto the edge of the bed and wandered over to the cell bars, digging her nose through them, attempting to catch a glimpse of the advancing company.

'Hey, when can I make my phone call and get a lawyer?' She

yelled as the prison guard escorted a robust beefy woman who was painted in menacing tattoos and restrained in handcuffs, eventually stopping in front of Sharon's cell entrance.

'Shut up, you'll get your chance. Stand back', The hard-edged guard stated as he unlocked the gate and thrust the macho prisoner into the cell, slamming the trapdoor shut as rapidly as he'd opened it. With a quick step, Sharon scuttled back towards the rear wall and inspected her fresh cellmate, who loomed over her like the Empire State Building. Not a word was spoken between them for an extended period as Sharon, upended and unmoving, anticipated what the powerful woman was going to do next.

'Hi, my name is Sharon', She finally announced.

'Agata', Answered the mannish woman in a low gruff voice.

'Hi, Agata, nice to meet you', Sharon chirped, nervously walking over to shake Agate's hand. 'Piss off', The grumpy cellmate stated as she walked over to where Sharon had been napping and picked her belongings, flinging them across the room, guaranteeing they landed on the secondary bed. Dumbfounded by Agata's outlandish behavior, Sharon stood there, her mind racing with vicious thoughts, finally sitting down on the undesirable inferior crib, with one side of the bed rails broken.

'You look like a porcelain princess, you know, the type of ornament they put on top of a wedding cake', Agata badgered and sniggered as she scanned Sharon's face, waiting for retaliation, but she didn't utter a word, which was entirely out of character for Sharon. But powerless to restrain herself, she finally bit back.

'Well, I'm locked up here with you, so I'm no princess but thank you for remarking on how flawless porcelain my skin

163

is', She smirked. Instantly Agata bolted upright, standing with her fists clenched and walking towards Sharon in a terrorizing manner.

'Don't get sassy with me, bitch, otherwise, I'll knock you through that wall you're so fond of leaning up against.' Sharon squirmed to the farthest end of the bed, evading Agata's threatening presence, and began screaming out for the indisposed guard to appear as the broad-shouldered woman roared with laughter at Sharon's emerging fright.

Returning to her own bed, she plonked herself down, all the while shamelessly glaring at the cowering woman on the other side of the room.

'Yeah, I didn't think so. You've got a big mouth with no guts to back it up with', Agata goaded.

'What are you in here for, princess?' She distracted, trying to unruffle the situation. Apathetically, Sharon contemplated her response; then after plucking up the courage to speak, she grudgingly replied,

'I'm here because they think I conspired to kill my sister.'

Agata burst into laughter at the thought of the porcelain princess being a cold-blooded murderer while Sharon deviously surveyed her every move.

'You? A murderer? Now I've heard everything. You wouldn't know how to kill a fly. No, really, why are you here?' She repeated, not believing a word of Sharon's revelation.

'I told you. If you don't believe me, then that's your problem.'

'There's that sassy attitude again. I've already warned you, princess, keep it up and I'll smack you into tomorrow. So? You are a killer? And your sister of all people? You must be one cold-hearted bitch.'

'Well, believe it because that's what they're charging me

with', Sharon aloofly reaffirmed. 'Who'd be vile enough to murder their own sister? You've got no feelings, princess. Were you hatched in a pod or something?' Agata sniggered as she persisted with her insults.

'What are you in for?' Sharon cagily reversed the discussion.

'Atacare Om ... how do you say in your English ... attacking a man' She communicated in broken English.

'You assaulted a man? Why?'

'It's like this, princess. He wanted to fuck me, so I knocked him into the next room, just like I've promised to do to you if you don't stop with your questions.' Agata carelessly lay down on the chosen bed and turned her back towards Sharon as she nuzzled into the flinty pillow and fell asleep; her cellmate regarded the broad-framed woman with repugnance. With arms enveloped around her legs, Sharon remained stagnant on the crib, her back against the wall that Agata had threatened to knock her through until she heard the accustomed footsteps of the prison guard approaching the chamber.

'You've got your phone call' The guard unemotionally informed and prudently unfastened the gate, grabbing Sharon powerfully by the arm while he padlocked her wrists in handcuffs and chaperoned her up the grimy hallway into another room. As Sharon placed herself nervously behind the desk, eyeballing the crucial phone in front of her, she picked up the receiver to make the anticipated singular call, which would ultimately hallmark her destiny. 'Use your best discretion and call someone who you're certain is going to answer the phone because you only get one chance' The accompanying guard warned. Sharon considered what he'd said, so with intensified desperation, she dialed the number to call home, trusting that her goal to be supported and released from the prison would succeed. The phone resonated five times, and just as Sharon's heart was plummeting to the bottom of her stomach in fear that no one would answer, William picked up the receiver.

'Karce residence' He remarked.

'William, it's Sharon, is Mama there?' She beckoned.

'No, Miss Sharon, she's at the hospital.'

'Hospital? What for?' Desperation and panic mounted in her voice.

'It's not for me to say, but seeing that your mother hasn't heard from you for some time and is extremely worried, I suppose she won't mind if I inform you that your father is unwell. Has Mr. Jenkins been in touch with you yet?' William asked.

'Mr. Jenkins? Who the hell is he?' Sharon was confused.

'A private detective your mother has employed to bring you and Annie home because of your father's illness.'

'What? No, I haven't even heard or seen Mr. Jenkins. How sick is Papa?' Sharon looked up at the guard as he was signaling her to end the call.

'William, I have to go, but before I do, can you please tell Mama that I'm in deep trouble and being held in a Romanian jail? I need a lawyer immediately. Please ask her to call me back on this number. I'll be able to tell her everything then', She pleaded.

'I will do that immediately. Are you alright? And where's Miss Annie?' Williams stated, overwhelmed at the worrying message.

'Annie's ... dead', Sharon uttered quietly and began to weep.

'That's why I'm being detained in jail, they think I had something to do with it.' Sharon paused for William's reply, but only silence occupied the end of the phone.

166

'Are you there?' And as soon as she voiced her last request, the prison guard snatched the receiver from her clammy hand and brusquely ended the frantic appeal.

'Why did you do that? I hadn't finished my call' She disputed furiously, with her tearful scam miraculously disappearing.

'You only get four minutes, and your time has ended. Now get up, you're going back to the slammer' He commanded in his broken Romanian accent as he replaced the cuffs, shoving her in the middle of the back, gesturing her to move forward. Sharon's ongoing destitution in the Romanian prison was going to test her egotistical resilience as the unavoidable level of suffering inherent with the country's detention system presented her with conditions she'd never experienced before. The unhygienic sanitary conditions, poor food, exploitation by the guards, and the presence of rats and insects were going to thrust her psyche to the parameters of craziness, and she would never identify with the meaning of a privileged lifestyle ever again. Sharon wasn't taken straight back to the original cell; instead, they conducted a thorough body search and performed a general clinical examination by the penitentiary specialty staff with the findings being documented in their medical records. They stripped her down, forced her to shower, and took pictures in order to operationalize the records. They obtained her fingerprints again and drew up a personal items inventory, finally briefing her about convicts' rights, obligations, and prohibitions as well as violations, disciplinary sanctions, and how that will be enforced. Dispirited and introverted after the degrading procedures, she was eventually ushered into an interview room where the guard powerfully sat her down behind a large empty table and lingered unwavering at the door behind her while she waited for two frustrating hours until the prevailing detective entered the room. 'Salut, Miss Karce', He broadcasted conceitedly in his Romanian enunciation as he settled himself opposite her.

'Oh, it's you. When am I going to be released? You haven't charged me with anything, so you can't detain me any longer. Why are you still keeping me here?' She commanded.

'You are being detained for quarantine and observation purposes, and we can hold you here for twenty-one days if needed ... and I have charged you with conspiracy to commit manslaughter at the moment ... if you remember correctly' He articulated, not looking at her as he flicked through the notebook in front of him.

'This is outrageous. They wouldn't treat me like this in Australia, I'm a lady of the Karce Province.'

'Yes, you've already told us that, and you're not in Australia, you're here in Romania.' He smirked as he recognized Sharon's escalating frustration and fear.

'Initially, I'm going to conduct an interview to determine your immediate needs and evaluate your psychological and social requirements' He announced coolly.

'Social requirements? I won't be here long enough to socialize with the scum you've got me incarcerated with' She screamed, leaning in towards the detective to antagonize him, but he kept his flat demeanor and casually glanced up at the surveillance camera, which was suspended in the corner of the room.

'Okay, we've received notification from the police in a small village near the Slovakian border that they've discovered the remains of a body who's allegedly been identified as your notorious friend Liam Cartwright.' He paused for a few seconds to analyze Sharon's reaction to the news.

'What? Liam? Near the border of Slovakia? No way, he wouldn't leave me in the lurch like this. He said that he'd ...' Her voice trailed off like a puff of smoke in the wind.

'He said what ... Miss Karce?'

'Never mind,' She muttered.

'Aren't you even a bit concerned that he's been found dead?' The detective probed inquisitively, regarding her for a hint of compassion.

'It's not Liam, he said that he'd never get caught.' Sharon bit her tongue as she suddenly realized that she'd just implicated herself and Liam even further.

'Caught for what? If he was innocent then why would he be heading for the Tatras Mountains? He certainly wasn't equipped for the hazardous weather and perilous terrain.' Once again, he silently gazed at her expression.

'It's not him' She bluntly denied the accusation.

'Yes, it is, I have his identification right here with me.' The detective reached into a large envelope and slid out a blood-smeared passport. Sharon looked fixedly at the document in silence, and without moving it, she vaguely identified Liam's picture through the desiccated blood, rapidly placing her hand to her mouth as she gulped with horror.

'What happened to him? How did he die?'

'They found his mutilated remains scattered in a dense forest. Not a strip of flesh left on his bones. His blood-splattered carcass was all fractured and partially consumed, with only his severed head completely intact. He was probably eaten by wolves while he slept.'

Sharon heaved at the explicit narrative the detective provided, and for the first time, the detective saw tears brimming in her eyes.

'I have an earlier self-proclaimed record that you and Mr. Cartwright collaborated to drive your sister crazy and that you did this by administering her with lethal drugs and that you were also going to pay him a quarter of a million dollars for his services, so stop with the guiltless humdrum and tell me what you both did ... oh, and by the way ... your associate Liam is also guilty of murdering a man by the name of Gary Jenkins ... just thought you should know' He continued not tolerating her sorrow.

'Mr. Jenkins? Our butler mentioned a private investigator by that name. He said Mama and Papa employed him to bring Annie and me back home.'

'So you know of him?'

'No, I don't. Like I said, our butler mentioned him when I was on the phone.' Sharon was annoyed by the lead detective's barefaced smugness. He deliberately persevered with every twist and turn of the blood trail, and her obvious frustration at this made it favorable for him to keep any complications from blurring the truth while he assessed her emotional response. He had already concluded that the homicidal act against her sister wasn't because of an unexpected strong urge, such as impulsive rage, but a well-planned and deliberate crime. He looked for signs of compassion, guilt, or for some kind of empathic pain that would cause her to feel a mark of sorrow for her sister; but she displayed no shame or tangible sentiment, so he began to judge her for who she really was: a cold-blooded murderer without consideration, regret, or mercy.

'So, this is what you've told me ... You strategically planned to murder your sister because of the combined inheritance, and you engaged Liam Cartwright to help because of his knowledge in chemistry and that you promised to pay him a quarter of a million dollars once the deed was completed ... Gary Jenkins, on the other hand, is a man who was referred by your parents to bring you and Annie home and was tracking your accomplice but ended up being murdered by him. You say that you didn't know Mr. Jenkins, but the way I see it, if yourself and Mr. Cartwright colluded to eradicate your sister, who's to say that you didn't conspire to murder Mr. Jenkins as well ... I think you're just telling me lies?'

'No, that's bullshit. I wouldn't be able to identify Mr. Jenkins. This is the second time I've heard of him. How could I devise to murder someone if I don't even know who they are?' She screamed with rage.

'That's what you say. I believe that you and Mr. Cartwright realized that Mr. Jenkins had already discovered your sister's death, through the local police and hotel staff, and figured out the scheme you had with Liam Cartwright, and knowing you were already being scrutinized by us, he decided to follow Liam to question him, but of course, your associate brutally stabbed him to death instead ... actually, he completely disemboweled him ... charming friends you have, Miss Karce.'

'No, no, no ... I told you that I didn't want Annie dead, just wanted her to go crazy, and I've never heard of Mr. Jenkins ... and that's the truth. Liam never mentioned anything to me about Gary Jenkins ... Liam said he'd wait for me.'

'Well, he didn't. He was trying to escape over the Tatras Mountains, so he was leaving you behind—as you Americans say—holding the bag ... It's a shame you don't have anyone around to confirm your story, Miss Karce ... you are all alone.' He sat at the table in silence for what seemed an eternity until he finally declared Sharon's perilous fate.

'I am charging you with the murder of your sister Annie Karce and the manslaughter of Mr. Gary Jenkins.' He informed her, smirking as he stood up from the table and walked over to the door, then he casually turned around to face Sharon.

'We will talk again, Miss Karce. Thank you for your cooperation. Have a nice evening.' He disappeared through the access door while the attending prison guard abruptly seized her, crudely hauling her up by the arm.

'I'm an Australian citizen ... you stupid fuck ... I didn't kill my sister or Gary Jenkins.' Were the last words she was able to shout at him before being funneled back to her prison cell and the awaiting Agata.

Returning to his office, the detective slumped down into his chair and casually opened Sharon's file, perusing through it like a cherished manuscript. He was a hardened investigator and had the ability to analyze complex problems of any case and find a solution. His critical thinking to reach logical conclusions based on the evidence was significantly practiced, and these skills allowed him to remove any personal prejudices and opinions and objectively make sound decisions. He could read people like a book and perceived things that most people would miss while possessing flawless attention to detail and the patience to work through cases, however tedious and slow they were. He'd already categorized Sharon as a dishonest self-entitled shrew and understood that her manipulative routines were the outcome of a lifetime of gluttony, which had matured her into a narcissist, and he wasn't going to allow her scheming ways to influence his case. Surging over the compiled data, he pondered over any weaknesses that would make Sharon's charges less credible, in regard to the judge's final sentencing, as his decisions were often supported with detailed facts and objectives, and he wanted to achieve a solid and warranted ruling at her trial. Once he was satisfied with the presenting evidence, he reached for the phone and called a criminal defense lawyer in the region, who was also an acquaintance of his and had been for many years.

'Salut, Adrian. I have a very motivating case awaiting here at the moment. The woman involved has been whining for a lawyer since she's been taken into custody, and I was wondering if you'd represent her. It's an open-and-shut case, my friend.' He listened intently for his associate's response.

'Grozav (great) and multumesc (thank you), I appreciate your interest. I'll send the file to your office and then you can make an appointment to meet with her. La revedere (goodbye), Adrian.' Smiling to himself, the detective placed the receiver down into its cradle. His strategy was going according to plan and was delighted that Sharon's unlimited insolence and self-proclaimed superiority were going to be finally destroyed and her deteriorating circumstances tougher to dispute. Opening the cell gate, the prison guard flung Sharon back into the slammer and sharply padlocked it behind her without saying a word. Brushing herself down with disgust and regaining her poise, she sat down on her bed and reflected on the detective's looming retaliation, and with her mind whirling with conflicting decisions, she secretly regarded Agata, who was snuffling and snorting as she slept on the other side of the room. With arms cuddling around her legs, Sharon propped herself up against the discolored wall, like a frightened child, until the sun peeked its first rays over the skyline; and by that time, she had fallen into a profound sleep. Her dreaming was restless and disturbing as she lashed back and forth from the feverish nightmares until she was abruptly awakened by Agata standing over her, salivating and foaming at the mouth, her gigantic frame obstructing any sunlight that endeavored to penetrate the bleak cell. Scrambling out of bed and onto her feet, Sharon quickly backed herself into a corner and began yelling at Agata.

'Hey, what are you doing?' But the monstrous woman continued to linger over the bed, and that's when Sharon understood that Agata was sleepwalking.

'Agata, wake up.' Sharon strolled up to her, nudging her shoulder, and Agata instantly turned around and spat directly at Sharon's forehead, the spume from the slobber trickling down her victim's face. With a robotic impulse, Sharon clouted Agata in the mouth, while rubbing the drool away with a sleeve of the putrid jumper she'd been wearing for days, and simultaneously paced backward, not wanting to collect another mouthful of sputum as she watched Agata awaken from her nocturnal trance.

'What? Where am I?' She groaned.

'Agata, you were sleepwalking and hovering over my bed. Does that happen often?' Sharon enlightened, standing immobile from a protected distance.

'Yeah, sometimes', Agata replied in her drowsy Romanian twang.

'Well, it scared the shit outta me, Agata. I wasn't sure if you were going to attack me or jump into bed with me.' Agata didn't utter another word and turned around leisurely, resting back onto the bed; she settled herself flat on her back and began snoring once again. Sharon stood there, absorbed with what had just happened, and started to feel a rush of anxiety escalate from her stomach as a thousand opinions raced through her mind:

'Is this a common occurrence with Agata? Will I have to sleep with one eye open from now on? I'm afraid of this woman, will she attack me next time? She looks like trash ... I could catch a revolting infection from her. I wish I was back home ... where is my fucking lawyer?' Squatting in the corner where she'd found refuge from Agata, Sharon bowed her head down into the covert of gathered arms and concealed her forsaken expression, as a result of the hopelessness she was feeling and remained assembled there for hours until a guard appeared at the gate.

'Get up, someone wants to see you' He demanded as he unlocked the entrance. Slowly lifting her fatigued head, she unwillingly stood up as commanded and walked over to the guard and routinely turned around for the handcuffs to be fastened on to her wrists, and once the officer was assured that she wasn't going to cause him any concern, he lugged her out into the corridor and guided her to the interrogation room. Sitting at the discussion table was a thickset overweight man in a crinkly suit with extended jowls sagging down his face like an exhausted time-worn basset hound. His disheveled black hair stuck out in every direction as if there was a deceptive gust of wind propelling around the room; and as she entered, he viewed her with a calculated disregard from the pulpit of his chair.

'Salut, Miss Karce' He grumbled in a deep raspy voice as she sat opposite him.

'Who are you supposed to be?' She quizzed.

'My name is Adrian Dalca, and I'm your appointed lawyer for the murder charges against you. I will be defending you in court when the time comes.' He opened her file and reorganized the documents, viewing them carefully.

'Bullshit ... no way are you going to defend me. I want my family's lawyer from Australia. He knows me', She barked.

'That isn't possible. Your family have been informed of your circumstances and your sister's death by the Romanian police yesterday. As you can appreciate, they are in shock and haven't reacted positively to the news, so I'm not confident that they'll be spending the money towards transporting their personal lawyer to Romania anytime soon. Besides, there is a time limit for us to work together and build a defense case for your court hearing. Your sister's body will be returning home after your trial ... if you are interested.'

'I want to make another personal phone call ... now.'

'Yes, I'll arrange that for you, but first, I need you to tell me what happened. You've been charged with the conspiracy to murder your sister and the manslaughter of Mr. Jenkins, is that right?'

'Yes, I've been charged, but as I keep telling everyone, it wasn't my intention for Annie to die, and I didn't know Mr. Jenkins', Sharon mumbled, not facing him, her head hung low as she didn't want to gaze into the chubby face of her substitute lawyer.

'Maybe so, but your sister did die because of the poisons you administered into her drinks. How long have you been doing that, Miss Karce?'

'Since the beginning of our trip' She admitted.

'Where did you purchase the substances for your blend of drugs? Did you have someone helping you?' He spoke as he hastily scrawled down her replies.

'Yes.' She meekly replied

'And? Who is this accomplice?' 'Liam Cartwright.' 'A friend of yours from where?' 'Australia.'

'Come on, Miss Karce, you've got to give me more information than one-word answers. I can't build a defense case if you don't tell me the whole story.' He encouraged.

'Did he travel with you and your sister?'

'No, I bought his airline ticket for him. He was broke, and he wanted to help me with my proposal to make Annie sick, so I purchased the ticket and gave it to him on the night of our farewell party. His flight departed Sydney Airport not long after ours', She exposed, finally realizing that there was no point in time-wasting as her fate was sealed.

'So what was in it for Liam? I mean it's a long way to travel and help a friend out with a deceitful plan.'

'He loved Annie, and she rejected him, so he wanted to teach her a lesson.'

'Really? That's the only reason? You can't expect me to believe that was it? You mentioned that he was broke. Did you offer him any money to assist you?'

'Yes', She answered timidly, knowing full well that she was digging a deeper hole for herself with every despicable fact she disclosed.

'How much money did you offer him?'

'I promised him $250,000 for his help.'

'Did you pay him?'

'Yes ... via electronic transfer.'

'Okay. So another question. Was he the one to furnish you with the substances, and if so, where did he get them from?'

'Yes, but he mixed the drugs, not me. He was a chemistry student at our University, and he knew how to make hallucinogenic potions. He gave me the stuff already mixed and told me to put it in Annie's drinks. I don't know where he got the drugs from ... and that's the truth.' 'You know that

177

they found Mr. Cartwright's remains high up in the Tatras Mountains?'

'Yes, I know.'

'Unfortunately, they didn't recover his head, just his upper skeletal and limb bones' He said solemnly as Sharon began to laugh at the thought of the runaway head.

'Why are you laughing?' Mr. Dalca asked, bewildered at her frivolous attitude.

'Liam always said that he'd never get caught, so even in death, his rebelliousness still endures. How do you know it was him anyway? If you can't find his blooming head, you're unable to make an ID.' She began to feel her chutzpah flowing back

'We have him captured on a grainy surveillance camera prowling around the village closest to the Tatras Mountains, with Mr. Jenkins sighted trailing closely behind him, and our forensic pathologists examined samples of his remaining tissue, the blood left on his bones and his femur bone. You're a doctor, Miss Karce, you should know all of this.' He began feeling exasperated at her idiocy.

'Maybe, but you can't identify him without him being in the system in the first place, I mean he's never committed any crimes before' She contested back.

'Actually, he had, he was convicted of theft in Australia four years ago and was sentenced to 12 months community service and a good behavior bond, so his DNA was in the system from the initial mouth swab they collected. Don't you just love technology? It's a wonderful thing, makes our investigations so much easier these days, and your Australian Federal Police have been very cooperative too' He ridiculed.

Sharon placed her hands over her face in an overwhelmed

gesture of the inescapable demise that was spiraling out of control, and with the feeling of absolute loneliness, she sighed deeply and didn't say another word.

'Who is Mr. Gary Jenkins? Do you know of him, Miss Karce?' Mr. Dalca continued to analyze, and while observing Sharon's every move, he waited for a long while before she responded.

'No, I didn't know him. I only found out who he was when I called home and our butler William told me he was a private detective employed by my parents to bring us back to Australia.'

'You realize that Liam Cartwright murdered Mr. Jenkins in cold blood?'

'Yes, but I had nothing to do with that.' She protested.

'The thing is, Miss Karce, the evidence they have against you is solid, and you have nobody to endorse your story. You've already admitted to conspiring with Mr. Cartwright to get rid of Annie, so why would the court believe you refuting ever knowing Mr. Jenkins? Plus the forensic team have identified your fingerprints on the bottle of wine you left for Annie at the café and on the discarded syringe you dumped at the railway station. Forensics did not discover anyone else's fingerprints on those two items, only yours. Unless we can prove beyond a shadow of a doubt that you weren't acting alone, the jury could settle with the opinion that Gary Jenkins knew about Annie's unexpected death and Liam told you he was pursuing him, so you mutually plotted to kill him too.'

'Stop, just stop! You're only speculating' she screamed.

'Well, Miss Karce, our justice system is very harsh, and you're not in Australia anymore. I suggest that you prepare yourself for a ruthless court battle. I'll request that you're able to make another phone call soon. I will be in touch. Please wait here.' Mr. Dalca's chair made an ear-piercing screech as he pushed it back from the table and collected the paperwork in front of him. Prudently watching Sharon, he stood up and casually departed through the exit, directly entering the viewing room where his friend had been witnessing their entire dialogue, while she just sat there, furiously raking both hands through her unkempt sinewy hair.

'What do you think of her?' The detective probed.

'She's very outspoken and conceited ... and she's as guilty as sin', Adrian established.

'I have a verbal and videoed transcript of her confession. Will you be able to build a reasonable defense for her in court?' The detective continued to explore.

'I will do my best, but the evidence is stacked up against her. She doesn't have anyone to collaborate her story with either.' They both stood there, silently observing Sharon as the prison guard escorted her out of the room and back to the jail cell. As she arrived, Sharon instantly smelt the pungent aroma of heavily spiced food and gawked at Agata as she quaffed into a bowl of congealed lumpy stew as if she hadn't eaten anything for a week. Once the handcuffs were removed, Sharon felt a dense queasiness accelerate in her stomach and instantly scrammed over to the toilet. Heaving violently, she had not an ounce of nourishment to eject and felt as though the pit of her stomach was about to dislodge while Agata just sat there, observing her convulsion, laughing hysterically.

Eleven

Chapter 11

E dna sat in the bright parlor, resting quietly in
her favored chair, feeling isolated and unassisted
with the recent burdensome tragedies that had
been communicated from Romania. She reminisced about
beautiful Annie, her smiles periodically turning into a cycle
of unbroken tears as she mentally detailed every moment
of her young daughter's life and amongst her inconsolable
bereavement, she wavered between sorrow for Annie and
absolute loathing towards Sharon. Annie's death aroused an
overpowering sense of injustice within her as she reflected on
her daughter's unfulfilled dreams and her senseless suffering.
She felt responsible for her child's death as she had always
noticed Sharon's resentment towards her younger sibling and
had never intervened and settled it once and for all, fearing
that she would only intensify Sharon's bitterness if she'd done
so. Ultimately, without Annie in their lives anymore, Edna felt

as though she had lost a vital part of her own identity. William stood motionless at the entrance of the parlor and cleared his throat urgently as he waited respectfully for Edna to notice him.

'What is it, William?' She asked.

'It's Miss Sharon, madam, she's on the telephone and wishes to speak with you urgently. She says that her call time is limited' He advised.

Edna stirred from her chair and wandered towards the house phone, reluctantly picking up the receiver, which was positioned on the counter.

'Hello' She expressed quietly, struggling to disguise her grief.

'Mama? Oh, thank God I've finally contacted you. I'm in deep trouble. They have incarcerated me here in Romania, they've charged me with Annie's death. I need you to fly our family lawyer over to defend my case. They've appointed this shonky attorney for my defense, but I've got the impression he's a friend of the detective who's heading my prosecution, so they're colluding against me. Can you please do this for me, Mama?' Sharon begged.

'The Romanian police have notified me of what's occurred, so if they've charged you, Sharon, then they must have evidence to support those accusations'. Edna found it extremely challenging to speak with the assassin who butchered her precious Annie

'It's all fabricated evidence, Mama. I wouldn't hurt a hair on Annie's head. You believe me, don't you?' Sharon sensed the distrust in her mother's awkwardness towards her. There was deliberate silence on Edna's part as she anticipated what to tell her criminal daughter.

'Sorry, Sharon, I'm unable to … your father is seriously ill in the hospital, and I can't make that choice until he is well enough to help me decide.'

'But, Mama, I'm your daughter, and how long before Papa is well enough to give his consent? I'll end up rotting in here', Sharon screamed down the phone.

'Did you do it, Sharon? Did you conspire with that vulgar Liam Cartwright to hurt Annie? Did he share in your wicked plan?' Edna courageously posed the inescapable question.

'No, Mama, I didn't murder her, I'll be truthful with you. Liam and I did put something in Annie's drink to make her sick, but we didn't think she'd die. I mean, we didn't want her dead', Sharon foolishly confessed.

'So you've lied to me, and everything I've been told about your treacherous activities are true? You're no daughter of the Karce family, Sharon. You have no morality, and you're a self-centered and materialistic woman. Even though you say that you didn't want her dead, your hand was in it when you poisoned her. I don't know who you are anymore. As far as I'm concerned, when Annie died, you died with her. You're on your own.' Edna curtly hung up the phone, listening to the dwindling echoes of Sharon frantically screaming verbal abuse down the receiver. Lifeless, Edna lingered at the counter for some time, shocked at the heart-rending confirmation she had just received; so without saying another word, she turned and apathetically climbed the staircase while William stood covertly nearby, observing his mistress's gradual emotional decline.

William had been a loyal and confidential butler of the Karce family for thirty years and was an essential part of Annie and Sharon's nurturing, so as much as it was distressing for Edna, he was plunging into an unacquainted melancholy of his own.

He had detected Sharon's ruthless and antagonistic nature towards Annie in the past, but he never imagined that she was capable of murdering her and questioned where it had all gone wrong for the two little girls who giggled and frolicked together in the large manor otherwise uninhabited of such innocent jollity. Entering the kitchen, he placed himself down wearily on a chair at the lengthy staff dining table and gestured for the cook to fetch him a cup of tea.

'Are you alright, William?' The housemaid enquired as she delicately placed the cup and saucer on the table, unswervingly sitting down beside him.

'It's all going downhill, Tilly, this lovely family is being destroyed at the hands of one person—Sharon. I can't believe that she could do something so despicable, and it's breaking my heart. If Mr. Karce doesn't pull through his illness, then I'm afraid that this estate will be sold, and then we'll be out of a job. I'm too old to be starting again with a new domiciliary.' He groaned as he placed the palm of his hand over his eyes, as though he felt pain searing through it.

William was the key element in the household's domestic team, and he always endeavored to deliver a professional service for Warren and Edna. His flawless technique to providing a very personal, detailed, and seamless service to his employers and their guests always exceeded their expectations as he took gentle care of them, responding to all of their needs and requests without imposing himself upon them and he had a reputation of striving to create a specialized atmosphere so that when Edna entertained her guests, they always experienced a sensational event.

'You'll get another job, William', Tilly comforted him, placing her hand on his shoulder.

Chapter 11

'I don't want another position, I've watched the girls grow up here, and I love this family ... I'm a part of their antiquity.' The two domestics chit-chatted in the kitchen for a long time, reassuring each other and discussing strategies on what to do, if and when they lost their positions at the distinguished Karce Estate.

Arriving at her bedroom, Edna closed the door behind her and lay down on the enormous bed that she and Warren shared; and with feelings of desperation battling around in her thoughts, she began to gently weep. Even though her trepidations were consumed with the overpowering events regarding Annie's untimely death and Sharon's imprisonment in Romania, she was dedicated to Warren's recovery from his brain surgery and identified that once he had learned about his daughter's fraught circumstances, she would have to be the strong one, which was a role she was not accustomed to. He would undoubtedly look to her for strength and she desperately wanted him to heal and return to the resilient and eloquent man she loved and depended upon, so she mentally prepared herself for the support and decision-making he would need her to do. She was mindful that his recovery was going to be a lengthy one, and the doctors had already educated her that he could struggle with phases of depression and confusion, so they instructed her not to focus on any negative aspects but constantly reinforce the positives, which would assist with his recovery going well. Immersed in her feelings, she heard an unexpected knock at the door.

'Yes, who is it?' She stifled between her episodic weeping.

'It's William, madam, the hospital just called, and they asked if you could go down there. I've already instructed the chauffeur to bring the car around the front.' He verbalized through the closed door.

'Thank you, William.' Within half an hour, Edna descended the stairs and observed William, who stood patiently by the door. Her appearance was fatigued as she never had minutes that seemed like an eternity as she walked in slow motion towards William, her thoughts clouded with worry and her eyes heavy from the strenuous effects of crying. She had not prepared herself for such helplessness, and the inconsistency of her judgments made her wish she could just lie down and die, as it took every bit of her strength to act as though she was in command of the tormenting state of affairs.

'Are you alright?' William examined as she passed him in the entryway.

'Yes, William, thank you for your concern' She lied before giving him a feeble smile as she walked towards the awaiting car.

Warren had been convalescing in an intensive care isolated room, and his induced coma had lasted for just over a week; but before Edna entered his room, the presiding doctor approached her.

'Hello, Edna, how are you?'

'I'm alright ... under the circumstances. How's Warren today?'

'He's doing well. We began bringing him out of the induced coma early yesterday afternoon and overnight, and he is responding well to the Glasgow Coma Scale. It's a status we use to gauge his perception after unconsciousness. He's having a little trouble focusing his eyes, so he looks as though he's staring off into space at times. When you go in, he may not be able to respond to you but his movement is good, and this is a positive sign of his improvement. He is self-aware

186

and is reacting progressively to sounds, so he'll be able to hear your voice.' The doctor informed.

'That's great news, thank you, Doctor, may I go in now?'

'Yes, certainly, I just wanted to prepare you.'

As Edna tiptoed into Warren's room, she gingerly pulled up a chair and sat closely at his bedside, embracing his hand as she made herself comfortable.

'Hello, my darling, it's Edna. I'm here for you, sweetheart.' She crooned, and as her words were articulated, she felt Warren feebly press her hand in response. His puny and deteriorating form still persisted, and as she studied his physique, Edna's attention rambled between the distress for her husband's disintegrating health and the catastrophic predicaments with their daughters; and as though Warren recognized her despondency, he ejected a drawn-out moan and sporadically uttered four words.

'Are … the … girls … okay?'

Mysteriously, during his coma, Warren had experienced wild, vivid dreams and night terrors, hearing and seeing everything that had befallen with Sharon and Annie, and the revelations tortured him. The realistic visions were so frightening, and he believed that he'd been living his everyday factual life, which summoned up powerful emotions and strong physical responses like he needed to fight with their culprits and save the day. Edna leaned in closer and gently caressed her husband's crop of dark hair.

'Yes, dear, the girls are fine. Don't worry about anything and just concentrate on getting better', she fabricated. There was a long silence before Warren exhaled two more words amidst another extended moan.

'Not … true.'

Edna sat there, astonished at her husband's reply. She'd never lied to Warren before and wasn't very skilled at it, so she selflessly persisted with the fib, wanting to protect him from the potentially upsetting information, as she believed that the appalling circumstances justified her dishonesty.

'Yes, it's true, darling. They're on their way home as we speak.' The lie instantly clutched at her brain as she listened to its sensibility and recognized that what she'd just told him was completely immoral. Warren heaved an intense sigh in defeat, as though he knew that her remark was deceitful; the lie was as obvious as a pimple on a pumpkin, but he didn't have the vitality to dispute it, so he closed his eyes and visualized the hallucinating terrors of his daughters' carnage in his mind. Edna continued to scrutinize her husband's overpowered expression, his face shadowy tinged, hollow, and emaciated, and presumed that what she'd just done was for his own good, not fully comprehending that the story she'd vowed was true would be irreparable. Abruptly, Edna felt her mobile phone vibrate in the uppermost pocket of her jacket and instantaneously walked out of the room to answer it.

'Hello, Edna Karce is speaking.'

'Hello, it's the Romanian police calling about your daughter Sharon.' The detective spoke in his fragmented English.

'Yes?' Edna calmly paused for more information.

'After your phone conversation with Sharon, she went berserk and spiraled into a complete rage. The guard heard noisy grunting and howling coming from the prison cell, and when he went to investigate, he found Sharon choking the other prisoner who she's been locked up with. Our warden got there just in time but not before the inmate received terrible injuries. We have no other choice than to charge her with assault and restrain Sharon in solitary detention until she settles down. It is our duty to provide you with an update of your daughter's situation.' He waited for Edna's reply as she quietly reflected what he'd just told her and without a smidgen of compassion in her voice, she answered,

'Thank you, Officer. I appreciate your obligation to inform me.' Edna ended the phone call and stood unmoving for a long time before wandering back into Warren's room, and upon witnessing him asleep, she silently turned around and left the hospital without even giving her husband a farewell kiss. As she arrived at the manor house, William stood dutifully by the entrance, indicating for Edna to deliver him her coat; and while she moved past him, he detected the concealed heaviness she exhibited, carved on her gentle face.

He needed to advise her that Mrs. Simpson had visited the house earlier in the morning and required Edna to get in touch, as she hadn't heard from her longtime friend during Warren's spell in hospital and felt concerned. William waited until the lady of the manor had settled in, rewarding herself with an accustomed pot of tea and biscuits, before he approached Edna as she absently stared out the window, inattentive of her surroundings.

'Excuse me, madam. Your friend Mrs. Simpson called in this morning and instructed me to ask if you could phone her at your convenience' He briefed.

'Thank you, William' Was all she could reply as her mind was deep within the confines of her family's dilemmas. She continued to sit for another hour before reaching for the phone to make the call, and on the third ring, her beloved friend answered.

'Hello, Grace, it's Edna.'

'Oh, my dear, thank you for calling. I've been very worried about you, how's Warren?' Grace Simpson probed.

'He's been quite ill, Grace. After the operation, they had to put him into a medically induced coma. He's come out of it now and is improving.' She strained to play down any seriousness. 'Well, I'm glad he's improving, Edna. Is he allowed any visitors yet? We'd like to go and see him', Grace explored.

'No, not at the moment', Edna's remarks were short and factual, as though she was being cross-examined by an arbitrator.

'Are you alright ... you seem very elusive, dear.' Her friend detected that Edna wasn't giving up any preventable information easily.

'Just tired, Grace, it's been a demanding time.'

'How are the girls then? Are they back from their trip? I suppose they're frantic to be by their father's side.' Edna sat there with an eerie silence, the fear of telling the truth threatened to consume her; and the longer she hesitated, the thicker the silence became, and she sensed her hands begin to tremble. The apathy in their conversation lay naked for her friend to pinpoint as the confrontation of what to say next left Edna solidified while disputing the impulses that whirled around in her head ... *The truth is the truth ... there's no changing it, and dressing up the bad news with a pretty bow isn't going to make things any easier ...* 'Should I tell her?' She thought. Then impulsively, she boldly fabricated ...

'The girls are fine. Even though they're concerned for Warren, they'll be extending their trip. I'm keeping them up to date on how he is.'

'Really? I thought they'd be in a hurry to get home?' Grace expressed her astonishment. 'Well, you know young people these days. Lovely speaking with you, Grace, and thank you for your concern. I have to go, William has just come in with some more news.' Edna briskly hung up the receiver.

Assembled in the chair, she sat, staring at her mobile phone, trusting that Grace wouldn't have the ambition to hunt for the truth, and a mood of panic descended as she realized that once the actuality about her girls surfaced, the bond she had between her husband and her longtime friend would be ruined. She understood that her dishonesty was going to require constant maintenance, and this was already beginning to feel like an exhausting charade, and the pretense was incredibly isolating. Covertly hidden behind the vestibule, William eavesdropped on Edna's conversation and was mystified why she hadn't told Mrs. Simpson the truth. He knew that someday, it would all come hurtling down on her in a most disturbing way and doubted her capability to survive the fallout of the deception. While Edna lingered in the parlor, mesmerized by her confusion, he roamed into the kitchen and sat at the acquainted dining table, not uttering a word. He felt passively angry, even paralyzed by the fear of maybe losing his job, and strained to protect himself against the agony he felt as the raw experience made him feel vile. Tilly turned around from the sink, customarily wiping her hands on the overused apron she wore, and regarded William with uneasiness.

'What is it, lovey?' She asked.

William stared at her with a foretelling expression.

'I just heard Edna lie to Grace Simpson about Sharon and Annie, which means that she's not coping' He supposed.

'How do you know she's not coping, William? You only heard one side of the conversation, and eavesdropping doesn't give you the whole picture on what's happening', Tilly detailed logically.

'She's not asking for support from anyone ... not even her best friend.'

'William, she's probably disgusted and ashamed. She's a principled woman, and we all know how honored she was of those two girls ... they were her life', Tilly simplified.

'Yes, well, like it or not, Tilly, if she doesn't pull herself together, we'll both be out of a job.' 'I understand how scared and angry you're feeling, but everything happens for a reason.'

'I'm too old to be looking for employment ... I thought I'd retire from this job' He objected. 'And you've got a wealth of experience and that amounts to a lot. Like my mother used to say ... Don't worry about worry until worry worries you.' Tilly fronted the sink and continued with the food preparation as William remained at the table, hands clasped together in front of him, deep in perplexity. Without saying another word, he suddenly proceeded from the kitchen into the doorway of the parlor, where Edna remained seated in her chair, and visually dissected her for more than five minutes, only returning to the kitchen with more antipathy in his heart.

'She's still sitting there, like a bloody statue' He blurted out at Tilly.

'Maybe she's deep in thought, William.'

'Or maybe she's turned into a zombie because she's not coping. Remember, she's a kept woman, Tilly ... never known a tough day in her life.'

'You're being unfair. Don't forget the years she struggled with those miscarriages and the difficult pregnancy she had with the girls. Now her husband is badly ill, and the only children she was able to deliver full-term—well, one of them is dead and the other one is in jail overseas, facing a murder charge ... and it's all happened at once.'

William sat quietly and considered Tilly's insightful reasoning, but even though he knew she was right, he ultimately huffed out a groan, still annoyed at Edna's reluctance to seek support from anyone. In his mind, he presumed she was being egocentric and reckless.

'Why don't you go and ask her if she's ready for lunch', Tilly coached, and as she busied herself fixing up a plate of fresh sandwiches and a pot of tea, William strolled back into the parlor and located himself beside Edna's lounge chair.

'Madam, would you like for your lunch to be served?' He asked graciously as he looked down at her with conflicting judgments... and he waited for her reply. Edna stared blankly out into the transparent void of the window with an empty look, her eyes unblinking and stagnant, the cold gaze indicating that her brain was suffering from an enormous short circuit, then she turned her head slothfully towards William and automatically answered.

'No, thank you. That will be all.' William took three steps rearward, and with a formal gait, he hurried back into the kitchen where he saw Tilly placing the food on a silver tray.

'Is she ready?' Tilly quizzed.

'No, she doesn't want anything to eat. She's just sitting there like an animated corpse. I told you, she's losing it, and there's the proof.' He snapped, with panic in his voice.

The hospital room was dark and silent and, in some way, gave Warren refuge from his unbearable nightmares as the fantasized terrors involving his daughters robbed him of his common sense and replaced it with crippling fears, depriving him of his strength. He slowly opened his eyes, narrowing

193

them in an attempt to sharpen the distorted images before him. And as he lay there, he could feel himself growing weary, physically and emotionally. He had this emerging anxiety come over him, a dread that nagged at his awareness, telling him that everything was not okay and that something unavoidable was coming. Alongside the dim light, which projected from the nurse's station outside his door, Warren evaluated the shadow people that flickered, then merged into one another on the adjacent partition, as the staff passed in front of the light, creating a peculiar atmosphere in his room. He turned his head towards the entry several times, to identify the transient persons occasionally moving back and forth, then slowly looked back at the partition again, struggling to determine if the shadows were just ordinary shadows and not something else. As he gratified himself with the assumption that the obscurities were meaningless and he was safe, from his peripheral vision, Warren unexpectedly sensed a manifestation located beside his bed; and as he turned around to look at the lurking entity, it was gone, as though the shadowy apparition was fearful of him and trying to hide. With panic intensifying in his body, he rang for a nurse to appear.

'Yes, Mr. Karce, what's the matter?'

'There's someone in here' He muttered despairingly.

'Yes, there's you and me in this room and no one else. It's very late, Mr. Karce, so I suggest that you get some sleep' She reassured him.

'No, there's someone else in here ... it's waiting for me in the shadows' He persisted.

'Mr. Karce, you have a neurological condition, and this can give you hallucinations. You might need a sedative to help you sleep?' She offered.

'No, thank you.' Warren refused the narcotic, needing to keep a watchful eye on the skulking revenant in his room.

'Okay, Mr. Karce, have a good night's rest, I'll see you in the morning.' The nurse dismissed his trepidations and halfway closed the door behind her so the outside light could marginally penetrate in. He lay stock-still in the bed, his heart pulsating a nervous and dreadful feeling of uncertain agitation as he meticulously watched the dark and the uninhabited crooks and crevices of his room. Time passed gradually, and just as he was about to fall asleep, a phenomenon so mysterious progressed through the wall, its movement unnaturally fast and disjointed. It wasn't bound by physical limitations as it prowled in the background then quickly transported itself from one location to another, crawling along the floor, up the walls, and along the ceiling, the dark figure deliberately fixing its evil stare on Warren. With its red fiery eyes, lifeless and frozen, endlessly leering at its victim, the shadowy specter progressed in a chaotic manner towards the end of his bed and perched itself upon the bottom railing, unwaveringly squatted and balanced, like a bird on a branch, and a crumbly demonic cackle steadily erupted from its barren disguise. It paused for a moment as its eyes tightened and scowled, then the satanic creature spoke.

'You have reached the point of no return You and your loved ones are ordained for decay It's the pendant's burden. Should never have taken it from its boundless dwelling.'

Directly, the apocalyptic creature took one giant leap backward and entirely vanished, morphing into the blackness of the room from which it came, as Warren frantically pressed the call bell for someone to show up.

'Yes, Mr. Karce' The nurse asked irritably as she entered the room again.

'There was an evil thing just here ... it sat on the railing at the end of my bed, and it spoke to me.' His voice was trembling and guttural.

'I told you that you're just having some delirium from the operation, plus you've been in an induced coma, so your brain is trying to adjust to the post-trauma.'

'No, no, no ... it was real' He implored.

The attending nurse rapidly breezed out of the room and called Warren's presiding doctor where she discussed her patient's worsening mental disorder and alleged he was capable of injuring himself, so she was advised to administer him with an antipsychotic sedative and to inform his wife immediately. Once the phone consultation had ended, she regarded Warren's medical plan and drew up 20 MLS of Mephobarbital to induce and maintain his sleep and re-entered the critical care unit.

'Mr. Karce, I have a sedative to help you sleep' She informed him.

'I don't want it' He demanded.

'Doctor has told me to give it to you because of your distress.'

'That hideous thing will come back and kill me ... I know it will. You should've seen it ... its eyes and the way it snarled at me. It said that I was ordained for decay, and it was the pendant's fault' He jabbered inconsolably.

'It's alright, Mr. Karce.' The nurse moved in closer and reached over to adjust his pillow, and that's when she craftily injected the tranquilizer, withdrawing it out of his sweaty arm before he even realized what had hit him. She stood back from the bed, observing him plummet into a stupor, his body amplifying into a drooping calico puppet as the minutes passed, and when she was satisfied with the result, she departed and called Edna as instructed.

'Good evening, Karce residence ... William speaking.' The respectful butler pronounced. 'Hello, it's Nurse Watson from Richmond Hospital. May I speak with Mrs. Karce, please?' 'I'm sorry, but she's unavailable at the moment.'

'This is urgent, are you sure she's unable to speak with me?'

'Mrs. Karce has retired for the day, it is late, Nurse Watson.'

'Well, can you pass on a message for me then?'

'Yes, I will, but it won't be given to Mrs. Karce until tomorrow morning', William educated her.

'Very well ... just let her know that we've had to sedate her husband tonight as he was experiencing a delirium from the post-trauma of the induced coma. He's resting peacefully now, but the doctor requested that I inform her of the imminent circumstances.'

'Thank you, Nurse Watson, I will inform madam as soon as possible.' William hung up the phone and dashed into the kitchen where Tilly was scrubbing the dishes.

'Tilly, it's becoming more apparent that things are getting worse for this family.' He announced as soon as he reached the doorway.

'What are you referring to now, William?' She uttered as she placed the last wet cup onto the drying rack.

'That was the hospital. The nurse just told me that Mr. Karce has had some sort of frenzy and they've had to sedate him.' William slapped the palm of his hand up to his brow.

'He's being looked after, and he's in the right place', Tilly huffed out of frustration from Williams's constant hissy outbursts.

'If he's going to have these episodes, he won't be coming home soon' He continued.

'Oh, can you stop with the hysterics, William ... you don't know that. They could supply medications when they bring him home, and the doctor is always on call for this family. When are you going to tell madam?'

'First thing tomorrow morning ... while she's having breakfast. She's very fragile at the moment, so I'll have to be tactful.' William positioned himself at the table while Tilly moved towards the stove, and with a water-filled jug in hand, she placed it upon the gas and boiled the kettle so the two of them could sit down and enjoy a cup of tea together as they chatted about their future strategies, if and when their employment status happened to change.

As he slept, Warren felt the top of his head being caressed, a merciful touch, as though a gentle breeze was stirring in the room. He opened his eyes, blinking a few times to focus on the image he saw standing beside his bed, and immediately gasped at the beautiful, enchanting face that radiated down at him.

'Oh, it's you' He spoke tenderly, reaching up to touch the side of her face.

'I thought something terrible had happened to you' He continued.

'I'm alright', she spoke with a voice as delicate as snowflakes. 'Come with me ... I need you.'

'How can I? I'm bound to this bed' He replied.

'Just kiss me, Papa.'

'Yes, I want to, and I will' He surrendered. Annie bent down and placed her lips upon her father's mouth and kissed

Chapter 11

him compassionately for an extended time, and while they embraced, Warren felt his life slowly recede away, comforted by her adoration. He drew one last breath, and in a room perfumed with the scent of fresh flowers, he quietly and softly perished.

Twelve

Chapter 12

~ ❧ ~

The secluded cell was like a prison within a prison and was no bigger than a horse stable. Her food was presented through a small door slot, and the entire time Sharon spent restricted in the tiny room that only contained a bed, a sink, a toilet, and no window, the feeling of losing her mind intruded as she began committing acts of self-harm, carving numbers into her limbs with her fingernails. She went without any human contact at all, which increased her disobedient behavior. So very desperate for interaction with someone and with thoughts that the walls were closing in on her, the only relief was to scream hysterically until a guard entered the cell and administered pepper spray into her face. To Sharon, this was a positive experience, especially when the alternative was zero interaction; and combined with the lack of sunlight, it created the perfect setting for her to become vicious, which made her feel alive. She'd been isolated for ten days, and by the time Sharon was taken back to her original cell, she had trouble concentrating, was depressed, and suffered hallucinations, especially in the dark. Her appearance was undernourished through extreme hunger, and unreadable symbols were engraved into her arms and legs, the marks made more distinctive by the dried blood that caked around them. As she arrived back in the former lockup, Agata was gone, leaving Sharon sitting unaccompanied in the resolute cell, droning a sequence of numbers, monotonous and repetitive, like she was chanting a prayer until a prison guard stood at the gate.

'Get over here' He commanded Sharon as she stared vacantly at the floor, still verbally pulsating the numbers. She reared up submissively and turned around so the guard could lock the cuffs on both wrists.

'Where am I going?' She muttered

'To the infirmary. Look at you, your cuts are bleeding all over the place' The guard proclaimed, revolted at the impressions she'd inflicted upon herself.

Once in the medical wing, the nurse analyzed Sharon's injuries and began to wash them clean with a saline solution as her patient sat motionless, regarding the numbers as they emerged from under the desiccated blood.

'Why did you do this to yourself?' The nurse asked.

'It's the numbers' fault', Sharon answered.

'What do you mean? I don't understand?'

'The numbers ... 58 equals 13, 733 equals 13, 184 equals 13, 49 equals 13 and 67 equals 13', Sharon enlightened the nurse.

'Okay? Where do these numbers come from ... what do they represent?'

'Number 58 was our gate number at the airport, 733 was

our plane number, 184 was our room number in Paris, 49 was our room number in Bucharest, and 67 was the room number that the hotel staff transferred me to after my sister was found dead.'

'And you think the numbers had something to do with your troubles?' The nurse continued to investigate.

'Yes, of course, they do ... 13 is a demon's number ... You know it's unlucky?' Sharon looked astonished that the nurse didn't realize what she was referring to.

'In our country, 13 is a divine number ... it looks after the passage between life and death.' The nurse smiled.

'What a load of rubbish.' Sharon ignored the medic's positive message

'You couldn't be more wrong ... 13 represents fresh starts and new beginnings, but it's usually a momentous choice that you have to make. One important aspect of this number is that it relates to you and you alone. Whatever choice you've made, it's going to be yourself who's responsible for it. Although the number 1 doesn't always represent a major change in your life, in the case of the angel number 13, it usually does.' The nurse spoke positively.

'What are you? Some sort of universal bunny hugger?' Sharon ridiculed.

'No, I'm not. Just remember this though, by keeping your thoughts focused on your wishes and the positive aspects of your life, you will attract the confident results you have always hoped for.' The nurse ignored the mockery of her patient.

'Well, my wish is to be represented by my family's Australian lawyer and to be acquitted from the crimes I've been charged with and get out of this Godforsaken country of yours.' 'Okay, well, your wounds have been cleaned and dressed, so you're alright to leave.' The nurse finally realized that she was talking to someone who wasn't open-minded enough to listen to her optimistic words of guidance.

The guard entered the room and strictly handcuffed Sharon for her transfer back to the cell when another prison officer verbally directed him to take her to the interrogation area. Under Sharon's protest, the guard forcibly sat her down at the table; and after releasing the manacles, he stood steadfastly by the door until the leading detective appeared and positioned himself adjacent to the murderer. Sharon glared at the detective with extreme distaste, as he deliberately ruffled through the papers in front of him before lifting his head, regarding her back with the same disfavor.

'What do you want now?' She rudely blurted at him.

The detective didn't answer straight away but mutely frowned at her for what seemed like an eternity.

'Well? Are you going to say something, or is this a staring competition?' She continued. 'Miss Karce ... I received a phone call from Australia last week.' His voice was apathetic and droned. Sharon loafed unemotionally in the chair but instantly sat to attention when she heard him mention Australia and moved her body forward, intently listening to what he was about to say next. She secretly yearned that Edna had reconsidered her appeal to send their family lawyer over for the court hearing.

'Your father died last Monday, Australian time.' He curiously watched Sharon for her reaction.

'What? Papa is dead? I knew he was sick but not enough to die. How did it happen?' She sounded uncaring and arrogant, but there was a quality of importance in her voice.

'He died peacefully in his sleep' The detective replied, still evaluating her every expression and move.

'Why did you take so long to tell me?'

'You were in solitary confinement, and it's not our procedure to interconnect with you while in lockdown.'

Sharon didn't reply; she sat diligently and reflected on her childhood and how her father had been intensely career-driven and fully in charge of every aspect of the family's regime. She wasn't pampered or treated as extra special by him ... that was Annie's honored prominence, as she was adored, her joy and laughter enthralling her parents who reveled in her ability to so easily please them. This made Sharon believe that Annie's life read more like a fairy tale, which was a polar opposite to her own, and she had real feelings that her father derailed her life. One thing was certain though, he did teach her that she could be her own protector.

'On your behalf and because it's a mandatory requirement as an overseas visitor, we have contacted the Australian Consulate in Bucharest, and they're going to pay you a visit sometime soon' The detective informed her, breaking the painful silence.

'Okay, when? I need to get home. What can they do for me?' Sharon muttered.

'Understand that your Australian nationality is not a shield. You're still bound by the laws of Romania, and you will have to face the consequences of your actions under our laws. The consulate will provide you with information about their facilities and relevant procedures of our country and that assistance can be the difference between life and death for you. But you could always choose to willingly admit to both the murders and throw yourself on the mercy of the court.' He shrewdly combined the optimism of a written confession from her.

'Oh, and by the way, as a result of your father being such a predominant man in Australia, his death has attracted a lot of media attention … and so has your law-breaking … so the world is going to know that you murdered your sister and Mr. Jenkins' He sneered as he stood up and moved towards the door.

'I keep telling you that I didn't mean to kill Annie, and I didn't even know Mr. Jenkins', Sharon exclaimed again in frustration at his barefaced refusal to accept the reality. The guard hauled her back to the cell, irritably locking the chamber gate and when he had vanished, she lay on the dirty thin blanket of her bed; and facing the wall, she wept quietly for her father. Drifting between the state of being awake and asleep, her reality began to warp with rigid consciousness dissolving into gentle lapping waves of early dreaming, and her world became a little hallucinatory. From the dimness of the cell, Sharon heard something mildly scratching and rustling around in the farthest corner and decided that it was probably a stupid rodent searching for bits and pieces of food. Casually rolling over, she confronted the irritating sound when a silhouette of something jutted out from the wall, taking on the ability to visually appear. The head was animalistic and particularly disgusting with its boar skull whitewashed, its mouth blackened, and its eyes sullied, cadaverous, and sinister. And as it advanced further, it salivated large globules of crimson mucus, dripping from its tusks as though it had just finished devouring gore. It began to laugh like a hyena, its voice sharp and cruel, sporadically breaking into a high-pitched falsetto, and it fed upon Sharon's excessive emotional energy. She felt instant hopelessness encircling her as the beast began to speak its accusations in a deep, emotionless, and calculated tone, attempting to intimidate her.

'You cry, but you have no heart ... you are a deceiver and a conspirator ... you kill for greed, and that greed will kill you.' And then it snorted, immediately disappearing into the void of wickedness from where it came. Sharon stared blankly at the declining image. She didn't yell out or feel any concern about the demon she'd just encountered and calmly turned back to her original position, facing the wall, without a grain of fear in her exhausted body.

In the early hours of the following morning, she was awakened by a prison guard pounding on the chamber bars.

'Get up, there's someone here to see you' He commanded as she slowly stood up, adjusting her visually distinctive prison outfit, and walked over to the bars, placing her hands through them while he fastened one handcuff around her wrist. He directed her back to the interrogation room, and there she observed an unacquainted visitor sitting on the opposite side of the large table. He raised up from his chair as she entered, extending out his hand to welcome her, but Sharon didn't participate in his good-natured offer of pleasantries and tamely sat down.

'Hello, my name is James Pickett, I'm a representative from the Australian Embassy in Russia. How have they been treating you here?'

Sharon mutely eyeballed James, and as he glared back with imagination, he noticed that she was once an exquisite-looking lady but had now deteriorated into a gaunt and fatigued version of herself.

'Okay, so you don't want to talk? That's alright. I'm going to outline your rights and what the consulate can do for you.' He broke the prickly silence, slanting his eyes up at her to check if she was focusing.

'You're going to be subjected to all of the local laws and penalties in Romania, even those that appear harsh by Australian standards. Privileges and immunities are not absolute, and the police officers here retain their fundamental responsibility to protect you, but they also enforce the law and expect you to conduct yourself in an orderly manner. Do you understand this?' He paused for a couple of seconds and looked at Sharon, who just sat there, glaring at him without voicing a word.

'Right, well, if you've got nothing to say ... I'll continue. I can provide you with legal advice and interpret documents for you, intervene in any court proceedings, make sure that you receive good treatment and post bail or pay your legal expenses, depending on your financial status. Any questions so far, Sharon?'

'When do I get my family's lawyer to represent me?' She quietly asked

'We've been in touch with your mother, and under the circumstances with your father's death, she isn't approachable to any suggestion of financing your legal representation. There's something else you should know ... your father's passing has attracted a lot of media attention, especially when he was such a predominant man with his substantial wealth ... This has unfortunately turned the media's attention towards you and has highlighted your murder charges.'

'How peachy ... so now I'm a superstar' She pooh-poohed, shaking her head with loathing towards Edna's unwillingness to fund her defense.

'I suppose you could see it that way, but you do realize that it's not an optimistic image they're depicting of you, Sharon.'

A sense of alarm rose up in him, as for the first time, he recognized her smug and apathetic boldness.

'I couldn't care less what they say about me ... it's all lies anyway' She huffed.

'Okay? ... let's continue ... The criminal militia here tries to suppress any exposure of criminal offenses that requires a preliminary investigation, and Russia has an antagonistic system where the constitutional rights doesn't allow for a jury trial in all capital offenses, as in your case, aggravated murder, and they can exclude any evidence for your defense. In the Romanian system, there are no juries—trials are "bench trials", meaning it is the judge alone or a panel of judges who hear the evidence and render a verdict. You may present appropriate evidence, obtain professional legal representation, have a full discovery of the contents of the preliminary investigation, and appeal a judgment of either an acquittal or a conviction. If you are convicted, you'll be sent to the women's section of Bristol prison. Do you have any questions?' James concluded.

'Yes ... where's my Australian lawyer? That Adrian Dalca is biased, he's an idiot and friends with the lead detective.'

'They're all acquaintances, Sharon, they've worked together for a long time. Dalca is a reputable solicitor here, and he got that way for doing what he does well, and he takes all things personally. He does everything just inside the rules ... They call him the subtle beast.' James evaluated what she was saying.

'I know that ... Why do you think I want someone who isn't a colleague here? Are you as daffy as the rest of them? Oh, that's right ... you're probably in on the bloody conspiracy as well.'

'I'm not conspiring against you Sharon, I only want to help. I can see that you're angry, but don't you want the best outcome for yourself?' James alleged.

'I don't give a rat's arse … don't you know I have no heart? Take me back to my cell' She ordered the guard who was securing the door, and as she exited, Sharon dissected James with a penetrating look. Lying on her bunk, she studied the gloomy corner from where the creature's head had appeared earlier and belittled her, so she began fearlessly calling out, 'Here, piggy, piggy, piggy, come and get me … you ugly fuck!'

Sharon had lost all emotional connection with everything around her and had subconsciously muffled her feelings. Being so cold made her appear as though she was emotionally unavailable, and her out-of-control anger was the only indication that she still had any emotions at all. The continual anxiety of her overwhelming situation gave her the feeling that she just wanted to 'shut off' in an effort for her psyche to save itself. Exhausted from the unending misery, she eventually floated into a deep sleep and visualized Annie as a child, playing in the gardens around their home. She regarded her from a private distance, as her sister danced around, winding through the lush greeneries, humming a song, and giggling as she occasionally stopped to cherish the perfume of the surrounding flowers. Jealousy rose up in Sharon as she envied the little girl's lighthearted attitude and how she enjoyed her life. She was always smiling, which made her instantly likable, attractive, and approachable; and the gentle way she'd naturally listen to other people's rainbows of sadness or happiness uplifted them. But it made Sharon sick to her stomach. Persistently observing Annie's garden frolic, Sharon abruptly witnessed their father enter the charming image, rushing in and scooping the little girl up into his arms; and even though he whispered something into her ear as they both sniggered, Sharon heard his words as loud as a chapel bell.

'My precious, Annie, I will always honor you and keep you safe. Know that you're loved and that I'll defend you regardless of the cost.' Infuriated, Sharon dashed towards her father, struggling to grab his attention by tugging on his trousers and, as she gazed up at them, Warren continued to fuss and cradle the adored child in his arms; and it seemed the more she yanked on his leg, the more trivial her existence became as she dwindled away like a withered-up leaf from the garden. Feeling increasingly disfavoured and insecure, she boldly shouted at him, demanding his comfort and affection, but he only looked down at her with disgust imprinted on his face; and then he spoke to her in a slow, deep voice,

'Defiant child ... you have no heart ... you're a schemer ... you have killed for greed and your gluttony will turn on you.' And as soon as his last words were uttered, he immediately transferred his attention back onto Annie, continuing to shower her with his love and affection.

Isolation and abandonment amplified in Sharon's subconscious as her body began to thrash about on the cold hard bed, her skin likening to a blistering broth, bubbling and searing, the pain struggling to leave her blood, searching for freedom. Feeling lost and overcome, she bolted upright, bawling out; the sudden awakening caused a disturbing emotional response as she erratically recited,

'It's been revealed there's a larger power at hand, some entity devoted to my eternal struggle.' Realizing where she was, Sharon sat on the edge of the bunk and hung her head low. She lucidly re-examined the intense nightmare and the significance of what she'd done to her little sister, but instead of allowing the excruciating shame and guilt to penetrate

210

her, she put her conceited mask back on and fabricated a misleading image of herself, deflecting any blame, turning it into added resentment as she believed that her motives for executing Annie were justified. Before another minute passed by, a guard fronted the cell gate.

'Get up and walk over', He commanded. Sharon did as he requested and was guided back to the interrogation room where another odd-man sat patiently alongside James Pickett.

'Hello, Sharon, please take a seat', James instructed.

'Who's this bloke?' She announced brazenly.

'You wanted an Australian lawyer, so here he is Mr. Paul Riddick. I've thoroughly acquainted him with your case', James informed her.

'Okay, can you get me acquitted, Mr. Paul Riddick?' Sharon openly faced him.

'Your charges are very serious, Miss Karce, we will do our very best to see you get a fair hearing. Your father's death has put a lot of media exposure on your criminal statuses, which haven't been positive ... and to answer your question ... no, it doesn't look optimistic for an acquittal. The evidence against you is severe', Paul Riddick responded.

'What good are you then?' Sharon probed offensively.

'I know all about the media frenzy ... James has been kind enough to express that, so I'm totally up to speed. What have they been saying about me anyway?' She continued.

'I don't think you need to know. You're at a massive disadvantage in the media, Sharon.' Paul tried to shut down the cynicism.

'It's about me ... so I want to know' She claimed as she glared down at the table with its large scratches gouged out from previous felons waiting to be grilled.

211

'Okay. The present investigation has scrutinized the nature of the coverage you've received, and this has been based on your ethnicity and your relationships with the female deceased. The prominence of who you are and the stories in the media have been framed around your background, your motives, and the opinions of those who have known you. They've been saying that women who kill are extra deviant and that you don't possess a nurturing or emotional bone in your body and what you have done profoundly challenges your ethical state. You've been labeled as a mad and wrathful bitch. So there you go.'

'Hmm ... that's cool. They've described me to a tee.' She reacted unruffled by the condemning news.

'Well, you should be concerned. This bad news has a negative influence on your trial, and it can distort the public's interpretation of you. It doesn't help your case at all. Anyway, there won't be a bail hearing as they consider you as a potential flight risk, so you'll be going straight to trial in a week's time ... I'll see you then', Paul concluded as he'd had enough of Sharon's disdainful attitude, and both men stood up; without saying another word, they exited the room.

Jock sat in front of the overly stacked fireplace, staring into the flickering inferno as he bathed in its warmth and pondered about Liam's fate, when an abrupt and powerful knock thundered on his cottage door. He jolted upright, feeling an immediate panic rise up in his body, so he cautiously walked over to the entry, opening it within an inch, and observed two men presenting their official police badges.

'Yes, can I help you?' He timidly asked through the minuscule crack in the door.

'Have you seen this man before?' They debriefed, holding up an old picture of Liam.

'No, I haven't', Jock replied.

'Well, one of the townsfolk saw a man of this description entering your cottage. How do you explain that?' The officer quizzed.

'When?' Jock reacted nervously.

'About a week ago.'

'Oh okay, now I remember him. He was scavenging through the garbage bins, I felt sorry for him, so I offered a warm bed and some food,' Jock rattled off as he viewed the photo more thoroughly.

'Would you come with us to the station then?'

'What for?' Jock uttered, surprised.

'We just want to ask you some further questions.' Jock reluctantly picked up his jacket that was hanging by the door, and the trio entered a police car, driving back to the station. Upon arrival, Jock was immediately taken into the integration room, where he innocently sat down at the table with an associate detective and began answering questions while Sharon stood behind a one-way mirror accompanied by a guard and the lead detective, ready to pinpoint Liam's accomplice.

'Do you recognize this man, or does his voice sound familiar to you, Sharon?' The detective probed as they all scrutinized Jock.

'No ... I've never seen him in my life ... why should I know him, who is he?'

'Alright, take her back to the cell' The lead detective ordered, and Sharon was whisked away in silence as he continued to witness the cross-examination behind his secretive mirror.

'So you saw this man rummaging through street bins? Then what did you do, Jock?'

'I approached him and asked why he was so poor? He had an Australian accent and was polite, so I offered him a meal and a bed for the night. I felt sorry for him, and I was just being kind ... that's all', Jock lied.

'You're enrolled at the University here and you're studying for a bachelor of science ... is that correct?'

'Yes ... why?'

'And you've never schemed with anyone so they could acquire chemicals from you?' The subordinate detective grilled.

'No? What for? I'd get kicked out of Uni and lose everything I've worked so hard for' He implored.

'So that was the first and last time you saw the man ... after he spent the night at your house?'

'Yes ... I did give him some cans of soup and beans and a sleeping bag for his journey ... but that's it. I could see that he didn't have anything to keep warm. He left sometime during the early hours of the night, and I never saw him again. What's this all about? Do I need a lawyer? Are you going to charge me with helping a vagrant?'

'You're a very kind-hearted om (man) ... do you help all the gypsies that pass by your house?' The detective ridiculed.

'Okay, that's it ... I've told you everything I know and if you're not going to charge me with anything then I want to leave', Jock said, infuriated with the extravaganza of senseless questioning. Jock desperately rubbed his hands over his face in frustration as the detective glanced at the mirror and nodded his head at the hidden onlookers, in a gesture that he'd finished with his interrogation. He unexpectedly stood up and exited the room, directly re-entering the secluded chamber behind the looking glass, and conversed with the lead detective, finally returning to Jock after ten minutes, with a decision.

'You can go' He acknowledged.

'Thank you', and as soon as the words passed his lips, Jock unswervingly made a hasty departure out the door.

Sharon wondered who the man was, sitting in that room, her brain spinning like a top, finding more questions than answers as there seemed to be an acquaintance to him she just couldn't shake, not a memory but an echo that called to her insight. She stared at the dark wall, a thousand-mile stare, her gaze clouding and going distant, as she took a deep breath and let it out slowly, shaking her head and repeating the word *'no'* like she was warding someone off. There was something familiar about his flat, hard voice she had trouble remembering, flashes of evoked memories stirred in her head, vivid and briefly recalled, as she fought to identify him. She paced the diminutive floor of her cell the entire night, and just as the sun was rising and its rays infiltrated through the window, like a light bulb switching on in her head, she captured the essence of who he was. At the time, she hadn't focused hard enough to think it was important, but now, recollecting Liam placing a phone call on loudspeaker for a moment while he spoke to his 'associate', she was frantic to get his co-conspirator back. Desiring instant gratification, Sharon relentlessly hammered on the cell bars, endeavoring to attract a guard's attention, as the neighboring felons screamed at her to shut the hell up.

'What is going on?' The prison officer remarked as he casually wandered up to Sharon's cell gate.

'I need to see the lead detective right this minute' She

demanded.

'Well, you'll have to wait. It's early, and he doesn't sit around his office 24 hours a day. I'll let him know when he comes into headquarters' The guard replied smugly with no urgency in his voice.

'But it's crucial that I speak with him now' She shouted through the bars as he apathetically walked away, only stopping momentarily to threaten the verbal rebellion; he broadcasted, 'Shut up or I'll put the lot of you in solitary.'

It was past midday when the lead detective visited Sharon's compartment, hanging stealthily at the gate, inspecting her as she catnapped on the bed.

'Sharon, Sharon, wake up' He asserted while the guard rowdily unlocked the cell gate. Sharon stirred and wearily sat up on the edge, her brain buzzing as if it was a flat battery. She felt hungover as though waking up no longer held the pleasure as it once did, and as she viewed the detective standing in front of her with his superior authority; there was a passing moment when she felt whole again, but it vaporized faster than summertime rain off the scorched earth.

'You wanted to see me?' He questioned.

'Ah ... yes ... I have something to tell you. I remembered it last night' She said hazily.

'Well ... spit it out' He barked intolerantly.

'That man you brought in for me to identify ... I know who he is. He's Liam's accomplice. I heard his voice once when Liam placed his phone on the loudspeaker. Took me all night to recall it.'

'Are you sure?' The detective badgered.

'Yes, I'm sure.'

Tersely, the detective exited the lockup and quickly paraded into his office where he immediately grabbed his identification and firearm, and with four other constables, they made a swift departure for Jock's place. As they cautiously knocked on his cottage door, the officers flaunted their guns and clustered against the wall of the building.

'Jock, it's the police ... open the door' The police ordered, and as they briefly waited, only stillness retorted back.

'Break down the door' The detective instructed the attending officers, but once they'd stormed inside, all they found was an extinguished fireplace, filthy dishware, and nothing else; Jock and all of his meager belongings had completely vanished.

'Set up a perimeter and keep it going until it's proven that the fugitive is outside that perimeter ... and check the street surveillance cameras' He initiated.

'Do you want us to get the tracking dogs in ... just in case he's headed for the woods?' One of the constables queried.

'Yes ... alert the dog squad. Those dogs are outstanding at tracking a human scent.'

The one thing Jock had become skilled at was a heightened awareness of police officers, what they looked like, how they moved, where and when they were likely to appear. He learned the models of their undercover vehicles, the way they held their bodies, and even the cut of their hair. His awareness had never left him as he would see them sitting in plain clothes in the street and could detect them coming up from behind him as he walked through the town. Sometimes, he found his body would anticipate their arrival with sweat and a quickened heartbeat before his mind consciously registered any signs of their appearance, so if his escape was to be successful, not only did he learn how to identify the police, but he also learned how to run and his escape had to be a solitary one.

The police started searching the nearby grounds for whatever Jock may have tossed before absconding, as one of the neighbors had told them, he'd seen Jock heading up towards the Tatras Mountains the morning before and thought it suspicious. The first 48 hours were crucial in finding Jock, so once the surrounding areas were investigated, the police search party broke up into two groups. The first group covered the primary areas while the second group began their exploration beyond the original search range and up into the mountains. 'Find this nelegitim (bastard)' The detective shouted at the troops, frustrated that he'd foolishly allowed Jock to getaway. So the search party diligently coiled their way up the ascending mountain track, hot on the heels of the determined, wailing hounds; but all the while, peering down at the scrambling display of police, high in the church bell tower, Jock artfully waited for his strategic gamble to emerge and that was to pull a disappearing act and dissolve into thin air ... for good.

Since the beginning of the entire Liam, Sharon, and Annie saga, he had wisely calculated his termination as 'Jock' and knew exactly what to do and how to do it.

'Goodbye, cruel Romania' He deceitfully sniggered as he pulled a blanket up over his head and shoulders, squatting down behind the ancient boulder wall; he finally found the chance to catch up on some much-needed sleep while listening to the vanishing howls of the dogs as they followed his misleading trail.

Thirteen

Chapter 13

The sky was eclipsed by rolling clouds, grey, misty, and silver as the rain drizzled down, and it felt like a court of conscience to those who mingled around Warren's gravesite. The magnitude of hopelessness flooded Edna's eyes as she stood there, dressed in modest black, with simple makeup and jewelry, emotionally devoting that her love will live on for Warren and as the crowd began dispersing, Edna lingered, a solitary figure against the backdrop of the desolate, tranquil cemetery. William moved towards her, gently touching her arm in an attempt to entice the grieving widow from the grave, encouraging her to leave.

'Come now, madam' He whispered, and she obeyed without uttering a word.

Her grief felt like she was climbing a spiral staircase, where things seemed as though they were going around in circles, and the restrictive suffocation she sensed from the sea of never-ending tears made it hard for her to draw a breath. As they strolled towards their awaiting cars, Edna grimaced at the assembly of journalists and photographers as they tousled about in a cluster, elbowing each other to get a better view of the grieving family, shouting her name and focusing their merciless questions at her.

'When are they going to leave us alone?' She quietly asked William.

'I don't know, madam. Unfortunately, it's not only Mr. Karce's death they're fascinated with, it's also the difficulties that are emerging with Sharon's charges.'

'I know ... the whole thing is an absolute mess ... there is no privacy, and they're victimizing us.' She began to cry.

Once at the manor, things were no different as the paparazzi hovered at the gate entrance to the property, with dozens of light bulbs flashing so close to the car windows, while Edna's limousine and the adjoining procession slowed down to creep their way through the anticipating horde. The low-key social gathering who knew Warren, or knew of him, were ushered into the parlor for their opportunity to grieve privately and pay their respects, as handpicked catering staff, who had signed confidentiality agreements, fussed about, making sure that everything was flawless. Masses of fresh white lilies and rose arrangements decorated the room, representing majesty, purity, and sympathy, creating a relaxed and friendly atmosphere for grieving friends and relatives. They felt comfortable chatting to one another, swapping their stories, some humorous and some serious, which compensated for the sorrow of losing Warren, with the joy of knowing him in the first place. The food that Edna had ordered entwined with the events and memories of Warren, as they symbolized and honored his love for scrumptious dining; delicious finger sandwiches of leg ham with cheddar, poached chicken breast with walnuts and homemade mayonnaise, smoked salmon with horseradish cream, capers and cucumber, creamed organic egg with chives, and warm salmon pinwheels were offered to the visitors, representing just a small percentage of his favorites. As the afternoon carried on, Edna began to feel exhausted. Never had a few moments reflected like an eternity as she felt her mindfulness fading away, with her thoughts sluggishly coming to an end. Her eyes grew heavy from the vigorous effects of the day's anxieties, and she hadn't prepared herself for such an unexpected weakness. Sitting on the sofa, she beckoned William over to her and gestured for him to bend down as she needed to whisper something into his ear.

'I'm very tired, William. I feel this awful, heavy feeling pulling me down. I've tried fighting it, for my guests' sake, but it pains me, and it's robbing me of my breath.' She complained

Instantly, he beckoned another staff member to assist him, and they collectively shepherded Edna up the stairs, to her bedroom door, as a handful of guests looked on with pitiful condolences and others, ignorant of her misery and unexpected departure, continued to chat. She temporarily stood at the closed door with her hand on the knob, reflecting on the oppressive situation that she was fronting. The world she'd known had suddenly dissolved away as she felt hollow and her heartbeat at her chest so hard that she thought it would break through. A black hole consumed her head, and it had swallowed all of her hopes and dreams as the awareness of the vacuum in her soul raided her existence. Leisurely, Edna wandered around the room, intuitively disrobing, leaving a trail of abandoned clothes scattered all over the floor while she randomly picked up framed images of her cherished family as they embraced each other in happier times. Plunging her attention into one specific photo, she remembered the day it was taken and smiled, as she enjoyed the fleeting moment, allowing it to penetrate her; but the jubilant feeling disintegrated and the panic-infused anticipation of her emotionally tormenting future engulfed her again, and she finally collapsed.

The following morning, Tilly knocked lightly on Edna's bedroom door, steadily poised with a breakfast tray on one arm.

'Madam, it's Tilly' She announced and listened intently for Edna's instructions to invite her in, but nothing stirred behind the solid wooden door, so she repeated the message.

'Madam, it's Tilly, may I come in? I have your breakfast tray.' Immediately, she opened the door and discovered Edna, lying in her underwear, unmoving from where she had fallen the previous night. Placing down the tray, she dashed over to evaluate the comatose woman and discovered that her skin was pale, cool. and sweaty; so she took her pulse, and it was slower than a wet week.

'William, William' She screamed, and within a few minutes, he appeared in the doorway. 'What happened?' He asked.

'I found her like this, she must have been lying here all night ... quickly get the doctor' She instructed, so William hurried down the stairwell and made the call.

Dr Bartlett arrived at the manor fifteen minutes later with William impatiently waiting at the accessible lobby; he guided the doctor up to Edna's room and directed him to where she was lying.

'How long has she been here?' Dr. Bartlett investigated.

Chapter 13

'I think all night ... can't be sure ... we didn't want to move her just in case she'd sustained an injury', Tilly informed, while the doctor methodically assessed his patient.

'Okay, put her on the bed' Dr. Bartlett instructed after he was satisfied she wasn't physically harmed, so William picked Edna up and placed her gently on the double bed.

'What's wrong with her?' Tilly asked.

'It's probably stress and high anxiety' The doctor answered as he gently coaxed Edna awake with a small amulet of smelling salts.

'Edna, Edna, can you hear me?' He persuaded.

The ammonia gas irritated Edna's lungs and triggered her to immediately inhale. She began coughing and spluttering as her alertness and consciousness increased.

'Sit up, my dear' The doctor ordered.

'Where am I?' Edna spoke in a disoriented and confused manner.

'It's alright ... you're at home. What happened to you last night?'

'I'm not sure. One minute, I was looking at our family photos and the next thing, everything went blank.'

'Okay, you're fine now, but if this happens again, don't hesitate to call me. I'm going to write her a script for some valium. I think she needs a few good days of rest.'

Dr Bartlett spoke to William as he scribbled out the medication request.

'Tilly, go make madam some fresh tea then dress her in that nightgown', William asked and took the script from the doctor as they all exited the room.

'With Sharon's murder trial approaching, you'll have to keep a close watch on her', Dr Bartlett whispered to William. 'And get that script filled as soon as possible.' He continued. 'Yes, Doctor, I will do that right away', William obeyed.

Edna remained in bed, with watery eyes and an excruciating headache; she sipped orange juice and nibbled at a piece of toast and marmalade that Tilly had delivered to her.

Pallid and very tired, she identified that her own body odor smelt somehow different, sour and unfamiliar as though her anatomy was launching volatile substances into the air, in protest to the anguish she'd been suffering. With her eyes locked on the precious framed memories that propelled her into oblivion the night before, Edna instinctively placed her hand on the bedside drawer, methodically sliding it open without even looking and reached in, her fingers pushing aside unwelcomed items, groping about until she found what she was searching for. Pulling out the hip flask, Edna unraveled the cap and poured two shots of 17-year-old Scotch whisky into her orange juice and gulped it down in two swigs before ringing the service bell for Tilly to bring her some more nectar.

'Yes, madam, what do you need?' Tilly asked respectfully.

'Could I have some more juice please, Tilly?' 'Another glass, madam?'

'No, I would like a jug of it ... if you don't mind', Edna wished.

'Oh, you must be thirsty madam ... I'll fetch it straight away.'

'Thank you, Tilly ... oh, and after you bring it, could you please close the door behind you?' 'Not a problem, madam.'

After receiving the additional pitcher of orange juice, Edna perched herself back onto the bed cushions, and with the whisky flask in hand, she consumed the entire decanter, attempting to self medicate and forget the pain of certain events that were torturing her and she completely failed to recall the time of day. Her increased isolation and loss of

Chapter 13

interest in daily life made her ignore other important areas, and she refused to indulge herself in friendly gatherings, even those she once loved and enjoyed. By midday, William returned with Edna's medication and politely knocked on her bedroom door, prudently listening for a beckoning response; and when she didn't answer, with pure unadulterated dread, convinced that something terrible had happened, he swiftly opened the door, only to find Edna napping serenely in her bed. Returning to the kitchen, he placed the medication down and leaned up against the counter with a sorrowful look on his face before Tilly exited the pantry carrying a large vessel of flour in her arms.

'Oh, you scared me, William. Why are you standing there with that wretched look on your face? Did you give Edna her pills?' She asked.

'No ... she's asleep' He murmured.

'That's good, but what's the matter? You look like the cat that swallowed the canary,' She said playfully.

'It's this whole state of affairs, I can't believe how everything is collapsing around us so fast. I'm going to ask the chauffeur to get me the daily paper. I need to know what they're broadcasting about this family. I'm not going away from this house, it's a media circus out there.' William promptly left the kitchen and phoned the driver, asking him to fulfill his request, as Tilly continued to knead the bread dough she'd started making.

She was enormous in every way, wide and tall with legs solid as a rock, breasts big as melons; but even though her size was immense, she was extremely lithe and light on her feet. Tilly had a dual role in the Karce manor. Her main job was

225

that of head chef, and when Edna prearranged dinner parties, she'd employ casual kitchen staff to help out with the volume of the food that needed preparing, making sure Tilly wasn't overloaded. The other position was as Edna's lady's maid where her specific duties included helping madam with her appearance, bringing breakfast to her room, and drawing Edna's bath. Tilly wasn't required to do any house cleaning as Edna employed freelance domestic workers to come in twice a week and painstakingly scrub every inch of the manor, while William persistently strolled around, inspecting their quality of work and studying their every move.

As Tilly proceeded to cut the bread dough into dinner rolls, William re-entered the galley with the newspaper shrouding his face as he flicked the newly printed rigid pages with his wet fingers, continuing to dampen them with his tongue while turning each sheet of paper. 'That was quick', Tilly remarked as William finally sat down at the table.

'Hmm' was all he would say.

'What?' She continued to query.

'I thought it'd be on the front page ... where is it? Oh, here it is ... page 4.' He began to read the scandalous narrative out aloud. 'Are you ready for this, Tilly? It reads ...

'The renowned Karce family's unblemished reputation has been eternally damaged with the news of their eldest daughter Sharon Karce being charged with the murder of her younger sister Annie Karce and the manslaughter of Mr. Gary Jenkins. 'Mr. Jenkins, a private detective, was employed by Edna and Warren Karce to find the whereabouts of their daughters who were holidaying in Romania after communication with the girls became sporadic. This has come as a shock to the

Chapter 13

Richmond Province as it isn't a normal occurrence for a family with such social standing and financial means to be embroiled in this type of immoral behavior, and it has been labeled by those who knew them as particularly odd as they now consider that Sharon Karce's crime was a premeditated act on her part. Adding to the family's grief, Mr. Warren Karce died recently after complications from brain surgery, leaving his widow, Mrs. Edna Karce, to manage the forthcoming murder trial on her own. One hundred and fifty people attended Mr. Karce's funeral yesterday, including Prime Minister Beecham, which was held at Saint Joseph's Cathedral. The Australian Embassy is assisting Miss Karce with her defense, but at this stage, it's not known if she'll be represented by her own family's lawyer during the hearing. Miss Karce's murder trial begins early next week in Romania. She has been refused bail due to being a potential flight risk—and that's it.' William stopped reading and curiously looked up at Tilly for a reply, but they just stared at each other, suffering the exact same gut-wrenching feeling of being very afraid of the knowledge that was hitting home, and for an instant, they mutually accepted the terrible certainty of their doubtful future that was beginning to unfold. Mutely, William stood up and ambled over to Tilly, embracing her in a profound hug, and then he slowly walked out of the kitchen without exchanging another word. As he entered the parlor, brushing his index finger along the furniture and mentally criticizing the amount of dust that had accumulated, he glanced up to find Edna sitting lifelessly in her preferred lounge chair, gaping out the window and into the garden.

'Madam, you're awake. I didn't hear you come in ... may I fetch you a cup of tea?' He respectfully asked, walking up behind her then alongside, moving in front of her to make himself visible, but as he noticed her expression, he jerked backward at her cold white pupils, which filled up so much of her eyes that she looked fossilized, like a person without a soul. He looked away from her, turning his head in revulsion, as the feeling of anguish insidiously crept its way into his fiber, and despite his best efforts, he couldn't stop it from overriding him. Without taking another glimpse at Edna, William impulsively ran into the kitchen to alert Tilly of madam's illness.

'Tilly, come quickly ... there's something wrong with Edna' He beckoned.

'What's wrong?'

'Just come with me' He continued, and they both quickly advanced towards their mistress. 'She's like a bewitched zombie' He uttered just before they reached Edna, and as they stood in front of her, Edna looked up, her eyes had returned to their ordinary blue color, and she smiled modestly at them.

'What's all the fuss?' Edna questioned.

'Nothing, madam ... William just thought you looked a bit poorly', Tilly answered while William stood there, unable to speak, totally astonished, as every part of him went on pause while his thoughts caught up.

'Would you like a pot of tea?' Tilly continued as she simultaneously nodded her head towards the kitchen in a gesture for William to join her.

'Yes, please, dear, that would be lovely.' Edna smiled, so both servants paced rapidly back into the galley.

'What's the matter with you ...? There's nothing wrong with her', Tilly barked as soon as she was out of earshot.

'Well, there was something wrong with her a few minutes ago. I wished you had seen it ... her eyes were unoccupied, and their white color was really scary', William defended himself.

The pressure of the tragedies that surrounded him were beginning to pile up. The telephone was constantly ringing with journalists wanting an exclusive interview, attempting to add a new facet to the Karce's breaking news story; he was still grieving for Annie and Warren and the house was going to shambles, which wasn't proper and didn't fit in with his obsessive-compulsive disposition to have everything flawless. Each day was like a small century, and with Edna's recent episode, any more surprises would be more than his brain would allow him to imagine.

It was coming to nightfall as Edna sat placidly in her chair, sipping on the hot beverage, still looking out the window, when she spotted a luminous glow, like a shimmer of mist radiating from the garden. Mechanically, she stood up and walked towards the manor's front entrance, opening the large door and not bothering to shut it, as her eyes locked on the apparition, outstaring the pearly white translucent object, which pirouetted around the distant flowering shrubberies. As Edna got nearer, she saw it levitating a foot off the ground as it slowly came into focus, giggling and beckoning her closer. The girl clapped soundlessly, laughing like she'd seen something amusing; and she didn't appear forsaken, mournful, or lonely. Instead, she was alluring and delightful, skipping about with abundant happiness. The girl twirled around and abruptly poised, fronting her summoned guest; and as she smiled, Edna immediately recognized the beautiful face, so she called out her name.

'Annie, my beautiful Annie, you've come back to me!' She exclaimed as they ran towards each other with arms outstretched, but as the apparition got closer, Edna detected that the beautiful girl had suddenly distorted into a ghoul, with staring heavy-lidded eyes and a sagging mouth, its cheekbones accentuating a skeletal look, and its expression deprived of any emotion. Feeling intense astonishment, Edna stopped unwavering in her tracks, but the ghoul kept coming until it permeated her body, taking her breath away, and sending her falling to the ground in a lifeless heap. In his customary fashion, William attentively searched the parlor for anything out of place, finally arriving at Edna's empty cup and saucer and proceeded to retrieve it when he casually looked up and saw Edna lying outside on the cold hard ground, and his heart started pounding at an increasingly rapid pace. Screaming out for Tilly, he immediately sprinted outside and knelt down beside Edna, feeling for a pulse; he then lifted her up into his arms, carrying the limp body inside, and commenced ferrying the unconscious woman to her room, as Tilly met him at the bottom of the staircase.

'What happened?' She said, alarmed, staring at Edna's sagging form.

'I'm not sure. Ring Dr. Bartlett at once' He ordered and proceeded to climb the extensive stairwell. Once in the room, William placed Edna tentatively on her bed and walked out the doorway, peering down off the indoor balcony, waiting for the doctor to arrive when he overheard the gentle sound of a girl giggling, delightful as wind chimes, and just as pleasing. He turned in the direction of the noise and witnessed Edna alert, sitting up in bed, watching him.

'Madam …are you alright?' He said as he wandered back in, amazed at her unexpected recovery.

'Why do you call me madam?' She replied.

'You're the madam of the house.'

'No, I'm not … my mother is', Edna tittered.

230

'Who are you then?' William requested, confused at the childlike tone of her voice.

'Don't you recognize me, William? I'm Annie ... silly man' She mocked, her eyes fixed as though she was looking at an object behind his head. William attempted to yell for Tilly, but he could only muster a choked cry as it forced its way up to his throat and spilled out like a spineless coward.

'What's the matter ... cat got your tongue?' The demented woman jeered, her voice changing into a curdling deep hiss, as the black energy oozed out with every cynical word spoken. The twisted entity had a specific agenda, and that was to actively involve itself firsthand by controlling Edna's mind and intellect with the sole purpose of harming her and fulfilling its own desires. Speechless, William watched as the hideous evil spirit invaded Edna's body as though it owned her and had a right to be there, occasionally speaking in different languages, taunting him with brutality. It hurdled upright on the bed, squatting on its haunches like a toad, and started grunting in an animalistic, berserk rage, trying to deepen his fear, as it looked straight through him with its blackened eyes. It was the enemy.

Just as it began laughing, a low rumbling, sadistic gurgle, full of torment, William heard faint voices and approaching footsteps climbing the stairs. He backed away from the unrealistic menace and hurried towards the top of the stairs, where he met Dr. Bartlett and Tilly as they deliberated over Edna's impending breakdown.

'Come quickly ... something has possessed Edna ... she's delusional, crouching on the bed and talking in some sort of demonic voice' He informed, marshaling them into the bedroom. As they entered and gazed upon her, Edna was lying on her bed, wrapped in a profound sleep, the distinctive soft echoes of her peaceful slumber filling the room as if she'd been there unmoving for hours. William halted at the sight of her tranquil behavior as Dr Bartlett and Tilly scrutinized him for his far-fetched deception while the doctor proceeded to lean over Edna, taking her pulse.

'Her heartbeat is racing' He declared, and as he turned towards the others, Edna's eyes suddenly opened, as wide as saucers, her pupils revolving backward, only displaying the whites of her eyes; and with the same maniacal voice as before, she stated with an unemotional insolence...

'You have reached the point of no return You and your loved ones are ordained for decay.

It's the pendants curse' The creature warned

Alarmed at the satanic expression on Edna's face and what she had just vowed, Dr. Bartlett bounded rearward and scowled at her, his mind competing with a logical explanation for her change, as Edna seethed at them, her mouth foaming with slobber.

'She's completely traumatized from all the exposure to the shocking ordeals she's experienced over the last few weeks. Her personality has transformed from psychological distress ... it's the most extreme case of posttraumatic stress disorder I've ever seen' He admitted.

'It's like she's demon-possessed', William indicated.

'Yes, it can manifest like that. With her suffering implicit flashbacks, we can mistakenly believe someone, or something, is controlling her, and this has triggered these hostile and intense feelings', Dr. Bartlett believed, feeling self-assured with his swift analysis.

'She said she was Annie before' William added.

232

Chapter 13

'The altered characteristics can embrace those from a close relationship with a loved one and can transform their mood and particular stressors can cause the alter to emerge'

'This identity may deny knowledge of the other, so when Edna awakes from this episode, her memories, personality of Annie, her convulsions and fainting as if one were dying will be erased', Dr. Bartlett continued.

'What's she talking about ... the pendant's curse ... what pendant? What does that mean anyway?' Tilly interrupted.

'I don't know ... just another part of her delirium.' The doctor shrugged off Tilly's unease. By this time, Edna has lapsed into her former stupor and was unmoving once again as the three individuals relocated themselves just past the open doorway and discussed Edna's remedial treatment.

'When she wakes, give her the prescribed amount of Valium and make sure this door is locked so she doesn't escape and hurt herself. Sometimes, these alters can induce feelings of desolation and suicide to the host. I'll be in touch after I investigate her dissociative identity disorder further. Keep a close eye on her', Dr. Bartlett drilled and exited down the stairwell alone, seeing himself out.

William and Tilly stared back into the bedroom where Edna lay quietly, sleep pooling in her eyes, so with crippling edginess rising in him, William crept towards the door and closed it, securely locking it behind him.

'This whole scenario is getting worse by the minute' He confessed again to Tilly as they descended the staircase, making their way through the parlor and into the kitchen.

'I told you we'll be looking for another job, and the lives we're accustomed to will be finished if Edna doesn't pull herself together' He continued, sitting himself at the table.

'Just follow the doctor's order and everything will be fine', Tilly consoled.

'Tilly, you're a lovely woman, but please get your head out of the clouds and stop dancing around with the butterflies … Just face the reality … everything is not going to be fine' He derided as his head lowered in dismay.

'As soon as Edna's awake, I'll give her the medication. That will keep her sedated and settled.' Tilly ignored William's perpetual miseries.

As soon as the trio had left the bedroom, Edna lay on her back, staring at the ceiling, awake and fully alert, as she contemplated why she was in her room with the door fastened shut.

A few minutes before, she had tested it and realized that something terrible must have happened for her to be padlocked inside like a prisoner. The last thing she remembered was seeing Annie frolicking around in the garden and feeling the desire to embrace her, but whatever occurred after that was a haze. The heartache she felt from missing Warren and Annie scorched her soul, and as she continued to lay there, she discovered the bed becoming cold and lonely as she missed Warren's muscular arms lovingly wrapped around her as much as she missed the smell of him. Their absence induced an agony that knotted in her gut like a dense lump of rock as she wanted so much to have them close, to talk and laugh with them like she once did, and the yearning of those past encounters left her feeling isolated and with little hope. Edna sat up on the side of the bed and began crying, face lodged into the palms of her hands until she heard a man's voice tenderly calling her name from beneath the window. She lifted her head and walked over to it, drawing the curtains back to gain a clear view of the garden below, and to her amazement, Edna saw Warren, looking up at the window with a pleasing smile showing from his handsome face. Waving at her to come join him, Edna showed no reluctance with opening the shutters and climbing out onto the windowsill, balancing her tiny figure on the insignificant ledge as she felt the eagerness to join Warren coursing through her veins. Without a sound, she took one mighty leap from the six-meter high window and landed hard on the ground, her legs crumpling from beneath her; but instead of worrying about the danger of injuries, her weird emotional state counteracted the severity of impact and she instantly stood up, robust and able-bodied, surviving the bewildering fall and ran off still wearing her snowy nightdress and vanished into the security of the blanketed gardens, calling after Warren.

An hour had passed before Tilly decided to go and check on Edna, clasping the bottle of Valium in one hand and a glass of water in the other as she ascended the staircase. Stopping at the closed door Tilly knocked and waited to be summoned into the bedroom, but Edna didn't answer, so Tilly rummaged around in the pocket of her apron, salvaging the keys, and finally opened the door.

'Hello, madam' She routinely welcomed as she viewed the bed, but discovered it empty, so her eyes frantically scanned the room and noticed the shutters wide open with the drapes wafting in the breeze. Tilly's knees bowed from under her as she tried to sit down, but it was more like a stumble, and the fall left her in a trembling heap on the floor while her mouth gaped open as she staggered to find the words to scream out for William.

'Help, help', She repeatedly shrieked until William appeared at the doorway.

'What's wrong?' Was his immediate question when he saw Tilly sitting on the floor with the jar of pills and water spilled out alongside her.

'She's gone', Tilly whimpered.

'Where did she go?'

'Look at the window ... it's open, and it wasn't before...she's jumped', The astounded maid said pointing at the moving curtains. William dashed towards the window and scrutinized the distant ground below, but he couldn't see Edna's body anywhere.

'She couldn't have jumped ... it's too high, and with her tiny frame, she'd be either lying there severely injured if not dead', He concluded.

'Check the rest of the house ... she couldn't have gone far ... and call Dr Bartlett immediately.'

'Okay, I'll do it straight away', Tilly complied as William helped her up.

'I'm going to search the outside grounds, I just hope none of those bloody journalists at the main gate see her and start taking photos ... she's still wearing her nightie', He added before Tilly gathered herself and exited the room. Placing on his coat, William scurried outside, his eyes darting around wildly with each passing second as he constantly looked for a glimmer of Edna's pale nightwear, repeatedly calling her name until his voice almost cracked. He ran through the gardens, which were obscured by a shroud of thin mist; with his adrenaline pumping, he felt the desperation of no hope finding her escalating in his being when unexpectedly, he caught a brief flash of white, moving swiftly, passing behind the shrubbery approximately four meters away. 'Edna ...

madam ... it's William', He announced as he raced towards the location of the abstract figure, but when he reached the spot, it had vanished, as if it dissolved into the very mist itself and was carried away with the breeze. Bewildered, William retraced his steps, eventually, finding his way back to the manor, and just as he was approaching the enormous house, he witnessed a hooded man in the distance, stagnantly fixed with his back towards him, gazing upwards, carefully monitoring Edna's bedroom window. William stealthily advanced on the stalking culprit, gaining in on him with every hurried step and as he reached the individual, he attempted to place his hand firmly on its shoulder, only to have the man impulsively turn away, and without showing his face, it brushed past him and evaporated into nothingness, like he never existed. Inactivated with terror and disbelief, William's shock was interrupted when he heard Tilly's voice.

'William, come quickly!' She yelled, bidding him to the house. He entered the foyer, panting as though his lungs were pushing up a lead weight on his chest, as he noticed Tilly standing in the doorway of the parlor, her attention preoccupied and completely engrossed on whatever was in there.

'What is it?' He wheezed, finally gathering the strength to walk over to where she stood, and as he stared into the parlor, he saw Edna sitting on the chair, her head drooped, looking emaciated and disheveled with strips of mud smeared on her face and twigs sticking out of her grubby messed-up hair.

'How long has she been there?' William asked Tilly.

'I don't know ... I just found her there a couple of minutes ago.'

'Edna, are you alright?' William asked softly as he knelt

down and observed her face, but her eyes were blank, indicating a lack of emotion, and she didn't answer him.

'How long before Dr Bartlett gets here?' William turned his focus on Tilly.

'He's at the hospital, so he'll be there for a while.'

'Okay ... let's clean her up and put her to bed ... I'll fetch the Valium, and this time, we'll make sure she takes it ... before anything else weird happens.

Fourteen

Chapter 14

⁓ ◦◦◦◦ ⁓

Sharon couldn't think straight. The day she'd been dreading was finally here as the dawn edged its way into gradual daylight. She had stayed awake most of the night, but it didn't make any difference to the heaviness she was feeling; and as she sat on the edge of her bed, she realized that the sheets were all tangled due to her erratic, fitful night of vivid dreaming. She refused to eat the food that was brought to her for breakfast, and she found herself masticating the inside of her cheek, as the bitter taste of blood filled her mouth and her pulse pounded inside her head. When the prison guard came to fetch her, she jumped with mounting anxiety as the nagging voice in the back of her mind spoke of nothing but disaster ahead.

'You're wanted in the conference room', He demanded, and as she routinely offered her hands to be cuffed, Sharon felt the trepidation of the daunting day ahead. The guard escorted her to the consultation room where Paul Riddick stood, locking his briefcase, as he prepared to have Sharon transported to the courthouse via a prison truck; and when they arrived, it was quite busy, with reporters tussling against one another to improve their chance for an exclusive snapshot. Handcuffed, shackled, and wearing a prison robe, Sharon was taken to the holding cells situated behind the courtroom'; and as she waited, the odor of decades of panic suffocated her, and she secretly hoped that her trial would start on time and the real truth of her case would play out before the judges. As Paul Riddick entered the detention area to go over the information they'd chatted about for weeks in the lead up to her hearing, Sharon studied him with harsh judgment as she had no respect for him and saw him as a second class lawyer ... and he undeniably felt the same apathy towards her.

'Okay, Sharon, they'll be calling you soon. You will get to hear everything that goes on in the courtroom, but at the time of others giving evidence, you won't be able to speak to me, and all witnesses will be kept outside until they have given their testimonies. There's a panel of three judges hearing your case today. Are you ready?' he communicated.

'Yes ... time to bite the bullet and get this over and done with', She concluded.

Paul visited the restroom before appearing in court, and while he was washing his hands, the prosecutor's lawyer walked in.

'How does your prosecution case look ... strong?' Paul badgered cheekily.

'Sorry, Paul, you're not going to make any fame or money out of this one ... it's going to be quick', He answered hastily, then picked up his briefcase and exited out the door. Arriving in the courtroom, constrained in manacles, Sharon appeared cool, composed, and unruffled as she regarded the overflowing chamber, while everyone was taking a hard look back at her.

A small number of journalists gathered at the rear of the courtroom, pen, and paper in hand, ready to jot down every detail of her character and the impending trial. She assembled herself on the chair at the bar table, and subsequently, the leading judge addressed her charges in a demoralizing tone while Paul indicated for her to stand.

'When I call your name, stand up ... Case number 103... Sharon Karce you are charged with one count of murder in the first degree, one count of conspiracy to murder, and one count of manslaughter ... how do you plead?' His voice thundered.

'Not guilty, Your Honour', She announced shamelessly before taking back her seat at the bar.

'You have waved the reading of your rights but not the rights themselves. No bail has been set, so you will remain in custody until your sentencing', The judge sustained.

'Yes, Your Honour', Sharon's defense approved.

'See? Even my case number adds up to 13', She whispered to Paul and he glared back at her with a confused look.

'Ssshh', He instructed.

Then the prosecution stood up and consigned their opening statement as Sharon felt a soft panic growing, churning into a tornado of futility.

'May it please the court and presiding judges. This is a case of murder in the first degree and manslaughter in the second degree. This hearing is being undertaken because that woman, Sharon Karce from Australia, conspired to murder her sister Annie Karce by intentionally poisoning her over a period of weeks. Her accomplice, Mr. Liam Cartwright, also from Australia, colluded with her to murder Mr. Gary Jenkins, a private detective who was sent over by Miss Karce's parents. 'It is the burden of the prosecution to prove to you beyond reasonable doubt that Sharon Karce is guilty of murder in the first degree, conspiring to murder and manslaughter in the second degree. We are confident that the weight of the evidence we intend to present to you during the course of this trial will clearly establish the defendant's guilt. Annie Karce will never feel the sun on her face and will never have children or see her family again. Make this defendant responsible for her actions. There is a chance for justice here, based on this evidence, and at the conclusion of this trial, we will hope that you find the defendant, Sharon Karce, guilty of murder, conspiracy to murder, and manslaughter as charged in this indictment. Thank you.' And the prosecutor diligently sat down.

As Paul Riddick stood up to make his introductory statement, he defended his client with enthusiasm.

'May it please the court and presiding Judges that we are here today because on April 25th, 2018, Annie Karce died from exposure to a horrific incident that ultimately claimed her life. My client wasn't even in the proximity when this tragedy occurred, and this is nothing more than a case of misplaced blame. My client has no prior felonies here or in Australia, and she belongs to a reputable family. 'Only after the prosecutors have presented their case will Sharon Karce have an opportunity to present hers. We ask that you wait until you have heard from all the witnesses before deciding on a verdict. It's the prosecution's duty to prove, beyond reasonable doubt, that Sharon Karce conspired to kill her sister, but until this time, I ask you to withhold your judgment until you have heard all the evidence. Why would the defendant want to kill her cherished twin sister? I am confident that after all the proof is presented, you will render a verdict that will be fair. We believe that the prosecution will not be able to prove beyond reasonable doubt that Sharon Karce murdered her sister nor colluded with Liam Cartwright to slay Gary Jenkins. Sharon Karce is not the brutal killer that the prosecution wants you to see. We expect that after you deliberate and carefully weigh all the evidence, you will return the only possible verdict of not guilty. Thank you.'

'Bring in the first witness', The primary Judge instructed.

Inquisitively, Sharon looked at Paul then turned around to view the person that the prosecution had conjured up to testify against her, and to her shock, it was the young waiter from the café. He disclosed that Sharon had made a dedicated request that he give Annie the bottle of wine the day she absconded to the beach and that he'd seen the sisters at the café dining together before, and Sharon's behavior towards her sibling was offensive and intimidating. The next witness was an impeccably groomed hotel staff member, and he commented that he had witnessed the sisters' never-ending bickering as Sharon constantly harassed and implied that Annie was crazy. Paul instantly stood up,

'Objection, Your Honour, personal judgment.'

'Sustained', The Judge granted.

Another hotel staff member stated that she observed Sharon constantly leaving Annie by herself, venturing out with strangers she'd met at bars and cafes; but before she'd leave, she always brought Annie a bottle of wine and left it for her in their room. The following witness was a lady that

Sharon had spent those days at the beach with; she and Jenny testified that Sharon bragged about her wealth and how lovely it would be if her spoiled sister was to simply vanish and leave her to exclusively inherit the family's fortune. When each witness was cross-examined by Paul Riddick, their testimonies remained watertight as they insisted they were telling the truth. Paul was left feeling like a chump as he argued points with no significance, trying to discover a thread of perjury in each witness's testaments, and it appeared to Sharon that Paul was defending a case that was completely outside of his niche. There were witnesses coming out of the woodwork. Sharon was horror-struck as they strutted themselves in and out of the courtroom like fashion models parading on a catwalk. Some of them she'd never seen before, like a couple who had dined at the table next to her and Annie on their first encounter in the beer garden and commented that they overheard Sharon's belittling nature towards Annie's interest in mythology and how Sharon had said that her lust for those types of legends would eventually drive her sister insane and she'd wished that she would just 'go away'.

Again, Paul objected, citing 'speculation' from the witness, but each of the couple affirmed that they'd specifically heard what was said by the accused as Sharon shook her head with skepticism. The prosecution ushered in a lady who revealed that on one particular day, she saw Sharon entering Liam's place and removing her sunglasses and scarf before going in. Sharon twitched in her seat as she outwardly scoffed at the witness's claims. Then there was the muscular hotel attendant who described Annie's hysterical and freakish behavior when she'd called and informed that there was a terrifying creature crawling up the wall of their apartment, but when he searched the place thoroughly, he couldn't find anything. While the witnesses spoke about Sharon in a harmful way, she comforted herself by repeatedly mumbling under her breath, *'Bloody wankers'*, while Paul constantly advised her to 'shut up' as he habitually looked down to scan his notes. The fascinated audience watched eagerly as forensic photos of the crime scene and CCTV footage were presented, displaying Sharon dumping the contents of her bag in a bin at the train station. Transcripts of phone calls made to Liam were reclaimed, establishing her relationship with him, while Paul erratically made preliminary objections to some of the material that to him seemed like improper handling of evidentiary issues. His cross-examination techniques were short and dense as he fought with what proof he could get from each witness, attempting to flag any errors in their inconsistent statements, hoping to strengthen his own defense case. Instead of coming across as though he believed in her case and what he was saying at that moment, he displayed negativity, which shouted at the judges that he was uncomfortable defending Sharon as he fidgeted about, unsuccessfully convincing the court of her integrity and diminishing her likeability.

At 3.30 pm, the court was adjourned for the day. The hearing had been lengthy and monotonous, and all Sharon wanted to do was go back to the encrusted jail cell, as she was tired and fed up with Paul's wretched attempt to protect her honor and stop her incarceration. As they walked out of court and into the foreboding atmosphere of the darkened corridor, which led to the holding cells, Sharon regarded Paul with extreme loathing.

'I knew it. You're not even a lawyer's bootlace. What the fuck were you doing in there? You were an indecisive idiot with no balls', She complained.

'Well, your case has many adversaries, and it's difficult to challenge them when their sworn statements are rock solid and consistent. I did warn you that the evidence was stacked up against you ... and we still have tomorrow's forensic testimonies as well as the lead detective's account of what you disclosed to him during the interrogation. Do you remember signing any documents at the time? Because he says he has a sworn statement from you.'

'I don't know ... Maybe I signed something in the beginning, but I was utterly confused ... everything was moving so quickly.' Sharon's mind raced faster than a speeding train as she labored to remember, the painful memories of her incarceration rising from her subconscious like a shadowy specter surging from its coffin.

'Am I going back to my original cell tonight?' She changed the subject.

'No ... you'll be staying here ... there's a deluge of media cameras camped outside the courthouse with satellite trucks ... journalists are nothing but commercial animals', Paul slated as the prison guard ushered Sharon into the grimy cell. Her nose immediately crumpled up with revulsion as the odors of vomit, human excrement, and mouse droppings intermixed into a stench that brought tears to her eyes. Fumbling about in the dimness, trying to find the bed, Sharon's fingers settled upon a dampish blanket, which made them suddenly viscid and gluey, and she impulsively heaved at the sensation.

'I can't believe you're making me spend the night in this cesspit. I'm sick of this. When do I get to tell my version of events in court?' She yelled at Paul before his departure.

'Tomorrow, after the prosecution finishes presenting their

evidence.'

'And then what?' She continued, striving to keep the discussion going, as she felt the twinges of self-doubt growing in her.

'Here in Romania, they have two types of prosecutors, the investigating one and the trial prosecutor. Once the investigation is finalized and the indictment is forwarded to the court by the investigating prosecutor, the trial prosecutor takes over the case. A different trial prosecutor will appear in court, depending on the stage of trial', He debriefed.

'Get some rest, Sharon, you've got a big day tomorrow', He instructed as he turned towards the door and left her, alone and isolated in the dilapidated cell.

The nocturnal hours dragged on, and around midnight, Sharon began hearing malicious whispering, the voices moaning nasty threats and sniggering as they badgered her with intimidations of despair, like *You'll never walk on grass again or feel the sun on your hair. This is where you'll spend your wretched life.'*

It was 9.00 am when Paul Riddick entered the holding cells the following morning, and as he looked in at Sharon, he saw her lying on the bed, her back curved, head bowed, and her limbs bent and drawn up close to her torso, as though she was a prenatal fetus.

'Sharon, wake up', He announced, motioning the guard to open the door. She woke as if there was an emergency, as though sleeping had become an unsafe thing, her heart beating faster as the revelations of the night before came flooding back into her incoherent brain.

'Huh? What? Where am I?' She stammered, disorganized in her thinking.

'Get up and have a shower ... here are some clean prison clothes ... court starts in an hour', Paul coached.

'Prison clothes? I don't wear prison clothes ... you must have mistaken me for someone else.'

'No games, Sharon ... get yourself ready now.' Paul was becoming annoyed with her hesitancy. The amenities consisted of a room with four showerheads, which enabled multiple prisoners to use at one time, but in this instance, Sharon showered alone. She placed her clothing and towel on the swinging door, and she stepped under the hot steamy water, allowing it to drizzle all over her body as the balminess washed away her feelings of loneliness and social rejection, making her feel better about herself.

'That's enough ... get out', The prison guard ordered, interrupting her spell of relief, so she got dried and dressed and prepared for the grueling day ahead. Shuffling along with her shackles affixed, she met up with Paul before entering the courtroom, and he noticed her stunned look with no intelligence or the slightest spark of interest in her eyes.

'Are you alright, Sharon?' He quizzed before opening the door for her, but she didn't react. As the trial proceeded, the next witness for the prosecution was the lead detective. He revealed to the court the complete testament surrounding Annie's death, Sharon's haughtiness to the actuality of being a suspect, her connection with Liam, the poisons detected in the wine bottles, the $125,000 transfer into Liam's bank account, and her eventual signed confession along with the recorded admission that reinforced his evidence. Utterly passionate during his testimony, he stated that he was never going to give up, as he had a gut instinct that allowed the evidence to guide him to the truth. His verbal proof was flawless, and

Sharon's forehead and hands began sweating, as she mutely sat there, terrified at his honesty. The next witness was a forensic pathologist who outlined the techniques determining Annie's cause of death from ultimate asphyxiation, but the poisoning and the chemical compounds that were found in her system substantiated her death. He also verbally charted how the main fields—forensic toxicology, biology, and pathology—pinpointed the proof of identity of the autopsied body found in the Tatras Mountains and how that established Liam's identity from his gruesome remains. The only defense witness called was the hotel supervisor, who affirmed that he saw Sharon visibly distraught from finding Annie's body in the hotel, but his testimony was short-lived and without any tangible substance, while the prosecution's response was the possibility that Sharon could've been staging the entire hysteria. Lastly, Sharon was called to the witness box; and as Paul approached her to ask his first question, she watched him with a spaced-out look, like the lights were on but no one was home.

'Miss Karce. Annie and yourself were fraternal twins, so you grew up together and established a close and loving relationship?'

'Sister Annie? Who is she? Oh, that's right ... my prima donna sister. Um ... she's back in Australia. She left me here to clean up this mess she's caused', Sharon huffed.

'Can you please answer the question Miss Karce', Paul repeated, glancing nervously up at the judges.

'Yes, of course, we grew up together, and we are close.' Paul Riddick approached the witness box and whispered his concerns to Sharon.

'What's wrong with you? Answer the questions the way

we rehearsed', He warned, then stepped back to continue his cross-examination, grabbing something off his desk.

'Is this a picture of your sister Annie?' He held up a photo for Sharon to inspect so she leaned forward, squinting her eyes to ponder over the image.

'Nope ... it's not her. My sister is pudgier and has blonde hair.' Paul immediately indicated to speak with the judges, and the trial prosecutor joined their huddle.

'There's definitely something wrong with my witness. I think she's suffering from partialities and is producing false memories. It's obvious she's confused and is having problems with her recollection', Paul established.

'Or maybe she's just playing you along ... She's a trisor (cheat).' The trial prosecutor disfavored Paul's attempt to justify Sharon's behavior.

'Call her what you want, but she is an unreliable witness ... her memory has been corrupted by some earlier occurrence.' Paul ignored the prosecutor's insolent remark.

'More like she's corrupt', The prosecutor's insults continued.

'Look, I'm not comfortable with your prejudices towards my client but under extreme stressors, witnesses can forget events that have happened to them and the people they once knew. She's clearly mixing up details across time and place, therefore citing errors in her evidence', Paul reasoned.

'This is her only time to testify ... if she can't comply now then we will have to rule against her. She doesn't get a second chance at this. Finish your cross-examination or remove her from the witness box. It's your plea, Mr. Riddick', The judges ruled.

Paul glanced at the trial prosecutor, who stood there grinning at the magistrate's condemning outcome, so he withdrew from the bench and reclaimed his position to continue Sharon's inquisitorial.

'Miss Karce, you're mindful that this hearing is for murder and manslaughter against you. If you don't openly convey to the court your details of events, then you will be convicted of both allegations and probably spend the rest of your life in prison.'

'Murder? Manslaughter? Who did I murder?' She cried.

'Remove your witness from the stand immediately, Mr. Riddick', One of the judges broadcasted, denying Sharon the pleasure of ridiculing his court any further; and as she stood up, she looked the judges squared in the eyes and commented out loud,

'The secret to life is knowing that you've worn out your welcome and when it's time to leave.' And as she descended from the witness box she muttered quietly under her breath, 'That's what I used to tell Annie' As her face simultaneously contorted into a mischievous deceitful grin.

'My client has obviously experienced a serious mental deterioration, so I ask the court for a psychological assessment to determine whether insanity is a viable plea and whether the defendant is able to withstand trial', Paul Riddick proclaimed.

The judges murmured amongst themselves for a few minutes then granted Paul's request while Sharon was escorted back to the isolation cell, where she claimed the corner of an aluminum bench, which was shared by six other female prisoners. She suppressed her natural curiosity to make eye contact with them, even though she felt starved for company; and lately, her coping skills with frightening situations seem to trigger her newly acquired phobia of the whispering voices. After an hour, Paul Riddick appeared at the lockup gate, and he gestured for Sharon to come closer.

'You'll be traveling back to your original holding cell tonight. I've been successful in ordering a mental health assessment for you, but it'll have to be completed within four days, and then you'll reappear in court. You'll be notified when this will happen. Don't stuff this up, Sharon ... this is your last chance', He counseled, and then he disappeared. Within two days, prearranged custodial guards accompanied Sharon to the psychiatric clinic where her appointment with Dr. Brevik was scheduled; and when he entered, she smiled an innocent grin, only using her mouth as the hypocritical smile didn't reach into her eyes. She shifted her gaze around the area rapidly, not maintaining eye contact with him, and Dr. Breivik observed this straight away.

'Hello, Sharon, my name is Dr. Brevik, how are you today?' Starting the dialogue, he gradually sat down on his large plush examination sofa. He studied her closed body posture as she waited with arms and legs crossed and her shoulders stooped.

'I'm alright', She answered, scratching her nose.

'Okay, do you know why you're here today?'

'Yes ... to find out if I'm mentally disturbed.'

'Well, I wouldn't put it that way ... but the court has ordered this assessment for your trial ... I'll be asking you some questions, so let's begin.'

'Is there any psychiatric illness in your family?' He sat composed with a pen and a notepad, ready to inscribe her answers.

'No.'

'Any substance abuse or suicidal tendencies?'

'No.'

'Okay. Describe your childhood in a word or two.'

'Despised, disfavored, and rejected. You know if you get rejected enough times you begin to feel as though you don't belong anywhere.'

'Rejected by whom?'

'My mum and dad ... mainly my dad.' She sat, leaning to one side of the chair.

'Was there any abuse during your childhood?'

'Yes ... emotional and mental abuse.'

'How so?'

'Dad favored Annie over me. He was far more affectionate towards her because she is pleasant and loving, and when I'd complain about it, he'd become defensive and call me resentful and abnormal.'

'How was your parents' marriage?'

'Very loving ... that's the thing ... they're all adoring each other except me ... Mum's very needy though ... always relying on dad for everything ... Annie's the same ... she always gets everything she wants from Papa', Sharon whined.

'You keep referring to your sister and father in the present tense. You realize they have both departed.'

'What do you mean departed?'

'They've died, Sharon ... your father passed away from complications of an operation, and your sister ... well, you've been charged with her murder.'

'That's bullshit ... Annie is a conceited little pain in the neck, but I would not kill her, she's my sister.' Sharon immediately picked up the glass of water that was sitting on the table and held on to it tightly, creating a barrier between her and the doctor. There was a deliberate extended pause in the conversation from Dr. Breivik to make Sharon feel uncomfortable, waiting for her to fill the void with words.

'I want you to understand that I do not have it in me to murder anyone ... let alone my only sister ... you can trust me on that', Sharon blurted as the doctor watched her take a large guzzle of water, draining the entire glass.

'Would it be possible to have another glass of water, please? I'm really thirsty all of a sudden.'

'Yes, certainly', The doctor obliged; reaching over, he clutched the water pitcher and walked over to his client, pouring more into the glass.

'Have you had any recent delusions or hallucinations?' He continued.

'Yes, most of the time. I saw this ugly pig's head come out of the wall in my cell, with balls of flesh saturating its mouth, and it grunted some threatening curse at me, and then I've been hearing whispering voices telling me that I'm doomed to spend the rest of my life in prison.' 'Other than those two times, have there been any more?'

'Well, that's enough, don't you think? They were both terrifying.' Doctor Brevik rested back into his chair and thought to himself,

'Is she faking it or not?' His extensive forensic psychiatry knowledge had experienced these types of felons before, and he questioned Sharon's integrity; and if she was scheming enough to fake a psychosis so she wouldn't be sentenced, what else was she capable of?

The extensive interview went for an hour and a half as Dr. Brevik tried to identify her symptoms of psychosis and prove that she didn't recognize at the time that poisoning and ultimately murdering Annie and colluding to murder Gary Jenkins was a serious crime.. Should she be detained in a mental institute rather than prison? This liability was his definitive decision.

Paul Riddick opened the office door, and as he placed down his briefcase, he instantly viewed a large white sachet on his desk. It had been another two days since Sharon's meeting with Dr. Brevik, so he anticipated that the report would be arriving soon. Assembling himself comfortably in the chair, he prudently opened the envelope. It was a thick and lengthy report, but in a nutshell it read,

An extensive interview was undertaken by myself, Dr. Brevik, with Sharon Karce to determine the state of mind of the accused. Combined with other relevant information from other agencies like the police and forensics, I have reached a final conclusion. We talked about not only the incident but also the time leading up to the incident and afterward. Did Sharon Karce, in some way, display psychotic symptoms like hearing voices and had a reduced level of consciousness motivating her to commit the crime? If Sharon had witnessed psychosis firsthand by a relative or in hospital, this would aid a more accurate performance, but this has never been validated. Miss Karce admitted to having continuous hallucinations, yet her description of symptoms were exaggerated. I guided her into saying she was experiencing a certain set of symptoms where she created an unrealistic picture of her supposed illness, which was not possible to have, ultimately directing me to the conclusion that she was fabricating. In closing, I reject her claims of innocence on the grounds of diminished responsibility and with her meticulous preparations to falsify a psychosis suggests a sane mind. Sharon Karce was within her right mind when she colluded with Liam Cartwright to eradicate her sister Annie Karce and the private investigator, Mr. Gary Jenkins. Her actions were premeditated and deliberate.

Paul slammed the report down on the desk, offended at Sharon's attempt to pervert the course of justice. His heart sank, and his anger built up from her deception as he'd sincerely believed that she'd suffered from some sort of breakdown, and now he knew the truth, he felt foolish in giving her the benefit of the doubt.

'Your goose is cooked, Sharon Karce, I can't help you any longer' He secretly stated.

The following day at the judicial bar, the judges glared at Paul Riddick as he stood to address the court while Sharon sat self consciously next to him.

'Your Honours. I have been in counsel with Miss Karce, and on behalf of my client, we have mutually agreed to enter a guilty plea without the need for the trial to go any further. We understand the court must ascertain the facts of both cases of murder, conspiracy, and manslaughter before it can pass its sentence.'

As he sat back down at the table, Sharon openly objected to the manslaughter charge, wanting an opportunity to address the court about the matter and its relevance to sentencing her on that allegation. She was granted the chance to make her statement.

'Your Honour, I didn't collude with Liam Cartwright to murder Gary Jenkins. I didn't even know him and that he was in Romania at the request of my parents. Liam said that someone was following him at one time, but he didn't go into any details about who it was. I plead with the court to believe me and not to sentence me with something I wasn't aware of or didn't do', She confirmed and began sobbing hysterically, placing her face in her hands.

'We have read the psychiatrist's report and heard your statement, and in relevance to changing your plea from not guilty to guilty and the fabricated performance in court of you falsifying a psychosis, attempting to pervert the course of justice, why should the court believe you now, proclaiming your innocence on the charge of Mr. Jenkins's death?'

'Because I didn't do it!' She shrieked at the judge.

'Control your client, Mr. Riddick. You have already tried to deceive the court, Miss Karce, so there's no trustworthiness in anything you say from now on. You and your counsel have willingly entered a guilty plea to the court. Do you understand that by pleading guilty, you give up your rights to an appeal to a higher court?'

'Sharon ... it's over and done with ... you've submitted your plea, you don't get a second chance. Please answer the judge', Paul whispered, touching her arm.

'Yes, I understand' She sniffled as she sat back down in the chair.

'The defendant has been found guilty on all charges, and the court will adjourn the case until tomorrow morning to deliberate on the sentencing. There will be no further attendance needed at this stage', The judges established.

The turbulent wave of emotions that Sharon felt—fear, anxiety, guilt, shame, and anger—overwhelmed her and fueled her absurdity that something had to be done about the wrong and these irrational opinions were well-rehearsed, habitual, and dominant. The court gradually emptied, and Sharon strolled back to the holding cell with Paul and a guard walking beside her. The passage of light in the corridor was vague, and the sounds of the two men talking slowed, as if they were underwater, with the only distinguishing sound coming from the thrashing beat of her heart. Unexpectedly, Sharon swung around and cracked her elbow into the side of Paul's skull, hitting him in the soft spot, high on the temple.

"You did nothing for me" She remarked.

Paul absorbed the trauma, swallowing the pain, as he grabbed the impacting arm with his left hand and punched her square in the nose with his right; and as she slumped, he pushed her away. Taking a deep breath, Paul exhaled and inhaled again while his head swam with the banging pain. His stomach tightened as he believed he was going to throw up; and as his eyes focused he could see Sharon being tackled by the guard, with a fistful of her hair, he propelled her into the holding cell by the back of the neck.

'She's like two scorpions in a bottle', The guard commented as he slammed the gate shut, while Paul stood there, establishing that his mortal danger had brought clarity on how treacherous Sharon Karce really was.

'Are you alright? You should charge her with assault', the guard advised.

'No ... I just want the crazy bitch out of my life once and for all', Paul answered, nursing the side of his bruised head, while Sharon crept into the murkiest corner of the cell, like a skulking louse, conspicuously analyzing him the entire time.

'See you in court tomorrow for your sentencing' Was all he said before forsaking her in the dirty, putrid cell.

The following day, the court assessed all aspects of the offense and the offender, aiming to arrive at a sentence that was fair and impartial, and explained to Sharon why the punishment was given. The prosecution outlined the facts of the case and drew attention to the issues that made it serious, including the impact it had on her victims. Then the defense responded, explaining her background and the circumstances, in particular minimizing the incriminating issues. Paul indicated for Sharon to stand as the judges passed their ruling.

'The court has followed mandatory sentencing guidelines that exist for the offenses and have taken into account the harm caused to the victims, the culpability of the accused, and any aggravating and justifying factors. The court's sentencing is final. 'Even though you changed your plea from not guilty to guilty, the court is not obligated to lessen your incarceration time. Sharon Karce, on the charge of murder in the first degree of your sister Annie Karce, the court sentences you to 50 years imprisonment. For colluding to poison Annie Karce and the manslaughter of Gary Jenkins, the court sentences you to 15 years imprisonment and, for the charge of trying to pervert the course of justice the court sentences you to 14 years imprisonment. You will be transferred from here straight to the maximum-security prison. The full sentence must be served consecutively with no parole. The court is adjourned.' Terrifying chills of panic surged through Sharon's veins, and as she was hauled out of the courtroom by two hefty prison guards, every footstep echoed the rhythm of her racing heart. The wooden floor planks beneath her feet rushed by as she hung her head low, feeling the blood leaching from her face and her consciousness receding away. It was like she was floating through space, and as she strained to call for help, the emptiness surrounding her filled with a dense ether, and she faded away until everything finally went black. When Sharon awakened, she found herself lying in a heap on the cold, hard concrete floor of the jail cell, and the unrelenting fear of her incriminatory future came flooding back, bringing about a wave of hot burning anger that sought to harm anyone in her path. She began shivering, her face swelled, and her eyes dilated as the fury accompanied the deafening howls of her ravenous self-induced rage.

'Shut up, or we'll chemically restrain you into compliance', The appearing guard hollered, but the mist of her breath reverberated like dragon smoke while she contemplated taking the life that stood before her as her continual sonic wails rang vibrantly in the ears of the posing challenger ... The berserker had arrived.

Fifteen

Chapter 15

The high-security prison was designed so that the inmates never knew their actual whereabouts within the facility as a small four-inch-by-three-foot slit of a window was their only source of natural light. The facility was intended to inflict misery and pain, and it was impenetrable. It was referred to as the 'local version of hell'. Sharon had suffered the humiliation of being stripped, disinfected, and subjected to a thorough body inspection again to make sure that she wasn't smuggling anything in.

'Prisoners, I'm here every day, and I like things nice and tidy, so if you throw up on my floor, you'll be the one cleaning it up' Was the primary verbal introduction to Sharon's new home base, as she lined up with ten other inmates, clutching her bright orange prison uniform, waiting to be processed. She briefly glanced at the residing inmates and saw that most of them were malnourished and looked diseased as this was due to the lack of running water and the appalling sewage system that sent toxic fumes into the prison. It created a myriad of health problems that were intensified by overcrowding. Sharon was informed that she would only receive one meal a day, which consisted of a bowl of rice and soup; and if she wanted any other meals, it had to be purchased through the canteen ... although she would come to realize that the poorer prisoners had to work for the wealthier inmates in order to afford the canteen's goods.

'Gate' Was the single word the guard repeatedly hollered as the large steel electronic doorway buzzed open then densely hammered shut behind each prisoner, letting them through one by one to their assigned cells. The maximum-security housed both local and foreign prisoners and had a reputation for being one of the worst prisons in the world due to inmate abuse, and it was compulsory for Sharon to wear shackles as it was common practice that a new inmate wears these for two weeks. The prisoners maintained their own kind of order in the form of rigid, gang-controlled hierarchy, and the lower-ranked inmates were required to pay the more powerful prisoners money just to secure some kind of protection; and later on, Sharon found out that if she was thirsty and wanted water, she'd be forced to drink straight from the rusty bathroom pipes. The perpetual conflict between rival gangs led to serious injuries such as bone fractures, deep gashes, and head wounds with most of those causing the assaults having been identified with a mental illness. And when the attackers were caught, they would be quarantined for fifteen days, isolated in small dark rooms with only a metal bucket for excrement and a wooden perch to sit on. Sharon's preliminary two weeks was unbearable as her restraints inflicted cuts to her ankles and wrists, which constantly bled and the restraints were never detached. She was allowed to move freely amongst the other inmates, and during this limiting phase, she spent hours observing and mentally separating influential prisoners from those that were the underlings, as she planned to launch her manipulative, devious plan. Straight away, she played the victim to everyone, always making others feel that they were the ones who caused her problems. When she did come in contact with 'others,' she would reveal her sugary side one minute, and the next she was completely standoffish, using her passive-aggressive nature to keep the other inmates guessing as she preyed on their fears and insecurities. Over time, it wasn't unusual for Sharon to become unexpectedly aggressive and vicious, resorting to personal attacks and criticism, utterly persistent in her quest of getting what she wanted. She used people as a vehicle to gain some control and wasn't interested in them unless she needed them as an unwilling participant in her plans. She was skilled at taking what they'd say, twisting it around so that what they had said became barely recognizable to them, leaving them feeling as if they were going crazy. She became skilled at invading their space— physically, emotionally, and psychologically. Relentless in getting what she needed, Sharon didn't care who got hurt along the way, even if it was herself who suffered assaults from the dangerous, hard-edged convicts that had developed a hatred for her constant bullshit. And when her attacks on the other inmates did happen, Sharon was chemically restrained with sedatives and exiled to a confined cage, with just enough space to stand in and pace back and forth. Even with the severe penalties she'd receive, again and again, Sharon saw nothing wrong with refusing to take responsibility for her actions, and the inmates likened her to a parasite, ultimately nicknaming her the *'bloodsucker'*. Nonetheless, that didn't stop her from creating scenarios and dynamics that nurtured intrigue, rivalry, and jealousy as her main goal was to promote disharmony ... besides, she'd developed a taste for the disciplinary narcotics and relished in the feeling of comfort, safety from worry, and the detachment it provided. She continued to seek power through her destructive means, and this reflected her underlying psychological disturbances as she continued to display problems with anger, dominance, and vanity, acting superior and judgemental when what she was really feeling was inferior and inadequate ... but everyone else saw her as vulgar.

'I hate my life,' She confessed to herself one day as she sat alone in her stony minuscule cell. 'It's Paul Riddick's fault, he should've fought harder for me ... and it's Mama's fault, she should've sent over our family lawyer ... and it's Liam's fault, he didn't have to murder Annie or Gary Jenkins and leave me here to take all the blame and rot ... now I'm the one paying the price for their inconsiderate blunders.'

'Fuck ... I've got to spend 79 years in this shithole ... and in Romania of all bloody places ... I'll never sleep in my beautiful bed and clothes or see the manor or any of my friends again or eat sumptuous food ... never live the beautiful life I once had' She grumbled.

A cold, light wind breezed through the cell as the room temperature suddenly dropped, and Sharon's warm breath misted up as she exhaled. Out of the corner of her eye, she detected a shadow passing by as fast as the blink of an eye, and goosebumps raised on her arms. At first, she sensed a vague presence, like she was being watched; but then it manifested into a flesh and blood entity, and Sharon instantly recognized who it was.

'Why are you blaming others?' The white iridescent vision asked, speaking in a soft crooning voice. Sharon sat unmovingly, her eyes captivated by the sanctified image, trying to fathom what was happening.

'It's their fault, that's why. My lawyer didn't try hard enough, Mama didn't help me in any way, and without my knowledge, Liam went and murdered Gary Jenkins and racked off ... and you ... you weren't supposed to die, Annie.' She whined

'Well, I am dead and you have to take the blame for it.'

'I am taking the blame ... look where I am ... to spend eternity in this snake pit!' She screamed, and just as the ghost was slowly evaporating, it replied, 'Death is eternity.'

'Don't go', Sharon pleaded, but the apparition dissolved without a trace. As she lay on the rigid bed, silently weeping, Sharon's remorse oozed into the forefront of her mind and commanded to be revisited again and again, but no amount of scrutiny was going to turn back the hands of time, and she was left feeling mortified of who she'd become. Loneliness clutched at her heart like a brace, with just enough tension to be a constant ache, taking whatever luster she ever had and replacing it with darkness that eclipsed every waking moment. Focusing within herself she began to talk about unrealistic things, framing Annie's character and imagining her as a real live person, conversing with her and making promises, wishing how her own life should have been, all the while feeling empty and lost inside. 'Annie, are you there? Come back to me, I miss you' She wailed constantly.

'Shut the fuck up' The other prisoners yelled at her in different languages until a presiding guard walked up to the gate of her cell.

'What are you wailing about?' He demanded.

'My sister is here ... she's gone now, but she was here a while ago', Sharon informed.

'Your sister is dead ... that's why you're in here—you murdered her ... it's all in your head ... stupid bitch', He cussed, irritated by her lunacy.

At the sound of the guard's damning words accusing her of Annie's death, she rushed up to the gate, hurling her arms out through the bars, attempting to choke him. He immediately drew out his weapon and tasered her with his stun gun. Electrified darts struck her in the chest, and Sharon felt a shooting pain course through her, rattling her entire body, shaking her brain like marbles in a jar.

'That'll shut you up', He sneered, walking away, leaving Sharon lumped on the floor as she distinctively overheard a hideous, spiteful laugh emitting from the darkest corner of her cell ... The sarcastic giggle filled the small room with a dreadful euphoria. Her mood plummeted as desertion and emptiness infiltrated her senses, and she remained on the icy floor while the grimness of her circumstances propelled her into a mysterious, dramatic, lucid dreaming—and that's where she stayed all night.

'Get up and get over here', The guard demanded before opening the cell gate the following morning.

'It's morning and time to get up. You can come out for an hour, then you'll be locked back into your cell.'

Sharon welcomed the chance to escape the confined box she called home, and still wearing the shackles, she cautiously edged her way out of the open doorway. It was daunting seeing the other women wandering freely about, and while she stood alone near the railing, Sharon instinctively stared down at the other inmates as they huddled together, talking roguishly amongst themselves, directly pointing up at the landing where she stood, and she knew they were talking about her with poisonous malice. But they lacked the nerve to confront her as they believed she was crazy.

'Everybody knows what you're in here for', A dull introverted voice resonated behind her. Alarmed, Sharon immediately turned around and saw a scrawny fair-skinned woman, with patchy hair on her scalp, and she was covered in a red to brownish-grey rash on her face, neck, and eyelids. The small obvious bumps leaked sticky fluid while the remaining sores were thickened, cracked, and scaly, and she looked infectious.

'What?' Sharon jerked backward at the sight of the ugly woman.

'You heard me. I've seen you and the way you manipulate people to get what you want. You think you've got it all worked out, don't you?' She squeaked.

'What worked out?' Sharon felt uneasy that this emaciated woman was so brazen towards her.

'What it takes to survive here. You look at me and you're thinking what does this puny, disease-ridden person know? I've been here for a long time.' She grinned.

'Good for you', Sharon reacted cynically.

'I can see that you've got secrets in you ... and some rage, plus you're very arrogant ... I like it', She continued.

'Look ... I just want to be left alone', Sharon informed her.

'We all know what you did ... killing your sister like that ... a bit of a cowardly act, don't you think, Bloodsucker?'

'I didn't do anything of the sorts, and it's none of your

business anyway ... and what did you just call me?'

'Yeah, that's what they're all saying about you. This place is full of "I didn't do it" motherfuckers, there are so many they're falling from the rafters. Oh ... I thought you knew ... that's your tag ... 'cause you're a fucking parasite.' She broke into a rasping cackle.

'Now that you're here ... it must be the season of the witch.' Shrewdly, the woman brushed past Sharon as she spoke her last words, lightly touching Sharon's arm, and she instantly felt a searing pain where a homemade shiv had met her flesh.

'You think you've got control ... watch your back, blood-sucker the best is yet to come", She remarked carelessly. Watching the infected harpy saunter away, blissfully humming a melody, in complete astonishment, Sharon cradled her arm while the red, sticky blood trickled freely from the four-inch gash and she instinctively rushed into her cell. Quickly covering it with a jumper, she raced back outside and found a guard patrolling the area of the wing.

'Guard, guard. I've been stabbed', She pleaded, offering her arm up for the prison officer to see.

'What are you bawling about?'

'Look, I've been knifed.' Sharon unraveled the jumper from her arm to show the officer the injury, and to her shock, the wound had completely vanished; there wasn't a drop of blood on the jumper, and her arm was perfectly unharmed, not even a mark to corroborate her accusation.

'So what were you saying about being stabbed?' The guard scorned with disfavor.

'There's this skinny, diseased-looking woman. She's Caucasian with hardly any hair, she's got sores all over her!' Sharon exclaimed.

Chapter 15

'I know all the inmates, and there's no one here who fits that description. Go away.' The guard dismissed her. Extremely frightened, Sharon ambled back to the lockup, her thoughts battling to comprehend the unnerving delusion she had just experienced, and rapidly collapsed down onto her bed in shock.

Edna studied herself in the tallboy mirror, criticizing her appearance, her eyes harsh and piercing as she evaluated her image. She had lost a lot of weight and appeared bony, and as she scrutinized the clothes she was going to wear for Annie's funeral, she mentally compared herself to a sallow thin scarecrow. The week after receiving Annie's body from Romania, Edna imagined an alien had invaded her body as she felt disoriented in the emptiness of Warren's and Annie's passing. Her actions and reactions became totally unpredictable and confusing while she strained to muddle through each day, trying to make sense of her life without them.

'Madam, are you ready? You have to be at the church in an hour', Tilly suddenly announced through the closed bedroom door.

'Yes, Tilly ... I'll be down soon.' As Tilly descended the staircase, she saw William patiently waiting on the ground floor.

'How is she?' He questioned as she met up with him.

'Well, she sounds alright ... she'll be down soon.'

'Another funeral, this one's going to be hard ... burying her child. I never thought I'd see the day', He continued.

'Have you read the papers? Sharon's court trial is over, and they gave her 79 years. She's never coming out ... she'll die in there', Tilly said soberly.

'I didn't have to read the papers, the Australian Embassy called here on Friday and informed me of the outcome ... I haven't told Edna yet ... I think she's got enough to deal with at the moment.'

'Why didn't you say anything to me?' Tilly sounded annoyed.

'By the time they processed the documents for incarceration, she'd already been in prison for nine days. They're bloody idiots— where's the importance of advising family first? We should've been notified straight away. They're slower than a snail', He cussed.

'Ssshh, here she comes now', Tilly cautioned.

Edna felt the growing tingles in her entire body, and she knew that if she didn't descend the staircase quickly, the pins and needles would make her legs collapse from beneath her. The black dress she wore draped down over her skeletal shoulders, hanging loose where it shouldn't; and her crepe-like skin was as pale as death, exposing her distorted cheekbones. 'Good morning, madam', William greeted as he assisted in putting on her coat, but Edna didn't respond.

'Madam, there's a media frenzy outside the gates in regards to Sharon', He gently added, testing her disposition.

' Have you heard anything about Sharon?' She asked in a dreary manner.

'Yes, she was sentenced late last week for her crime, madam.'

'What was her punishment?' She seemed detached from her daughter's fate.

'Life, Madam ... she got sentenced to life in prison.' William's eyes quickly darted towards Tilly as he prematurely unveiled the information.

'Good', was Edna's only reply.

'Where's the car I have to go and bury my other daughter today', She continued, sustaining her indifferent and emotionally remote façade.

The car drove down the red stone driveway and stopped when the wrought iron gates gradually opened, allowing Edna's chauffeur-driven limousine to pass. Six broad-shouldered security guards and a dozen police officers pushed the determined crowd back from the windows of the car as it surged its way through. Flashing camera lights from enthusiastic journalists continuously flared, blinding the occupants as they tried to obtain an exclusive photo of Annie Karce's grieving mother. The car temporarily stopped, and just as it did, a man broke through the blockade, plastering the latest newspaper headlines up against the passenger window, which displayed Sharon's withered and pallid face highlighted on the front page, and it read,

SOCIALITE IN TATTERS FROM GLITZY RICHES TO PRISON RAGS HOW SHARON KARCE BECAME A TREACHEROUS VIXEN

Edna rapidly turned her head the other way and summoned the driver to hurry up while tears flooded her eyes, and even though she shut them tightly, the image of her haggard daughter being hauled into the back of a prison truck was permanently trapped in her mind.

Once at the church, the magnitude of anguish was enormous. Everyone who was anyone attended, dressed in black with hoary elongated expressions on their faces as they regarded a large picture of Annie, her face gazing back at them with the innocence of a child, her beaming smile radiating like sunshine, even amongst the assembly of grief and despondency. Edna sat in the front row, struggling to hold back the tears that flowed steadily down her vacant face. She felt battered inside, empty and traumatized; her soul reluctant to acknowledge the finality of Annie's death, to be here on this day, saying goodbye to her beloved daughter, without Warren, even though she knew that her beloved daughter was already gone. The service was short. There were only two eulogies spoken: the first one was from William, who had known Annie since she was a babe in arms; and at first, he felt nervous and a little exposed because there were moments where he became overcome with emotion, needing to pause to take a few deep breaths to carry on. The second person to speak was a friend of Annie's from University who had studied for the same degree as they'd shared many hours together, side by side, assisting each other with exam notes and assignments. Her tribute enthralled every person there.

'Annie was the very essence of compassion, of style, and of beauty. She was my dearest friend, and we supported each other through many tough times at Uni. She was never ashamed about working hard, even if her efforts resulted in failures. Those of us who loved her and ache with her passing know that Annie Karce, daughter, sister, and a cherished friend had this attitude towards living—love your life, perfect it, and beautify all things you touch. Seek to make your life as long as you can and always show respect to all people, even if they are a stranger, and never forget to smile as every day on this beautiful planet is a good day.'

As soon the service was over, Edna boarded the limousine at the back entrance of the church, endeavoring to avoid the paparazzi and make a speedy getaway towards home. She'd decided that there wouldn't be awake dedicated to Annie's memory because Edna's resilience for putting on a brave face had waned, and all she wanted was privacy and didn't care if she became a prisoner in her own home. Shelter and respite from the constant tragedies in her life was, above all, her main objective.

The preceding week when Annie's body had returned home from Romania, it was necessary for Edna to view the corpse for identification purposes. The commanding police officer had said that viewing her daughter's body would help bring clarity to her loss and support the grieving process. Viewing the body, he alleged, would assist with severing the bond with the deceased, which was essential for Edna's well-being, but she flinched at the idea and sent William to undertake the grueling responsibility in her place. On that abysmal day, he stepped into the mortuary room where the human corpses were being held, awaiting identification from their various loved ones. As the coroner opened the cold locker, hauling out the block on which Annie lay, he pulled back the white sheet that concealed her; and Williams's skin became instantly pale as the blood drained from his face. He stood there unblinking, with his mouth drooped; he stared at her motionless body, shaking his head in disbelief, and the astonishment sent him stepping backward until his brain fought to make sense of it all. Ultimately, it rendered him speechless.

'Is this Annie Karce?' The coroner asked quietly.

All William could do was nod yes. Returning home to the manor, William observed Edna sitting in the parlor, and he carefully approached her. Before he'd even reached the sofa, she addressed him in a cold manner, the whole time her gaze was transfixed outside the window. 'Is it her?'

'Yes, madam, it's Annie', He answered gently with his head

lowered.

'Is there anything I can do for you, madam?' He continued.

'Just make the necessary funeral arrangements ... that's all thank you William', She answered resolutely. So the week leading up to the funeral, it was Williams's great responsibility to take on the duty of making preparations for the young lady he cared so deeply for, and his heart was heavy with sorrow. Ten dreary days had passed since Annie's memorial service, and all Edna could mentally visualize was the tragic picture and cruel headlines of her eldest daughter, featured on the front page news, which the intruder had so heartlessly mortared against the car window. Her desire for refuge and seclusion was like hunger, and she'd gratified this craving by residing in her bedroom for most of those ten days. The essential need to find out more answers to why Sharon had committed the shocking murder, infiltrated her every waking moment and she desired to actively seek reasoning of that unknown. Today, she'd decided that it was time to willingly cast herself into the mysterious waters of Sharon's sinister motives, and this hunt made her senses more alive and her instincts alert. Entering the parlor, Edna immediately called for Williams's assistance. 'Good morning, madam, how can I help?'

'I've decided that I'm going to Romania to see Sharon. I'd like you to make the arrangements as soon as possible. Not only the travel but with the prison as well', She instructed.

'Are you sure, madam? It may be too much for you?' He sounded puzzled by her request. 'Yes, just do as I ask please, and book two tickets because you're coming with me.'

Composed and polite, Edna and William progressed methodically into the Romanian maximum security prison, and their status was instantly identified by the apparel they wore. Edna donned a dark-emerald knee-length skirt, decorative buttoned-up chemise, and a tweed jacket, with a woolen shawl wrapped loosely around her shoulders, while William looked sharp in his dark-blue suit and immaculately pressed shirt, and tie. The mood there was one of despair and decay as eerie cries echoed from the distant chambers. They arrived half an hour prior to the start time as they presented their identification and were searched for prohibited items. Edna was required to leave her shawl behind as they were scanned by electronic metal sensors, and drug detection dogs sniffed them up and down.

'Turn out your pockets and open your mouths for inspection', A chubby, abrupt female guard demanded. Edna's self-worth plummeted as her pride and dignity were compromised by the shame she felt from the humiliation of being physically examined and having her daughter living in this place of squalor.

'Follow me please', Another guard instructed.

'Gate!' The guard yelled, and the heavy steel door opened and shut steadfastly behind them. The moments Edna walked down the menacing corridor, she felt the coldness of the surrounding emptiness, and it felt like a sinister veil over her skin as a creeping sorrow filled her heart.

'I'm sorry, this is happening to you', William compassionately whispered into her ear as Edna appeased him, touching his shoulder.

The guard opened a bulky, strong door, entering the room in front of them, obstructing their view of the person who was waiting at the bench; and as he moved to one side, Edna caught the vision of a gaunt woman, her short hair grubby and coarse like a mop of recycled steel wool and her exhausted face worn from prolonged suffering and exertion.

'Mama?' Sharon lifted her head off the table, hearing their footsteps come in.

'Hello, Sharon', Edna replied as William and herself pulled out a chair, sitting opposite her.

'I can't believe you're finally here. Have you come to take me home? I can do my punishment in Australia ... all I need is your approval', Sharon radiated. 'No, I haven't come here to take you home, Sharon. After what you've done, I can't have you living in my home anymore. How are you anyway?'

'Look at me, Mama, I've turned into a neurotic hag ... what do you think? It's a nightmare being incarcerated in this place.' Sharon's impertinence quickly presented itself.

'Well, you should've thought about the consequences before you murdered your beautiful sister. Why did you do it, Sharon?' Edna prodded.

'I didn't mean for Annie to die ... I just wanted to ...' Sharon's voice trailed off, and she took a deep sigh.

'What does it matter now anyway?', She continued.

'It matters to me, Sharon ... you murdered my baby ... your only sibling. That's why I came. I wanted to look you in the eyes and for you to tell me the truth.' Edna sounded irritated as William sat quietly, visually dissecting the bizarre woman in front of him.

'She was a constant pain in the arse ... you and father never loved me ...you only tolerated me, during my whole life, everything was all about Annie.'

'How can you say that? Both of you girls got the same love and attention from your father and me.'

Chapter 15

'That's what you think, but it's true. So you've come all the way to Romania to hear my honesty? OK? Here it is. Do you know why I wanted Annie gone? I wanted all the inheritance to myself ... it's the least you could do for me ... call it compensation for all of those wretched years I had to put up with your favoritism towards the hallowed Annie— there, you have your answer.' Sharon sat back, pleased that she'd finally spat out the reality for her naive mother.

Edna hung her head in despair and sighed deeply.

'Alright, I've heard enough. You're a delusional and greedy woman Sharon and I feel very sorry for you. Look where your arrogance and bitterness has led you" Were the last words spoken to her eldest daughter.

It's time we left', Edna then directed her dialogue towards William.

'Guard, could you let us out', William instructed.

'No, don't go, Mama ... I am angry. I didn't mean what I just said', Sharon implored.

Edna and William stood up without saying another word, and as they were walking out the door, Sharon shrieked after them, repeatedly banging her fists on the table like a ruined child. 'I want my money ... give it to me ... it's legally mine.' The door padlocked shut, and Sharon never saw them again.

'I have no more family. Warren and Annie are dead and Sharon ... well, I don't know who that woman is ... so my eldest daughter is gone too', Edna indicated forlornly to William.

'You still have Tilly and me', He replied.

The afternoon Edna and William arrived back in Australia, they were both shattered and drained from the curt awareness of Sharon's cruel insanity and from the long trip home.

277

'I'm going straight to bed, William ... I won't require any dinner, good night.'

'Good night madam ... try to sleep well. I'll see you in the morning', he replied, giving her a weak smile.

The following morning, Edna awoke and informally placed on her robe and slowly descended down the staircase. Every time she closed her eyes, haunting mental images of Sharon sitting in front of her at the Romanian gaol, emaciated and resentful of the privileged life she once had, battered her and it left a nauseating pain in her stomach. Edna clutched the stairwell railing with both hands as she attempted to manage the overwhelming dizziness that was inundating her. She drew a yawning breath before carefully descending the staircase and informally entered the parlor for breakfast.

As she sat down in her favorite chair, William approached her with a pot of tea, and with a cheerful demeanor, he placed a cup and saucer down on the table next to her.

"Good morning Madam, I hope you slept well" he greeted

"Actually William, I'm not sure how I slept. I don't feel very well this morning"

"That's a shame Madam ... especially when it's your birthday today"

"Is it? I completely forgot. Who cares anyway with everything that has happened to this family" Edna droned

William looked at her with confusion then walked back to the kitchen entrance where he beckoned for someone to enter the parlor. Edna turned to observe who he was talking to

and to her far-reaching bewilderment, there they all were, an entourage of people smiling at her, like dazzling lights in a dark room.

She felt instant happiness growing in her heart with the gift

278

of living and a penetrating relief that became brutally intense.

'Happy birthday!' they all hailed.

'Good morning, my dear', Warren greeted as he walked up to kiss Edna on the cheek.

'Good morning, Mama. How are you feeling today? You've been quite ill and asleep for three days, you must have been very tired', Annie and Sharon welcomed, displaying their affection for her.

'Oh my goodness ... I can't believe this, have I been unwell?' was all she could say, completely overburdened, attempting to comprehend what was happening.

'Yes, dear, you've been very strained lately with a fever. The Valium Dr Bartlett prescribed has helped you to rest', Warren informed her.

'Sit down, Mama, we have a present for you.' The girls beamed as they handed her the gift. 'We all chipped in for it', Annie radiated. Edna took the tiny parcel that was enfolded in bright-pink paper with an extravagant bow on the top and just stared at it.

'Oh thank you, dear, what could it be?' she quietly said as she skillfully removed the wrapping, still in shock at the sudden, incredible revelations before her.

'You'll see mama, you're going to love it.' Annie beamed

A petite carmine metal jewelry box appeared, and as Edna unfastened the lid, slowly drawing it back, there in all its glory, nestled in crimson velvet, sat the pendant. The blistered nugget lustered its bright-yellow glow, capturing the sun flickering within its belly and the handmade chain with its intricate vintage design crafted in silver that reflected light even in the dimly lit room.

'It's lovely', Edna remarked, hypnotized by the jewels' familiarity. While she stared at the pendant, there was a knock at the manor door, so William went to answer it and promptly escorted two young men into the parlor. Edna looked up as Annie greeted them both with a colossal grin on her face, interlocking her arm with one of the males.

'Hello, Mrs. Karce, and happy birthday?'The men acknowledged

Edna gasped at the sight of them.

'These are our friends, Mama ... Liam attends my university and this is his brother Jock ... Jock has just flown in from Romania. The same country that we're going to visit when we go on our overseas trip. What a wonderful coincidence! It's like an uncanny premonition', Annie revealed proudly, smiling from ear to ear while her sister Sharon, just loitered in the background, slightly behind the men, and leered at her mother with cold penetrating eyes and a traitorous grin adorning her smug face, as her thoughts were consumed with the shrewd, evil plan she would finally execute once abroad, with the help of her deceitful accomplices.

The End